THE DALLAS DECEPTION

Richard Abshire was with the Dallas Police Department for twelve years, and a private investigator for two, before becoming a writer-producer for the Law Enforcement Television Network, a satellite network featuring products, strategies, and technologies to law enforcement professionals nationwide. He is the author of the Jack Kyle mysteries *Dallas Drop* and *Turn-around Jack*. He lives in Dallas.

THE DALLAS DECEPTION

A JACK KYLE MYSTERY

Richard Abshire

PENGUIN BOOKS

PENGUIN BOOKS

Published by the Penguin Group

Penguin Books USA Inc., 375 Hudson Street, New York,
New York 10014, U.S.A.

Penguin Books Ltd, 27 Wrights Lane, London W8 5TZ, England

Penguin Books Australia Ltd, Ringwood, Victoria, Australia

Penguin Books Canada Ltd, 10 Alcorn Avenue, Toronto,
Ontario, Canada M4V 3B2

Penguin Books (N.Z.) Ltd, 182–190 Wairau Road,
Auckland 10, New Zealand

Penguin Books Ltd, Registered Offices: Harmondsworth, Middlesex, England

First published in the United States of America by
William Morrow and Company, Inc., 1992
Reprinted by arrangement with William Morrow and Company, Inc.
Published in Penguin Books 1993

1 3 5 7 9 10 8 6 4 2

PUBLISHER'S NOTE

This is a work of fiction. Names, characters, places, and incidents either
are the product of the author's imagination or are used fictitiously, and
any resemblance to actual persons, living or dead, events, or locales is entirely coincidental.

THE LIBRARY OF CONGRESS HAS CATALOGUED THE HARDCOVER AS FOLLOWS:
Abshire, Richard
The Dallas deception: a Jack Kyle mystery/Richard Abshire.
p. cm.
ISBN 0-688-10799-0 (hc.)
ISBN 0 14 01.7407 9 (pbk.)
I. Title.
PS3551.B84D34 1992
813´.54—dc20 91–39450

Printed in the United States of America
Set in Caledonia
Designed by Kathryn Parise

To big Dave McClure,
a straight shooter

THE
DALLAS
DECEPTION

CHAPTER
1

I felt like a peeping Tom, looking through the square of bluish light at the naked girl. She had spiky blond hair and shocking blue eyes, and a lean body. She was being mauled by a dark and furtive man, who had mounted her from behind. He had his fist in her hair, pulling her head back. Her mouth was open, showing white teeth between painted lips, and she might have been screaming.

But there was no audio, and the blue square wasn't a window. It was a television screen, and I was watching a video-taped replay of something I didn't care for. As I watched the man getting rougher and rougher with the girl, I wondered why I was being shown this.

The tape was playing on a rented TV with a VCR attached, the whole setup sitting atop a heavy metal tray on wheels in Eddie Cochran's hospital room. I had stopped by after hours to smuggle him a bit of booze and to give him a hard time about getting busted up in the Dallas police charity rodeo a couple of evenings earlier.

But Eddie had not been his usual self, and he hadn't even

offered me a drink of the whiskey I'd brought. He'd acted glad enough to see me, but it was obvious he had things on his mind. This tape had been one of them.

Eddie triggered a switch on his remote-control gadget, and the blue light went out, leaving us in the semidarkness of his room. There was a small lamp burning on the table beside his bed, but that was all.

"I guess that's enough," he said. "You get the idea."

"I guess."

"They call this stuff 'keyhole' porn. You know about it?"

"No."

Eddie was a homicide lieutenant, and what he knew about any kind of porn puzzled me. "What's the deal?"

"The creep there gets a kid like this in bed—usually it's behind some kind of drugs. He does his thing, and all the time there's a video camera getting it all down on the sly. The kid never knows she's making a movie, not unless somebody catches her performance somewhere and tells her about it."

"Who's this guy?" I asked.

"I'm not sure, Jack."

"And the girl?"

"That's what I want to talk to you about."

"Okay."

But he didn't start talking right away, so I lit a cigarette and took a seat in the chair at the foot of his bed.

"She's the daughter of a friend of mine," Eddie said.

"A friend?"

"More than that." Eddie quit fussing with the remote control and looked past his suspended left foot at me. "Give me a minute or two, Jack. I'll get it all out."

"Maybe a drink would help," I offered.

"I'm a little loopy already, from the dope they're giving me in here."

"I'm not."

"Help yourself."

I watched Eddie out of the corner of my eye as I poured myself a healthy slug of the scotch I'd brought in under my shirt past the desk nurse. He lay propped up on pillows, in a great cast that covered his waist and his left leg all the way down to his foot, which was hung from a frame over his bed. His toes stuck out, swollen and a couple of ugly shades of purple. He was frowning, his eyebrows furrowed and making shadows on his face in the dim light. I settled back into my chair with my drink and gave him a smile.

"Okay, shoot," I told him. Whatever it was, we could handle it.

"Her name's Carol," he said.

"The kid in the video?"

"No, her mother, my . . . friend."

"Your lover."

Eddie looked up at me, with a wry smile and a shake of his head.

"Yeah," he said, like he was confessing to a crime. "My lover."

"Christ, Eddie, you don't have to act so guilty about it. It's been a while. I'm happy for you."

"She's a widow."

"Okay."

"A widow with problems. Her son died a while back. Her daughter . . ." Eddie waved his hand as if he didn't know what to say about her. "You'll see."

"Oh?"

"Yeah. Her dad's a little irregular, too, in his own way."

"How'd you get involved?"

He gave me a look like he didn't think that was any of my business, but of course it was, and he knew that when he stopped to think for a second.

"Her son's death looked at first like it might be a suicide. I worked the case."

"Tough way to meet."

"You never know."

"I guess not. How does that saying go?" I asked, a little sarcastic. "'Never play cards with a man named Doc, never eat at a place called Mom's, and never get involved with a woman who has more problems than you do.' Isn't that it?"

"All right, I know better, but . . ."

He wasn't going to finish the thought, I could see that. Probably because his voice had that queer little squeak in it.

"You can't help how you feel," I told him. I meant it, too. I had some experience along those lines.

"No, I can't. She's had it tough, Jack. Her husband died young and sudden, left her to raise the kids."

"It's your business, Eddie. What about the daughter?"

"Her name's Elizabeth. Liz, everybody calls her. She's okay, but she's been running wild since her brother died."

"She's playing around with some rough folks."

"Yeah, I'm afraid so."

"Drugs?" I asked.

"Designer stuff—'ecstasy,' crap like that."

"Okay. What do you want me to do?"

"I wouldn't ask if I wasn't laid up. You know that."

"I know." Eddie was not the kind of guy to ask for help from anyone, especially on something personal like this. "So what do you want done?"

"I want the tapes, the original of this son of a bitch and any copies. I don't want anybody else to see her like that."

I nodded, and told myself it could have been worse.

"By the time I'm back on my feet, that tape will be all over the country, Jack. And I can't ask anybody on the department to get mixed up in something like this. You know that."

"I understand."

A cop could get fired for doing a friend the kind of favor Eddie was asking. An ex-cop private investigator, on the other hand, didn't have so many rules to worry about.

"You're sure that's the plan? This guy's in the business, I mean. He's not just in it for kicks, like a hobby?"

"I don't want to take the chance. Carol's . . . she's just worried sick over this thing. It's really tearing her up."

"You haven't said anything about blackmail."

"No."

"So how did you get your hands on a copy of the tape? If the porno prince didn't make any demands, where did the tape come from?"

"That's a good question, Jack."

"I could use a good answer."

"Carol found it in her house."

"Terrific."

"I know, it's a squirrelly deal, Jack. I hate to drop it on you, but . . ."

"Hey, what are friends for?"

"Jack, you know I appreciate this. I'll owe you one."

I finished my scotch and rinsed out the glass. This was not the kind of deal I wanted any part of. The kid sounded like trouble, and it's almost never a good idea to mix business and friendship, not in my business. But there wasn't much doubt in either of our minds that I'd do this for Eddie. The favor business works both ways, and I didn't have that many friends. Eddie had stuck with me through some pretty rocky times, and there was always the chance that this deal wouldn't turn out to be the fire drill it smelled like.

"Where do I find this guy?"

"Liz can give you that. If you're not busy tonight, I can call and set up a meet."

"Okay." I didn't have any plans. By my watch, it was a little after 11:00 P.M. I'd wrapped up a penny-ante surveillance job a couple of hours earlier after being up most of the night before. "I'd like Mom there, too."

"I don't blame you. Hang on a second."

He dialed a number on his bedside phone, and you could see it in his eyes when he got through to Carol. Eddie had it bad, and I didn't envy him.

I made a point of not eavesdropping on their conversation, all the hushed and whispered stuff a man and woman get into when they feel that way about each other. It occurred to me that another drink might be in order, but I thought better of it. Better have my wits about me when I sat down with Eddie's girlfriend and the kid. Like I said, I'd been up most of the night before, and it's been my experience that you can save yourself a lot of headaches in these deals if you pay attention to details going in.

"How's midnight at the Art Bar?" Eddie asked, his hand over the mouthpiece of the phone.

"The what?"

"Art Bar. It's at Main and Crowdus, right behind Club Clearview."

"Deep Ellum?" I asked.

"Yeah. It's kind of an art gallery with a bar included, or vice versa."

"Terrific."

"Okay, so it's not a friggin' Denny's. It's close, and it's a nice spot. You could meet people in nice places once in a while, it wouldn't kill you."

CHAPTER
2

It almost never rains in August in Dallas. August is when we have killer heat waves, thirty consecutive 100-degree days. It's the time of the year when even the weatherman gets it right, because every day's the same. But this had been an odd August, with two or three spells of rain that lasted for a couple of days or more. And when I stepped out of the Baylor Medical Center on Gaston Avenue, I walked into a coolish drizzle that gave the night a curious feel.

Finding Main and Crowdus wasn't much trouble, but I made the block twice before I spotted the Art Bar. It was part of a big building on the northeast corner, diagonally across the intersection from the more noticeable Flamingo Joe's. There were plenty of signs announcing the Blind Lemon Bar, and Club Clearview, which took up most of the building. The Art Bar, I finally noticed, occupied the corner of the building nearest the intersection.

It wasn't much longer before I was able to find a place to park my car. There was a lot of traffic for a late Wednesday, cars and people milling around in spite of the persistent misting rain.

Once inside the place, I was treated to a charming ambiance featuring a couple of what looked like Scud missiles hanging from the ceiling, with sharks' mouths painted on their noses. There were nine large oil paintings mounted around the two solid walls, in a style I've seen referred to as "Texas Gothic." But my favorite touch was the old TV set at the end of the bar. Where there should have been a picture tube was an aquarium, with big goldfish swimming happily across the screen.

The two sides of the place that faced Main and Crowdus were taken up with big windows for watching all the characters pass by outside. There were half a dozen round black tables huddled in the middle of the floor, attended by mismatched black chairs. Along the windows, red plastic booths faced more black tables. And the bar was a statement all its own, a curved thing with glaring images that looked like they'd been spray-painted down the front, and some kind of recessed lighting along its leading edge that must have warmed the heavily cushioned stools. I picked a stool near the end and said hello to the bartender, a cute kid with a healthy suntanned look and an engaging smile. I figured I could risk one more scotch, and told her I'd have one on the rocks.

There was a pretty sparse crowd in the place, five people huddled around one of the tables, all dressed in black except for one young man with a tuxedo shirt worn with the tails out and a tall pair of boots with buckles all the way up the front. There was one loner already at the bar, and a brace of young Asian guys in a two-man booth at the Crowdus window. They had the lean and hungry look that too often means trouble, but I had no reason to think that whatever they had in mind would go down in the Art Bar, at least not while I was on hand.

I waited from a quarter to twelve until a quarter after, killing time having a friendly bartender explain about the paintings. They were on loan from galleries around town, the bartender said. If I saw something I wanted to buy, she would tell me which gallery represented that artist, and I could call to close the deal. The art was changed monthly, and the system seemed to work out well for everyone involved. I told the bartender—her name was Bobbi—as she brought me a second scotch, that a particular nude on the wall across the way reminded me of her. I asked her if she'd posed for it, and she laughed, not offended. She seemed like a nice kid.

"Mister Kyle?"

Carol and Liz had no trouble picking me out from the description Eddie had provided. But then, I was the only old fart at the bar. The place catered to a pretty young crowd.

"Yes, ma'am," I admitted, rising. "And you're Carol?"

She nodded and introduced me to her daughter. There was a third member of their little party whom I had trouble making out. About five-three, with hair of a particular blue-black that does not occur in nature, the face pale and clean, with the kind of smallish, round dark glasses with wire rims that John Lennon made popular. The lips were thin, a straight line under a pug nose. It was hard to tell much about the body; it was draped in a couple of formless baggy black shirts, one open over the other. I wasn't sure if it was a boy or a girl, and when it introduced itself as "Syd, with a y," the voice was no help.

I suggested we move to a table, and we settled in at one not far from the bar.

The mother and daughter were interesting. Liz looked a lot different than she had on the tape, of course. She wasn't wearing her hair spiked up tonight. She was dressed about like Syd, baggy, layered stuff to make her formless. She looked awfully young. So did her mother.

Carol was a looker, but there was no family resemblance. Her hair was dark, cropped short in a way that only looks good on women with the right kind of cheekbones and eyes. It looked good on her. And she didn't dress like the kid, either. Her sleeveless sweater and the gray pants didn't hide much.

They were tasteful clothes, and probably expensive, but they made it obvious that Mom was still in shape. She had the kind of slim-hipped, leggy body you'd expect in a model, and I didn't think having a couple of kids had done her any harm.

She fixed me with an earnest look and began explaining things. Liz looked bored, and didn't seem to be paying me or her mother any attention. Syd sat between me and Liz, and looked at me like she thought I was there to make trouble.

"It was lying in the entry hall, along with the mail," Carol was saying. "I didn't know what it was."

"Or where it came from?" I asked.

"No."

"How about you?" I asked, meaning Liz. She turned to show me that she'd cocked an eyebrow. "Do you know how the tape got into your house?"

"I haven't a clue," she said.

"And don't give a shit," I offered.

"I beg your pardon?"

"Yeah, and you can kiss my ass for good measure, kid."

"Mister Kyle," Carol put in. "Please . . ."

"You can call me Jack, and don't worry about my language or my attitude."

Syd was giving me the eye like I'd just pissed on her leg.

"I thought . . ." Liz began.

"Here's the deal, sweetheart: You're in trouble. I'm going to try to get you out. I'll need some information to do that. If you don't care about this problem, then I sure as hell don't. Maybe you don't mind being a movie star."

"Leave her alone," Syd growled.

"And who the hell are you?" I wanted to know. "Her bodyguard?"

"I'm her friend, and you don't have to talk to her like that."

"Yeah? Well, where were you the night of the crime? Why didn't you keep her out of this mess?"

"It's not her fault. I did it," Liz said. "It's all my fault."

"You want to tell me about it?"

Liz nodded, then cut her eyes over at her mother.

"Listen, Carol, I need to talk to Liz here alone for a couple of minutes. Why don't you and Syd give us a little room?"

"I don't understand why . . ."

"It'll just be a couple of minutes."

"All right."

Carol got up, but Syd was not so quick to go along with my idea. She didn't budge until Liz assured her it was all right.

It wasn't clear to me which one of the two women Liz had been putting on her tough act for, but when it was just the two of us, I thought I saw a change in her. She put her hand to her mouth and looked down at the table. When she looked up at me, she looked more like a kid than before.

"How old are you, Liz?"

"Seventeen."

"Jesus."

"How old are you?" she asked.

"A good bit more than twice your age."

"Old enough to be my father."

"Kid, I'm probably old enough to be your mom's father."

"I don't think she's as young as she looks."

"But enough about that. Tell me what happened."

"I lost my cherry on videotape."

CHAPTER
3

She sounded pretty tough when she said it, tossed it off to shock me, I figured. But I didn't say anything, just let it lie there between us, and she started crying.

"I'm sorry," she said. "I don't mean to cry and everything."

"I don't blame you for crying, kid. You don't have to act tough with me."

"Have you seen it?"

"Part of it. Looked pretty rough."

She shook her head.

"I couldn't believe it was happening to me," she said.

"What's his name?"

"Freddy, that's all I know."

"Where does he live?"

She told me the best she could, which is to say that she had no idea what his address was, and only a general idea that it was an apartment complex off North Central Expressway near Meadow. There were a lot of apartments in that neighborhood.

"He was supposed to give me a ride home, but he said he had to stop off at his place first, on the way."

"A ride home from where?"

"One of the clubs. I don't even remember which one, for sure. Syd and I were just out clubbing. I got kinda bored, so I ditched Syd and a couple of our friends. I think that was at Club Dada. I partied with some more people, and then it was late and I didn't know where Syd was. She was driving, and I was broke, so I needed a way home."

"Were you drunk?"

"A little."

"The people at the clubs didn't card you?"

"Sure, but I have a really good fake I.D."

"Smart. Were you doing any drugs?"

"Why?"

"I'll take that for a yes. What was it, 'ecstasy'?"

"I think so."

"Christ, aren't you sure?"

"I got it from some friends of mine. I don't remember. They called it 'hug drug.'"

"Right. So Freddy invites you in at his place. Then what?"

"I wasn't feeling very good. I was kind of . . . coming down, you know? And Freddy said he had something that would make me feel better."

"What a guy."

"So I took a couple of pills, and then . . . it starts getting pretty confused after that."

"Yeah, I guess it would."

"I remember we started making out, and it was okay at first, but then he got a little rough."

"A little?"

"I told him I didn't want to do it, I wanted to go home."

"How old a guy is Freddy?"

"Pretty old. Twenty-five, maybe."

"Right."

"Finally, he said I'd got him in a hell of a state. He said I'd have to do something for him before he'd take me home."

"Did he rape you then?"

"No . . . not exactly." She looked at me, playing with a lock of her hair between her fingers. "He said he wanted me to suck him, so I did."

"That wasn't rape?"

"Nah, I do oral. I just didn't want to have sex with him."

"Oh."

"So, anyway, I blew him, and then I thought everything was cool. But the next thing I knew we were on his bed and he was tearing my clothes off, and . . . I don't remember much after that. I don't remember the ride home, I just remember he kinda woke me up and we were in the street out in front of my house. He got me out of his car, and then he left. I went inside and went to bed. That's all."

"What kind of car does he drive?"

"A blue Honda. I think it's a Civic, but I'm not sure. He has a CD player in it."

"Could you describe him for me?"

"Didn't you see him on the tape?"

"Not his face."

"Oh. Well, he's tall and thin. His hair is black, and he has a . . . what do you call it? A mustache and a little chin beard."

"A Vandyke."

"Yeah, he has one of those."

"Anything else?"

"I don't remember anything."

"Now I want you to tell me the truth. I don't care if you don't want your mom to know, or Syd or whatever, but it's important for you to level with me. How did the copy of the tape wind up at your house?"

"I swear I don't know!"

"Did he make a copy before he took you home? Do you think

he could have made a copy and put it in your purse or something?"

"I don't know. Like I said, I don't remember much after a point, but I didn't have a purse that night, and it wasn't in my room when I woke up the next morning. I'm pretty sure of that."

"Okay."

Carol and Syd had stayed away as long as they could stand it by that time, and they rejoined us. I told them I wanted Liz to come with me, to see if she could show me Freddy's apartment. Carol had no objections, but Syd really bristled.

"You can come, too, if you'd like," I assured her. Little Liz had a way of sending mixed signals, and I was none too eager to spend a lot of time alone with her.

As we made our way toward the door, I saw the two Asian kids get up and leave their table.

"Carol, we'll talk again when I bring Liz home."

"I'll wait up for you," she said over her shoulder as she preceded me through the door.

I held the door for the girls, and that was when I saw one of the Asians say something to Liz. She looked up to see that I was watching, and didn't respond. The man leaned close to her and said something else.

"Can I help you?" I asked.

The two of them looked me up and down pretty good, and I don't imagine the sight of me scared them much. I am almost always underestimated by people like that, and I wouldn't have it any other way.

"It's okay," Liz said, with a smile that was none too convincing. "No problem."

"No problem," the Asian said. He was smiling, too.

The two of them looked to be in their twenties, neither of them very tall. But they seemed to be the quick, wiry type, the kind I have the most trouble with in a fight. I have better luck with heavyweights. They were both wearing the high-dollar kind of faded-looking jeans rolled at the cuffs and Air Jordan sneakers, the type kids in some places have been known to kill each other for. One of them, the one doing the talking, was wearing a black satin jacket, the kind you can buy with team logos. There was something written in an Oriental script on the front, but it didn't mean anything to me.

The girls hustled through the door to join Carol outside, and I played a little gesture to let Ying and Yang know I'd be happy to hold the door for them, too. But they were having none of that, so I went next.

"My car's up the street," I said.

"I parked the other way," Carol replied, pointing.

"Come with me, I'll drop you off."

"That's not necessary."

"Don't argue."

So we trooped off up Crowdus Street toward the Art Bar parking lot. I checked to see if our friends were following us, but they were still standing at the corner. When they saw me look back at them, they both waved and smiled again, nodding.

No problem.

CHAPTER
4

It didn't take Liz much more than an hour to finally find her way back to Freddy's apartment. I made a note of the address, and we killed a little time looking around for a blue Honda Civic with a CD player, with no luck. It was almost two o'clock Thursday morning by the time I dropped Liz and Syd off at Carol's Highland Park home. It wasn't enormous, but a home in the Park Cities didn't have to be big to cost a bundle. It looked like a copy of something English, with a lot of ivy crawling up the front of it, and there were shutters alongside the windows. It was a two-story job. I walked them to the door, and Carol let us in. The girls went upstairs, and Carol and I talked in the entry hall.

"I don't know very much about you," she said.

"You know Eddie Cochran," I answered. "That ought to be enough."

"You worked with Eddie on the force. He told me that."

"Yeah, we go back a way."

"I get the impression you don't approve of me."

"What do you care, one way or the other?" She hadn't offered me a seat or a drink, so I didn't ask her permission before lighting a cigarette. I didn't see any ashtrays, and usually I take a hint like that. But it was late, and I was tired of being out in the rain and overdue for some sleep. "Eddie's a big boy."

"Yes, he's . . . an exceptional man," she said, with a coy smile that put a twinkle in her eyes. "He's . . . well, I care for him very much."

She wasn't my type particularly, but she had a way about her, and I could see how a man could look too closely into those eyes. The ash on my cigarette was getting pretty long, and I looked down at it so she would notice. She didn't though, or else she didn't care if it fell on the rich plush carpet we were standing on. The carpet was blue, with silver filigree, and it ran down the long entry hall to a spiral staircase. It was not an enormous house, but it was in a ritzy neighborhood, and it was well appointed, to say the least. I'd only gotten as far as the entry hall, but everything I could see had a shine on it, very clean. It didn't look like anybody lived there.

I tugged my notebook out of my pocket and handed her a business card. It had my phone number and address, and my P.I. license number on it. She didn't read it, and when I asked her all the questions I usually ask a client, she rattled off the answers without any argument. I got all her particulars, all the details you don't want to overlook because you never know what kind of people you're dealing with in my business.

When I finished and put my notebook away, she asked me if all that was necessary.

"All you're supposed to do is get the tape back, isn't it?"

"That's my understanding."

"Well, I suppose you know your business."

"I like to think so."

"Is that all?" she asked, stifling a yawn.

"One more thing," I answered.

"What?"

"Eddie mentioned that Liz's brother died some time ago. I believe he said Liz was a good kid, but she'd been acting up since her brother died."

"Did he? He told you that?"

"Words to that effect. I wasn't taking notes at the time."

"I see. Would you like an ashtray, Mister Kyle?"

As if she'd just noticed that I was smoking, now that my cigarette had burned down to the filter and there was ash on the carpet, she turned sharply away from me and went into a room off the hall. She was back in a couple of seconds with a brass ashtray that filled her hand. There was a design etched into the side of it, but I couldn't make it out because of the way her fingers curled around the thing. Like the rest of what I had seen of her house, the ashtray was empty and clean.

I put my butt in the ashtray and nodded thanks.

"May I have one of those?" she asked.

"Sure." I let her take one out of the pack and lit one for myself before lighting hers. "There you go."

"Thank you." She drew heavily on the cigarette, making the hot end glow like a beacon, and held her smoke deep inside before exhaling. "Alan."

"I beg your pardon?"

"Liz's brother. His name was Alan. He died last year, on his birthday."

"How did it happen?"

"A heart attack, or some kind of failure of the heart. I've forgotten the words the doctors used."

"How old was he?"

"Eighteen. Exactly."

"Of a heart attack?"

"There was something wrong with his heart, the doctors said. Something congenital."

"You hadn't known there was a problem?"

"I had no idea."

"I'm sorry."

"I beg your pardon?"

"I said I'm sorry. To bring this up. It must have been a terrible shock for you." She had an odd, distant look in her eyes that I thought might mean she was reliving her son's death, seeing the images again in her mind of a fatal eighteenth birthday. "I didn't mean to upset you."

"Yes."

"And you began to see a change in Liz after that? Her behavior?"

"Not long after. She started running around with different people, staying out all hours. I've been . . . worried about her."

"Were she and Alan pretty close? I mean, sometimes brothers and sisters can be especially close, or sometimes . . ."

"They were close. Liz idolized Alan. I think that would be fair to say."

"Is there any problem with her heart?"

"No."

"You've had her checked, and there's no problem there?"

"No. Liz is healthy as a horse."

"So she's not thinking that maybe the same thing will happen to her. I mean, she's seventeen and her brother died on his eighteenth birthday. You don't think she's acting crazy because she's afraid . . ."

"There's no reason for her to think that way, Mister Kyle."

"Maybe not, but we don't always think reasonably. When's her birthday?"

"In a few days. September fifth."

"I see."

"Is there anything else?"

We'd finished our cigarettes, and it was half past two.

"No, I think that's all, for now."

"Good night, then. And thank you."

"Good night."

I was out the door and across the porch when she called my name. I turned back to see her leaning on the door frame, the door ajar behind her, backlighting her silhouette.

"We haven't discussed your fee," she said.

"No fee."

"That's not necessary."

"I don't charge a fee for doing a friend a favor, lady."

"I see. I didn't mean to offend."

She had not offended me particularly. It's hard to do that, hurt my feelings by offering me money. Of course, there was no way I'd take money for doing this thing for Eddie Cochran. But that didn't mean money isn't important to me. It is, because I don't have any of it. Or not enough, by a long shot.

There are all kinds of private investigators, just like with any other kind of job. The ones who can afford not to worry about money usually have a couple of things going for them. For one thing, they're retired from something else—they're on pension from a police department or maybe the FBI. For another, most of them have one or two big clients on retainer, and that covers expenses. Usually something corporate, doing backgrounds or loss-prevention work, something like that. Or maybe a couple of law firms who need them on a pretty regular basis. With a setup like that, if you keep your overhead within reason, you can afford to be casual about money.

I was not in that category. When I left the DPD, it was well short of full retirement. I cashed in what I had in the pension fund and financed a divorce and a fishing trip in the Gulf of Mexico. That left just about enough to get my P.I. license and pay rent on a modest office. Since then, it had been pretty much a scramble to pay the rent and child support for my son, who lived in Paris, Texas, with his mom's folks while she was working out some problems of her own. Legal problems. I still lived in my office, being careful not to let my suitemates get wind of that fact, because I knew some of them would jump on a detail like that to have me tossed out of the place for violating my lease.

Such as it was, my little homestead looked good to me that morning, when I stumbled off the elevator and unlocked the door. I retrieved my army-surplus cot from behind my file cabinet, grabbed my pillow from the bottom file drawer, and got ready to turn in. All that involved, really, was kicking off my loafers and folding my sports coat neatly over a chair. Then, with my customary reverential glance at the framed photo on my wall of the charter fishing boat I'd fallen in love with on my Gulf trip, I tucked myself in.

It was three in the morning, and I'd have to be up and about by seven, before the rest of the folks on my floor showed up for work. That didn't leave much time to conjure up my favorite dream, the one where my kid and I are heading out to sea in the fishing boat in the photo, the big Bertram.

CHAPTER
5

Seven o'clock came early Thursday morning. I hadn't gotten around to investing in one of the nicer types of alarm clock, the kind that let you snooze a couple of extra minutes, then nag you again to get up. Mine's just the basic windup model with the bell-and-clapper arrangement, and there is no second chance. One reason I hadn't gone with any of the modern plastic jobs was that I was wont to slap the son of a bitch across the room, and I didn't think the electronic jobs could handle the abuse.

I didn't get all of the clock that morning, so even though I did punch it off my desk so hard it caromed off the baseboard, it kept ringing. It was out of sight somewhere underneath the cheap three-drawer office-surplus desk, lost among the paper clips and crumpled sheets of paper I had missed the trash can with after giving up on figuring a way out of my various financial binds. By the time I located the noisy beast, I was wide awake.

Della, the receptionist whose desk occupied the little foyer of our suite of offices, was usually the first one in every morning, and she already knew my little secret about living in my office. On the days I didn't answer the call, she would usually lure me out of my cot with a fresh cup of coffee, but still it was a rush to get things squared away before some of my less understanding suitemates showed up.

I was just finishing up in the men's room when I heard the elevator bell jangle, and I knew Della had arrived.

The coffee maker, an industrial-sized job we all shared support on, was located behind a partition in back of Della's desk, near the supply closet. Having stashed my cot and stuffed my dirty laundry in the bottom drawer of my file cabinet along with my pillow, I came whistling out of the men's room to wish Della a good morning and poured us both a cup. She took hers with a revolting amount of sugar and creamer, so I stopped adding things when the coffee took on the color of the gooey stuff in the middle of a Snickers bar.

"You're feeling pretty chipper this morning, Jack."

"Actually, I'm feeling like hell, but why should I burden you with it, kid?"

"Another all-nighter?"

"Practically."

"Still the surveillance job?"

"No, I wrapped that up. It's something else."

"Business is picking up."

"I'm afraid this one won't make much of a splash in my quarterly report."

"Something personal?"

"More or less. How was your evening?"

"Quiet."

"Sorry to hear it."

"There's nothing wrong with snuggling up with a good book once in a while."

"At your age? With those legs? What's the matter, did the dipshit forget your phone number again?"

She showed me her smile, a wondrous thing to behold, which is also true of the rest of her. I didn't have too hot a track record when it came to reading women I cared about, but I honestly didn't think this kid could hide a thing. When she was happy, which was almost always, her smile had a way of breaking out on her face and lighting up the room. When she was unhappy, and I'm afraid I've been on hand for a few of those occasions, it showed all over. That was one of her best qualities, her obvious sincerity, either way. It was also the main reason I had never taken her up on any of her many offers to help me with my cases. A person who can't lie doesn't have much of a future in my line of work.

"Dipshit" was my generic name for any of the guys Della got involved with, but only because I didn't think any of them were good enough for her. A couple of them had turned out to be trouble in spades, including one heavy-handed jerk I'd had occasion to muss up a bit. We didn't talk about him anymore, which suited me fine. The particular dipshit in question was a new guy. He also didn't deserve her, in my opinion.

"Bill's out of town for a few days, on business."

"Good."

"Don't be so hard on him, Jack. He likes you."

"Terrific."

"What's the new case? Anything I can help you with?"

"Maybe."

"Really?"

"Yeah, maybe. We'll see."

She was putting up her things and getting ready to get to work, while I was busy borrowing a neighbor's *Dallas Morning News* off the stack the deliveryman always left by the elevator door. I photocopied the crossword puzzle and returned the paper just about the time the elevator bell went off and Mrs. Farragut marched out.

"Good morning, Miz Farragut," Della sang out.

"Morning," she answered stiffly.

"Hi." I smiled.

"Mister Kyle."

She said it in a civil tone, and that was more than I had come to expect. She ran the corner office for some old fart who didn't come in every day anymore. I wasn't sure what kind of business it was, and Mrs. Farragut and I hardly ever chatted around the coffee machine.

Farragut and company had been in the corner office when I moved in three years ago. And the two of us, along with Della, were the only ones left out of the original occupants. There were half a dozen offices on my floor, and of course everybody who'd been in real estate was gone. So were a pair of investment brokers, who if I am not mistaken left under the cover of darkness. Now there was one vacant office, and a couple of CPAs, and one outfit that had something to do with insurance. Della handled the switchboard and made a good impression on anybody's customers who came calling, along with a little light typing. She did my contracts, when I had any. I hadn't exactly overworked her. If it hadn't been for some pickup work filling in on other investigators' cases, Kyle and Associates might well have gone under like the real estate magnates. As it was, I had no real associates, but I thought the name looked okay on my door.

Della was watching me when she thought I wasn't looking, and every time I turned her way, she'd look down at something on her desk, trying to hide a little smirk.

"What's the matter?" I asked her. "Is my fly open or something?"

"Don't be silly."

"Okay. Hold all my calls, I'll be in conference for a while."

"Right."

You can't always be sure Della knows when you're joking, but at quarter past seven, the odds against my having any calls to hold were astronomical. Nobody I liked would be up that early, and the nice folks down at the child-support office didn't come in until nine.

The crossword is my hobby, or the closest thing I had to one, not counting drinking. I'd always done the puzzle in the *Times Herald*, but they'd gone out of business, making Dallas the biggest one-daily town in the country. Lucky for me, the *Morning News* added a *New York Times* crossword to their regular no-brainer, and that was diversion enough.

It wasn't that I had forgotten about Freddy and his tapes; I was just killing a little time until I could do what I had in mind about it.

CHAPTER
6

Private investigation, at least down at my level on the food chain, consists of about equal parts of lying and loitering. Either you are hanging around keeping an eye on somebody or something, or else you are trying to get some piece of information that you probably are not exactly entitled to. That's where the lying comes in.

When I told the assistant manager of Freddy's apartment complex that I was "Mister Anderson of the Retail Services Corporation," calling to confirm Freddy's particulars, she was too helpful. She was probably new in the business, which often is the type of employee you get in most places if you call first thing in the morning. Yes, she was happy to assure me, Freddy Barksdale did live in apartment 118. I got the last name out of her by pretending I was having trouble making out Freddy's handwriting on whatever application for credit the assistant manager had inferred I was confirming. The apartment number I knew from my visit the night before with little Liz.

I told her I couldn't make out all the digits in Freddy's phone number, either, and she was happy to explain that to me, too.

That was what I was interested in. I thanked her and hung up. I hadn't asked her not to tell Freddy I'd called, but I did make it a point to use the word "confidential" several times, knowing that should impress or confuse her enough that she'd probably discuss it with her manager before mentioning anything about it to Freddy himself. She didn't think to ask for my phone number, in which case I would have explained that I was working off a phone bank and couldn't really take any incoming calls, or something along that line.

On my way out of the office, I asked Della to start trying to track down my erstwhile associate, Speed. He was a freelancer, and I had half a dozen numbers for him in my book. He was a good man with a camera, and I didn't know whom else to call to have a look at whatever I got from Freddy. I wouldn't know an original videotape from the third generation.

It was just a few minutes after eight when I arrived at Freddy's apartment complex. I had not seen a pay phone the night before, but I made a quick circle through the parking lot anyway, in case I'd missed one. No luck, so I withdrew across the street to another complex, which featured a pair of pay phones adjacent to the wall of mailboxes that served their residents. I was pleasantly surprised to find that one of them was still working.

Freddy answered on the fourth or fifth ring, and he sounded a little sleepy. From where I stood, I could look across the street into his parking lot, and I had my eye on a blue Civic that had not been there the night before. It was not parked at the curb directly in front of his apartment, because all the curb spaces were taken. The Civic was sitting a couple of rows over, near the middle of the lot. That would work out okay for me.

"Yeah, hello."

Freddy sounded pretty fuzzy, and I was glad he did not have an answering machine. If he had, it would have made things a bit more complicated.

"I know what you did, motherfucker," I snarled into the phone.

"What? Who is this?"

"You fucked up, little man. That blonde was a friend of mine."

"I don't know what you're talking about!"

"I'm on my way, Freddy boy. And I want those tapes, or I'm gonna break your fucking kneecaps. Then I start on your perverted fingers."

"Uh, really, man. I don't . . . who is this?"

"Don't make me have to chase you down, Freddy. You'd better be there when I come."

He finally hung up, which was what I wanted him to do in the first place. I was running out of threats, and growling low in my throat like that to sound like a movie mafioso was not easy.

It would take him a few seconds to shake out the cobwebs, maybe throw on his pants and shoes, and then he'd have to round things up. I figured I had time.

Freddy didn't surprise me. He came hustling out of apartment 118 just as I pulled my high-mileage little Reliant into a parking space near his Civic.

He was looking this way and that over his shoulder as he bolted out across the parking lot. He looked at me once, but I didn't look threatening enough to be the bad-ass he was worried about. Besides, I ignored him. I was looking at an apartment a couple of doors down from him, and checking a piece of paper in my hand like I was making sure I had the right address. I was so oblivious of Freddy that he passed within a couple of feet of me on his way to his car. I was glad to see that he was carrying something, a paper sack from the neighborhood Tom Thumb store. As we passed, he switched the sack from his left hand to his right, away from me. He was looking at me pretty close as we closed, but of course I pretended to have other things on my mind. And he bought it. That's why he went down so hard when I tripped him.

He banged face-first into the asphalt of the lot and threw his hands out to break his fall, but not quite in time. The Tom Thumb sack skittered in front of him, and he tried to scramble to his feet, but he couldn't get any traction. He was so scared, he was running too hard, working his feet so fast his slick-soled little slippers were doing nothing but working their way off his feet.

Freddy was cursing under his breath, and his blood pressure must have been soaring, because when he looked back at me his face was so red it looked like somebody had slapped him with a bloody towel.

A casual check of the area told me there was nobody up and about nearby, but you always have witnesses. I had worked enough cases where somebody happened to look out a window, or a maid doing the laundry just happened to look up, all that kind of thing. So I kept it casual, and just used my feet. In a lot full of parked cars, that wouldn't be nearly so obvious as putting my hands on him. I gave him a little nudge in the small of the back, and he sprawled flat on the ground for me.

"Take it easy, Freddy," I told him, keeping my voice nice and low. "You're going to hurt yourself scrambling around like that. Here, let me help you up."

One of the things you learn as a police officer is how to take somebody down without making a fuss. Like a protester interrupting a heavy hitter's speech, for example. You want to get the guy out of the auditorium, naturally, but there's always a school of pressies around, and too many of them turn their cameras on the asshole instead of the guy making the speech. So the last thing you want to do is make a hero out of this jerk by beating him up or choking him down right there on national TV. But still, you have to get him out of there. What you do is what they call "pain compliance." I've always been fond of euphemisms, and this is one of my favorites. What it means is, instead of hurting the guy overtly and making him go, you hurt him more subtly and make him *want* to go with you. That's what I did with Freddy. I helped him up, with a low-profile little grip on his right hand that put his wrist in such a bind that he would have done just about anything I'd asked him to do. But from any distance, it looked like I was helping him up, maybe giving him a hand in case he'd sprained his ankle or something.

When I told him to pick up his paper sack, he was only too happy to do that for me. He wanted to give it to me, but I told him I thought he should carry it, and he did. We went back to apartment 118, and he unlocked the door.

When we got inside, I didn't let go of him until I'd kicked over one of the two barstools sitting at a counter and looked at the underside of it to make sure he didn't have anything along the line of a weapon secreted there. Then he put the stool back on its feet for me, and I sat him on it.

"Put your hands on top of your head," I told him. "Interlock your fingers. Now rotate your hands until they're palms up."

I frisked him and everything he could reach to make sure there were no guns or knives lying around, and then picked up the sack he had left on the floor. There were four VHS videotapes inside, along with an old cash-register receipt from Tom Thumb.

"Who are you?" he asked.

"Edwin Meese. I'm committed to stamping out pornography."

"Well, look, Ed . . . there's been some kind of a misunderstanding here."

Sarcasm is lost on some people, even irony.

"I'd say you did the misunderstanding, Freddy."

"No, Ed, I mean it. I don't know what you've been told, but that ain't no pornography there."

"Isn't it?"

"No, man. It's just . . . you know, home movies."

"Let's see."

High tech I am not, but even I can operate a VCR. The first of the four tapes I played was a dead ringer for the one Eddie Cochran had showed me in his hospital room. The next one had more stuff on it, a couple of minutes of a football game at the start, and quite a bit of give-and-take between my man Freddy and little Liz. They walked into the picture and she was shaking her head, like she was dizzy or something, and they talked for a minute or two before old Freddy made his move. He yanked her around a bit, getting her out of her clothes, and then he pinned her down on the bed, making sure her face was turned so the camera would get it. From there on, it looked about the same.

Tape three was just like the second one, with the football and everything. Number four was a duplicate of the first, with the organized sports left out.

"Nice," I said, showing Freddy a disgusted look. He was so stupid I could see that he thought for a moment that I really meant it. "Is this it?"

"What?"

"Is this all of it? Or do you have some more of these stashed around here someplace?"

"Of her, you mean?"

"Yeah. For now, let's just stick to this young lady."

"Nah, man. That's it. I got this phone call, see . . ."

"Really?"

"Yeah. I thought maybe . . . it was you, right?"

"You catch on pretty quick."

"So I was . . . uh . . . I was . . ."

"You were hauling ass, Freddy. That's what you were doing."

Freddy looked down at the floor, or maybe his lap. And I found myself wondering how this dud managed to pull off the seductions his racket relied on. Maybe there was something about his looks. He was tall and slim, not bad-looking in a dark and slithery way young girls might go for. Or it might be he had good drugs, and that was all it took. Hell, maybe kids like Liz weren't afraid of him because he was so stupid.

"Stand up for me, Freddy. And keep your hands on top of your head just like that."

"You're gonna kill me, ain't you, Ed?"

"We'll see. It depends on whether you lie to me or not."

CHAPTER 7

I didn't carry a gun, because it's not allowed in Texas. Contrary to what a lot of people expect when they come to the Lone Star State, we do not normally go about on the street with six-guns strapped to our hips. Other than people on their own property, only cops, security guards on duty, and sportsmen in some cases are allowed to go heeled. P.I.'s are not included, and there's no such thing as a permit. So, once Freddy got up off his stool, if he wanted to take his hands down off his head and try something, it would have been an even chance for him. Maybe a little better than even, since he was a good ten or fifteen years my junior and looked to be in pretty good shape. I was pushing forty, had a birthday coming up, and I'd been nursing a bad back as a memento of my police service. But I didn't figure Freddy for a fighter, not when it came to a grown man, and he didn't disappoint me. Of course, if he thought I might have a piece in my pocket, I didn't go out of my way to disabuse him of the notion.

Freddy showed me around his place, and it didn't take long. There was just the little combination living room–breakfast nook with the portable TV and the two VCRs, along with the barstools and a beige sofa that looked like a rental, a small kitchen, and the bedroom. That part looked familiar, from looking at Freddy's videos.

The bed was full-sized, with a laminated pressboard headboard that showed too much wear and tear. I pulled back the mattress to check between it and the box springs, and saw that he had cotton clothesline tied off on either side of the headboard.

"You charge any extra for the bondage routine, Freddy? Or is that just a personal preference?"

"Aw, man . . ."

"Aw what, Freddy?"

"It ain't like you think, Ed. . . . Some of the girls, they ask for that kind of stuff. They like it. You'd be surprised."

"I'd be flabbergasted. What's that, your closet?"

"Yeah."

"Let's have a look."

That was a waste of time. There wasn't even enough crap in the walk-in to make a mess. That left a dresser that stood a few feet from the foot of the bed, up against a wall. It had a mirror on it. When Freddy lay in bed, he could see himself in the dresser mirror, and I imagined he liked that.

Freddy opened the dresser drawers for me while I watched his hands, in case he wanted to reach into one of the drawers quickly and come out with a surprise. But I had my bluff in on him, and he didn't try anything. Besides, there was nothing in the drawers that would have been of any use to him, just his collection of men's bikini briefs in every color you could imagine, some socks, and a short stack of girlie magazines, a couple of them the kind that specialize in what they like to call "bondage and discipline."

I'd already seen Freddy's rather limited wardrobe hanging in his closet, and a quick check of the bathroom turned up nothing more ominous than the usual shaving equipment and some very heavy cheap cologne.

That left the kitchen, with a refrigerator fully stocked with TV dinners and beer. In the cabinets, I found just less than a full set of cheap dishes, assorted glasses of the kind Tom Thumb sells, and several bags of potato chips.

I lit a cigarette and looked Freddy over. Doing a little figuring, I realized that the kitchen pantry shared a common wall with the bedroom, and opened that door. There was his camera, all set up on a tripod and ready to go. I motioned for him to go in ahead of me, and we just about had room to fit in the narrow space.

There was nothing very sophisticated about it. The camera looked like a run-of-the-mill consumer job, about eight hundred dollars retail. Freddy had bored a hole in the wall twice the size of the camera lens, and when I turned out the light and closed the door, we had a clear view of Freddy's bed through the mirror atop his dresser. It was one of those one-way jobs, a mirror on one side and a window from the other. I knew of three or four places in town that sold them, as "security mirrors."

With the light back on and the door still closed, I listened to Freddy breathing for a minute or so. There was nothing else in the pantry, no normal supplies or blank tapes, or anything else that made it look like he had any plans to use the rig again any time soon. I asked him to open the camera up, and he did. There wasn't any tape inside.

"You getting ready to move, Freddy?"

"Huh? . . . no. No, I ain't gittin' ready to move. Why would you ask me something like that?"

"Let's just say I find it hard to believe you're this neat a housekeeper. How long have you been living here?"

"Huh? Uh . . . about six months, I guess."

"Let me give you a little tip, Freddy." I blew smoke at him, and he ducked. "Every time you lie, you say 'Huh' first. It's kind of a giveaway."

"Huh? I mean . . ."

"Never mind. Let's step outside of your office for a minute."

I nudged him through the kitchen back around to the barstool and let him lean against the stool while I mulled things over.

"You gonna whack me now?" he asked.

"Whack you? Where'd you get that expression?"

"Uh . . . I dunno. TV, I guess. I watch a lot of TV."

"Really?"

"Uh-huh. Cable, mostly."

"I see. Where's your dope?"

"Huh? My what?"

"I'll tell you what, shithead. Just don't lie to me anymore until you learn to do it better. Now up your goddamned dope!"

"Huh? I mean, I don't know . . . I don't have any. . . ."

"I'll make you an offer you can't refuse, understand?" I figured he'd seen *The Godfather* a couple of times. "I said, do you understand?"

"I getcha."

"Okay. Here's the deal: I'm going to go into your bathroom and yank down your shower-curtain rod and look inside it. Then I'm going to take the lid off your toilet and look around. If I find drugs in there . . ."

"You're gonna whack me, right?"

"You said that, I didn't."

"Okay, okay. I'll get it for you."

I followed him into the bathroom, and sure enough, he had his stash wrapped up in a couple of sealed Baggies hanging on a string in the toilet bowl. A real mental giant. I let him unwrap the wet part, then took the little treasure from him. I found myself holding what must have been a couple hundred tablets snuggled in a plastic Baggie. The tabs were peach-colored, with a tinge of red at each end. I hadn't seen any like them before. I couldn't make out any lettering or logos on them, but I didn't have my glasses with me, and I wasn't going to take my eyes off Freddy long enough to eyeball them any closer. I palmed a couple of them, then handed the rest back to Freddy.

"What the hell are these?" I asked.

"I don't know," he said, without the telltale "Huh" preamble.

"Where did you get them?"

"A friend gave 'em to me."

"Of course he did."

"I swear."

"And you don't know what they are?"

"Some kind of designer stuff."

"What kind?"

"Ecstasy, I guess. Something like that. You know, like 'Eve' and stuff. There's always new kinds comin' out."

I knew he was right about that, but I didn't think these tabs were any of the ordinary street stuff. That kind of thing was usually a piece of shit, rough-looking, like somebody'd just pounded it out on a stovetop at home. These babies looked much nicer than that, well made, smoothly finished, like a real company somewhere had put them together. I figured somebody'd scored a diverted shipment of medical supplies somewhere along the line.

"What are you going to do with them?" I asked, looking stern.

"Huh? I, uh . . . I don't know."

"Think about it."

"I, uh . . ." He shifted from one foot to the other, then back. "I . . . I could . . . flush 'em?"

"You know, Freddy, I think that's a very good idea. Mind you, this is your dope, and I'm not telling you what to do with it. But if you decided to flush these things down your toilet there, I think that would be a good idea."

"Okay."

I watched him dump the tablets and push the handle, as tears welled up in his eyes. He wiped his eyes with the backs of his hands, and then he looked up at me as if he thought his life might be over, one way or the other.

"Now, let me see your driver's license."

He had quit trying to figure out why I asked him things, so he just took his license out of his hip pocket and showed it to me. I jotted down his full name and address, plus his D.O.B. and the D.L. number, just in case, and gave it back to him. Then I asked him what kind of car he drove, and he did not lie about that. He told me it was the blue Civic in the lot outside. The shaky tone of his voice convinced me that Freddy didn't think he would ever see the little blue Honda again.

"You understand I'm going to take these with me, don't you, Freddy?" I asked him, pointing to the videos in the grocery sack.

He nodded.

"And you don't have any problem with that, do you?"

He shook his head.

"Good. Then there's only one more thing to do."

I thought he was going to start blubbering on me right there. I patted him on the shoulder.

"Take it easy, Freddy. Do like I say and you won't feel a thing."

"Oh, Jesus," he whimpered. "I won't feel a thing."

"Go in the closet."

He let me show him the way to his own closet, and his knees buckled with every step. He was crying now, and there was snot blubbering on his lip.

"Put this on, Freddy," I told him, handing him a pillowcase. "Over your head."

"Over my h-e-e-a-ad," he blubbered, doing as he was told. "Now lie down right here."

When he was prone on the floor of his closet, I told him to count backward from one hundred. It was quite a while before he got started. I finally had to prompt him, but by about ninety-five he was getting the hang of it.

I interrupted him at eighty-five to ask him a question or two, because there was something about him and his setup that bothered me.

"Who's in this with you?"

He jumped like a fish, his hands covering his head, and choked off a half-assed little scream I was afraid a neighbor might have heard. Apparently, he thought I'd already left.

I got him calmed down and asked him the question again. I lost my patience when he started his usual stammering around, and gave him a sharp little toe-kick in the short ribs. He didn't complain.

"Guy's name is Lee."

"Lee who?"

"I honest-to-God don't know, Ed."

The poor son of a bitch was probably telling the truth. I mean, he was dumb enough to think I was Ed Meese, why should it occur to him to ask the man he's in business with his last name?

"How long you been in this racket?"

"I ain't much good at dates and stuff, Ed. We've done maybe four or five girls."

"How does it work?"

"When I get one, I call him. He tells me where to meet him, and I deliver the tapes. That's all."

"Does he pay you in cash or dope?"

"Usually cash. Dope the last time."

"How about this time, for the blonde on these tapes?"

"Special instructions this time. I'm supposed to sit on 'em, wait for him to call me back."

"And all you know is 'Lee'?"

"Swear to God, Ed. He's some kinda Occidental."

"What? He's some kind of what?"

"Occidental . . . you know, Chinese or something."

"You mean Oriental."

"If you say so, Ed."

"How did a copy of the tape wind up in this girl's room? That's not usually part of the drill, is it?"

"Nope. Special instructions, again. When I dropped her off, I put a copy of the tape in through the mail slot in the front door after she went inside."

"Do you have any idea why all the special instructions this time?"

"I swear to God I don't, Ed. You've got to believe me."

"Any more special instructions?"

"No, that's it."

"And there aren't any more copies of this tape anywhere?"

"You've got the whole works right there. Swear to God."

I hadn't known what to expect from this deal, but I didn't like what I'd found. Maybe I'd been hoping Freddy would turn out to be something simple, a pervert building a collection, so there wouldn't be any loose ends.

"One more thing, Freddy."

"Yeah?"

"If you do as I say and count and everything, I'm not going to hurt you. But I can't say as much for your Chinese friend, Mister Lee. So, if I were you, I'd be awfully careful for a while. He might be pissed at you over all this. Do you understand?"

"You're not gonna whack me?"

"Not if you keep counting."

"Aw shit, I'm a goner!"

"What's the matter, Freddy?"

"I've lost track on my count, Ed. I can't remember where I left off."

"Just start over at one hundred."

"Okay. Thanks."

"Don't mention it."

I closed the closet door and left him counting into his pillowcase, as confident as I could be without actually killing him that he wouldn't rush to a window and get my tag number as I drove away.

CHAPTER
8

I found a 7-Eleven on my way back to the office and checked in with Della from a pay phone. Surprisingly, she'd had no problem getting in touch with Speed, and my jerky little friend was supposed to be on his way to my office to meet me, she said. I told her I wouldn't be long.

It was a little after nine on a Thursday morning, so Central Expressway would have been almost passable if they hadn't finally started work on widening it. As it was, one of the two inbound lanes was closed, so I got off at University and worked my way down Greenville Avenue to Ross and finally over to Gaston and let Eddie Cochran know how things were going.

I found my way through Baylor's bustling maze of corridors and busy people without having to resort to any of the YOU ARE HERE computerized displays that are supposed to show you how to get where you're going if you'll just type in the pertinent information. I don't get along well with anything that's computerized, and when they say "user friendly," they do not mean me.

The whole trip was a waste anyway, because I found Eddie's

bed empty, and a nurse told me that they had him off in a body shop somewhere tinkering with his cast. She assured me he wouldn't be back for over an hour, and then he wouldn't be feeling like having company. I asked her to tell him I'd been by, that he could call me when he felt up to it. She said with a smile that she would give him my message, and suggested in a very friendly and helpful way that next time I might want to call before I came visiting. I made a note of the number on the phone in Eddie's room, and thanked her for the good advice.

All in all, I'd had a pretty busy and even productive morning, and by the time I got back to my office, I was already thinking about lunch. It was only half past ten, but I hadn't had any breakfast.

Speed and Della were deep in conversation when I stepped off the elevator, and I could tell they had been talking about me by the way they tried to act casual when they looked up and saw me. It's not easy to act casual when you're not, and they didn't fool me for a minute.

"Morning, Speed." I smiled as I watched him try to figure out what to do with himself. "Good to see you."

"You, too, Jack. You're looking good."

"How's Leslie?"

"Fine. Sends you her love."

"You two aren't spatting or anything?"

"Now and then, you know, keeping things spicy. And you?"

"And me what? Am I spatting? Who the hell with?"

"Guess that answers my question. Still going solo, huh?"

I was at the coffeepot by this point, and I gave Speed a bit of the eye.

"Speed," Della chimed in, "I didn't know you were trying to fix him up."

"Me? Not exactly . . ." Speed shrugged and showed us his palms, like he was pleading Not Guilty to something.

"Well, I think somebody should," she added, smiling impishly.

"I need fixing up?" I asked them both. "What am I, a bungalow? A little fixer-upper, a diamond in the rough?"

"A project," Speed offered.

"Yeah, well let's talk about something else," I insisted. "Because, for the record, I wouldn't go out with a woman who would be seen with me."

"Sounds like a torch song," Speed stage-whispered to Della behind his hand.

"The only torch I'm carrying is for old Della here," I announced, patting her on the head as she sat allegedly trying to type something. "She's the only girl for me. Fortunately for both of us, she's got too much taste to have anything to do with me."

"Ah, Jack," she teased. "How can you say that?"

"With a lump in my throat, kid. Now get to work. Speed, let's you and me get out of a working girl's way. Let's take a meeting."

Speed and Della shared a grin like they knew something I didn't, and Speed followed me into my office. As I closed my door, I heard Della's machine clacking away and what sounded like her humming something, but I couldn't make out the tune.

"What are you two cooking up?" I demanded of Speed.

"Who two? I just got here."

"Whatever it is, forget about it," I warned.

"Whatever you say, Jack."

"Right. Now, to business. You got a little time on your hands?"

"For you, of course. Besides, I could use the money."

"So could I, but there isn't any. I'm talking volunteer work on this one."

"How much time, and who's the beneficiary?"

"Not much time, and we're doing a favor for Eddie Cochran."

"What's the payback?"

"He owes me a big favor, I owe you a little one. Good enough?"

"Sounds right. What's the deal?"

"Some pretty nasty videos. I need to be sure I've got the original."

"That's it?"

"Far as I know. It's not a problem?"

"How sure do you have to be? Ninety-five percent, or metaphysical certainty?"

"Somewhere in between."

"You have the tapes?"

"They're in the trunk of my car. I don't like wagging them around."

"Makes sense. I'll make a couple of calls, Jack."

"Use my phone."

I let him slide into my chair behind the desk, and left him looking through an address book he pulled out of a jacket pocket while I stepped out into the foyer to have a word with Della.

She was still typing, but she stopped when she felt me standing behind her.

"Yes?"

"I want to know what you two are up to," I said. "You and Speed."

"Jack, he's your friend. I was just entertaining him while he waited for you. What are you talking about?"

"All this talk about fixing me up. It makes me nervous, and I don't like it."

"Then I won't talk about it anymore. Okay?"

"And you won't do anything about it, either. Right?"

"I don't know what you're talking about, Jack. But if it makes you feel any better, I'll swear an oath."

She went back to her typing. Maybe I had been wrong about little Della. Maybe she could lie with the best of them.

The door of my office opened, and Speed stuck his head out, my phone under his chin.

"Jack, when do you want to do this?"

"Now's good."

"Okay."

The door closed again for a second, and then Speed came bouncing out.

"I'm telling you, have I got contacts, or what?" he said, preening.

"I give up. Do you have contacts?"

"Only the best. Let's go, Jack. We can get this little thing taken care of before you buy me lunch."

CHAPTER
9

The place Speed took me was out at Las Colinas, the Communications Complex. I knew about the complex, generally, that they made movies there from time to time, but I hadn't been inside the place before.

We parked around behind one wing, in front of a tall, long building Speed told me was a soundstage. Then he led me, carrying my videotapes in Freddy's grocery sack, into what turned out to be a two-story office complex.

"Lots of producers, all kinds of movers and shakers, have offices out here," Speed assured me as we climbed a flight of stairs. "Talent agents, too. You'd be surprised how many big-time projects get done out here. Features, commercials, tons of industrial films. Dallas is third in the nation for making commercials, you know. Behind only New York and L.A."

"I didn't know. Where the hell are you taking me?"

"Hold your horses. We're going to see a friend of mine."

I followed him through a door that had no name on it, only some kind of a fancy-shmancy logo I couldn't make out.

"Anybody home?" Speed sang out as he made his way past an empty desk and through another door.

"Back here," came a voice out of nowhere.

Back we went, until we came to another door, this one marked with a sign that read POST. Speed knocked, and the same voice invited us in. It was a big, deep voice.

When we went through the door, I caught sight of the guy the voice belonged to, and it was no mismatch. He looked at us through a pair of glasses that had worked their way down onto the bridge of his nose, and then he started uncoiling out of his chair. By the time he was through standing up, I guessed he was all of six-six, a barrel-chested guy with a full blond beard and a friendly smile. A man that big can afford to be affable.

"Jack Kyle, this is my friend Dave MacDougal. They call him 'Big Mac.'"

"Makes sense to me. Pleased to meet you."

"Charmed. You guys bring the whiskey?"

"Speed?" I turned to my companion.

"All things in due time, Mac." Speed was smiling and shaking his head, like he thought this big guy was quite a kidder, all right.

Myself, I prefer to take big men at their word. If Speed had promised this man a bottle of whiskey for doing us a favor, I was all for making a quick dash to the nearest liquor store.

"Speed," I said. "If we owe Mac a bottle . . ."

"First things first, Jack. For heaven's sake. Mac, here's the deal. . . . Like I told you over the phone, we have some tapes, and we need to know if one of them is the original, the master. It'll just take you a second. It'll be fun, kinda."

"Fun I dub off and keep a copy for my personal amusement. Shit I have to give back, that's work."

I thought the big man had a point.

"Okay, okay. I tell you what. We'll do lunch as soon as you finish, and drinks till you drop. Jack's treat." Speed smiled. "Right, Jack?"

"I think I might come out cheaper if I just buy a fifth."

"All right, goddammit. Enough haggling. Let's see what you brought me," Big Mac growled.

Mac took the tapes out of the sack I offered him and popped two of them into slots on a machine in front of him. He punched some switches, and both tapes started playing at the same time on two screens.

With a couple of dials, he'd slow first one tape and then the other, freezing one for a couple of seconds to look at it, then reversing it and playing a scene through again. When he'd seen enough, he popped those two tapes out and replaced them in the two player slots with the remaining tapes. More of the same, back and forth, the two sets of images, until I lost interest.

I stepped outside the big man's workroom, and made sure there was an ashtray on the nearest desk before I lit a cigarette. There were only three of the ultralite 100s left in the pack, and I made a mental note to stop on the way back to my office to pick up a couple of packs.

I had just stubbed my butt out when the door opened and out stepped the big man, my four tapes in one of his hands.

"I marked the master for you," he said. "It's a piece of shit, looks like it was shot with a little home camcorder. From the grayish tint, I'd say whoever did this probably shot it through a mirror, or a piece of glass of some kind."

"Yeah," I said. "That all fits. You're sure that one's the original."

"That's what I said."

"Okay. Any way of knowing how many copies were made?"

"Sure." Big Mac gave me a patient smile as he lit a cigarette of his own. "Find the cameraman and beat the shit out of him until he tells you."

"Good idea. Thanks."

"No problem."

Speed wanted to show me all the equipment in the place,

but I had no time for that. Then he wanted Big Mac to show him all the crap he didn't know how to operate, and I made them an offer. I showed them a couple of twenties. Speed could stay and play as long as he liked, then Mac would drop him off at his car back at my office. It wasn't far. The Communications Complex is on Royal Lane just off Stemmons, and my office is in a little square on LBJ between Josey and Webb Chapel. With the forty bucks, they could do lunch, buy whiskey, or whatever the hell they wanted. The two of them agreed to my idea, and I left them squabbling over how to spend the money as I found my way out of the building and back to my car.

I broke a $10 bill at a 7-Eleven on my way back to the office to take advantage of their special three-pack offer that came to about $6.50 with tax. It was the last of my ready cash, and all I had left was the fifty bucks I try to keep stashed in the trunk of my car. I used to try to keep a hundred there for emergencies, but business hadn't been that good lately. I was owed about four hundred for the surveillance job I'd just finished, but the first of the month was only a week or so away, and that meant rent on my office was due and my child-support payment, too. My in-laws were much nicer about that than my ex-wife had ever been, and I knew that whatever I sent them probably went into a bank account for the kid. They could afford to pay for whatever Little Jack needed, and they were crazy about him. I'd have to take a look at my checking account and see how short I was going to be on the first. This thing I was doing for Eddie Cochran was not going to help my finances any, and besides, it was tying me up, which meant I wasn't available for a paying job if one came along.

Back at the office, Della handed me a couple of phone messages. Eddie Cochran had called, and wanted me to call him as soon as I got in. Carol had called, too, wanting to know if I had anything for her yet. I called Eddie first.

"How's everything going up there in the lap of luxury?" I asked him.

"Lovely, Jack. You ought to try it sometime."

"I'll put it on my list of things to do."

I'd spent my share of time in hospitals for this and that, one kind of trauma or another. I had a pretty good idea how restless and helpless Eddie felt.

"Have you come up with anything yet?" he asked.

"Is this phone okay?" I wanted to know. What I had done with Freddy was perfectly kosher by my way of thinking, but I knew that someone with a more rigidly legalistic view of things might think otherwise, and I wasn't interested in giving up any details on a party line. "You don't have somebody on a switchboard listening in, do you?"

"Nah, it's a direct line. Your line's more likely to be monitored than this one. What've you got?"

"Four tapes, and one of them's the original. I had an expert look at 'em to make sure."

"Christ, Jack, I didn't want you showing the damned thing around all over town."

"And I didn't. But we had to be sure we had the master tape, and it's hard to tell if I don't let anybody see 'em. I damned sure can't tell by looking."

"Okay, I know. Where are the tapes now?"

"I have them. You want them?"

"Nah. Give them to Carol. Or burn 'em in front of her. Have you heard from her yet?"

"She called while I was out."

"Yeah, it figures. This thing's driving her crazy."

"Really?"

"Of course, really. What are you getting at?"

"Nothing in particular. She just seemed pretty calm about the whole thing last night, that's all." Carol had seemed pretty calm, period. Almost disinterested. "Maybe that's just the way she is with strangers."

"I don't know about that, but I can tell you this hasn't been easy for her."

"What do you know about the brother?" I asked.

"Who?"

"Liz's brother. What was his name?"

"Alan. He died last year."

"Yeah. On his eighteenth birthday, I understand."

"That's right."

"Some kind of heart condition. Something congenital."

"Yeah, that was what the medical examiner ruled."

"Not a suicide?"

"No, a natural. Carol took it hard as hell."

"I can imagine. Why was there a question about it?"

"Pretty unusual, a kid that age dying of a heart attack."

"I guess it is."

"What are you getting at?"

"Maybe it has something to do with Liz playing the wild child. You said she'd been pretty quiet until her brother died, right?"

"Maybe. But she's been checked out, Jack. There's nothing wrong with her heart."

"How about Carol?"

"How about her heart, you mean?"

"Yeah," I said. But I was interested in more than Carol's heart. Put another way, I was interested in more about her heart than just would it keep beating. "The boy inherited the bad heart from somebody."

"Carol's healthy as can be, and so's her dad. Her mother passed away a long time ago. There may be a connection there."

"What does he do?"

"Who?"

"Carol's dad. Is he retired?"

"Hell, no. He's some kind of scientific wizard. Invents crap you and I've never heard of, stuff that's worth millions. He's got more patents than Bell Labs."

"Who?"

"Never mind, Jack. Just stick to business. Get those tapes to Carol and put her mind at ease. Do that for me, will you? And as soon as possible."

"Sure. I'll give her a call."

"I appreciate it, man. You'll never know how much."

"Don't mention it."

I called the number Carol had left with Della, comparing it at the same time with my notes from our conversation the night before. It was her home number, the one she called her "direct line," to distinguish it I supposed from the kids' phones or maybe the published main number. People with money fascinated me, and I was constantly picking up little things like that about them.

Carol answered and sounded relieved about the tapes. She wanted to know if I'd bring them right over to her house, and I assured her I would. It was almost noon, and I was thinking there might be a free lunch in it.

CHAPTER
10

Carol met me at the door at about half-past twelve and showed me into a study off the main hallway. The house was quiet, and there was no sign of Liz or her odd little friend, Syd-with-a-*y*.

Carol didn't look as if she'd been out of bed very long, but of course we all had been up late the night before. She was wearing a dressing gown that was probably real silk, with matching shoes, the kind I had learned from my ex-wife back before our problems got deadly were called "mules," backless, strapless high-heeled jobs. These particular mules had bows on them, and showed Carol's very nicely manicured and polished toes. Her hair looked okay, and I knew that wasn't as simple as it looked, even with her short do. She was wearing just enough of the right kind of makeup that she looked perfect in a natural, unmadeup way.

She sat in an expensive but comfortable-looking chair in front of a fireplace in which the firewood had been replaced with a brightly colored floral arrangement more in keeping with the season. And she offered me coffee, which I accepted and she poured into a china cup from a sterling-silver set on a matching tray. At her direction, I settled onto the corner of a sofa facing her across what looked like a very expensive Oriental rug.

"You have the tapes?" she asked.

"Yes."

"In that sack?"

"Yes. There are four of them, the original and three copies."

"You're sure that's all the copies that were made?"

"Counting the one you found in Liz's room, reasonably sure. There's no way to be positive."

"There isn't?"

"No, there's no way to tell from looking at the master how many copies were made. Not that I know of."

"I see."

She sipped her coffee and I drank mine, wondering if she'd already eaten. There was music, soft and unobtrusive, something with strings and not a lot of drama to it.

"The master's marked," I offered, Carol having lapsed into a silence that seemed oblivious of me and featured a bit of lip-chewing. "Freddy, the man who made the tape, had two VCRs in his apartment. That's all he would need to make the copies. There are no edits in the copies; he just left out some of the nonvital stuff that went before on the master. Kind of tidied it up."

"What are you trying to tell me?" she asked, studying the cup and saucer perched on her lap.

"That there's nothing in the tapes to indicate that anyone else was involved. No high-tech editing gear was used, so the logical assumption is that Freddy was the only one who'd seen the tapes. He hadn't delivered them yet."

"Why not?" she asked, looking up. As if realizing she'd asked the wrong question, or asked her questions out of order, she rushed to add, "Delivered them to whom?"

"An Oriental guy named Lee," I said, taking the second

question first. "That's all I was able to find out about him."

"I see."

"Does that name mean anything to you?"

"It's a very common name."

"How about the Asian angle, generally?"

"I don't follow you."

"The two men last night in the Art Bar, one of them wearing what looked to me like gang colors. They seemed to have some kind of business with Liz. You didn't know either of them?"

"Of course not."

"Or about their connection with Liz?"

"Of course not."

"Please, Carol, don't keep saying that."

"What?"

"'Of course not.' It implies that I'm asking dumb questions."

"Sorry. I hadn't realized . . ." Her voice trailed off; then she brightened a bit and looked up at me with a smile. "Are you hungry, Mister Kyle?"

"I told you last night, it's just Jack. And now that you mention it, I could do with a bite."

"Lois is doing the marketing, I'm afraid."

"Lois?"

"My housekeeper. I could make you something."

"I wouldn't want you to bother. Really, I'm fine. I'll grab a bite later."

"It's no bother. Let me just see what we have."

She set her cup and saucer down on the tray and stood, then swirled out of the room. If the look on her face as she went through a door into her kitchen meant she was surprised that I had risen and followed her, I didn't let that stop me. I was in no mood for a break in the action, because I had a couple more questions for her.

She padded across the tiled floor and tugged open the door of a refrigerator of the kind I thought only restaurants use. It was taller than she was, stainless steel, with more space in it than a couple of places I've lived in. There were only about enough groceries inside to feed a squad of hungry men after a hard day's work.

"Anything strike your fancy?" she asked, looking back at me over her shoulder as she bent from the waist in front of the racks of food. "Stir your appetite, I mean?"

From where I was standing, Carol was mostly the nice smile and her slender hips, the silk of her robe clinging and cleaving very nicely as she rested her hands on her knees and waited for me to say something. She gave the impression that she was in no hurry for me to make up my mind.

"The rump roast looks nice," I said.

She looked where I was looking and reached into the big box to withdraw a serving plate with some kind of beef wrapped in clear plastic. Straightening a bit, she examined it.

"I don't think it's a rump," she said. "A standing rib roast, I think."

"That'll do fine," I assured her. "I'm used to being ribbed."

I watched, still holding my cup and saucer, while she fumbled around unwrapping the meat, then pawed through a couple of drawers before finding a knife. When she put a finger to her lips and wondered aloud where the bread would be, I took over for her. The bread was in the bread-box, and I hacked off a slab of roast and made a sandwich. It went down all right with the lukewarm coffee, and she made a point of watching me eat the first couple of bites.

"So the two Asians in the Art Bar, the jacket with the logo, an Oriental named Lee—none of this means anything to you?" I mumbled around a mouthful of food.

"Of course . . . No. Not a thing."

"How about Freddy Barksdale? The name sound familiar?"

"No."

"He's a dunce, midtwenties. I don't imagine he ever went to

a school you or your kids would have heard of. If he's ever worked, it would have been something menial."

"I've never heard of him."

"He might possibly have been a deliveryman, maybe a gardener's helper, may have mowed your lawn, something like that?"

"No." She folded her arms across her chest. "Why all these questions?"

"I'm thinking maybe he knew Liz from somewhere, at least may have known of her, who she is."

"I don't see why."

"Because if he didn't, then his making the tapes of her is just a coincidence. A blind-chance kind of deal."

"What's wrong with that?"

"I don't care for coincidence. It makes me anxious."

"I see."

"I don't suppose he might have known your son?"

"Alan? Certainly not."

"Alan didn't attend public schools, I suppose."

"Hardly." She was gnawing her lip again. "Not because we had money, Mister . . . Jack. It wasn't simply that we're snobs, although I imagine we are, if it comes to that."

"Nothing wrong with snobbishness," I assured her. "I hope to be a rich snob myself someday."

"Alan was a special student. A special person, as a matter of fact."

She didn't look as if she planned to explain that, and I knew there were a lot of things that could make a kid special, some good and some bad.

"Special in what way, Carol?"

"A genius. His mind was . . . remarkable."

I'd finished my sandwich and would have liked a refill on my coffee, but she seemed to be pulling all her answers out of some deep well of thought or memory, and I didn't want to distract her.

"What kind of genius?" I asked.

"I beg your pardon?"

"There are all kinds. Was he a musical prodigy, a math whiz, what?"

"I'm not sure I understood it. But he worked with the Doctor even as a child. He understood what the Doctor was about, and by the time he was a teenager, he was working with him regularly. To see him in a normal school, even a very good school . . . it was like watching Einstein try to make change for a dollar. Do you know what I mean? So beneath him, he couldn't bring himself down to it . . . as if he didn't even understand why he was being bothered with something so pedestrian."

"Who's the Doctor?"

"Oh, yes. You don't know about him, do you? He's my father. That's what we call him, the Doctor."

"But he doesn't practice medicine."

"Not directly."

"I beg your pardon?" Now it was my turn to be confused. "What does that mean?"

"He does research. I haven't a clue what it's all about, but some of it has medical applications. I suppose I meant that he practices medicine indirectly. Something like that."

"Oh."

"Would you like some more coffee?"

"Yes, thank you."

Back we trooped into the study, me lugging the grocery sack full of videotapes.

"Thank you again," I said, as she poured me another cup from the fancy serving rig. "I hope I haven't imposed."

"Not at all."

"Is anything the matter? I mean, besides the obvious business at hand."

"Why do you ask?"

"You seem a little . . . distracted. Like you have something on your mind. Is it anything I can help you with?"

"Distracted . . . do I? How rude of me. I'm very sorry."

"You needn't be. There's nothing I don't know about that I need to know?"

"Of course not. I'm sorry if I've given you that impression."

"Stop apologizing. I was just wondering. I'm too suspicious sometimes."

We both heard a car pull into the drive outside.

"That will be Lois," Carol said.

"I hope she won't mind that I trespassed in her kitchen."

"Of course not."

"Well, you have the tapes, so I guess my job's done. What do you intend to do with them?"

"Destroy them, of course."

"Yes, I thought you would. Actually, what I meant was how do you plan to do that?"

"I hadn't thought that far ahead."

"Okay. You could yank out the tapes, take them out of the cassettes, cut them up, and burn them. Or you could just dump the whole works in a fire, for that matter. Would you like me to do it for you?"

"No, I'll do it. Liz and I will do it."

"Sounds like a good idea." I put down my cup and stood to go. "Well, then, if there's nothing else I can do for you . . ."

"No, you've done such a great deal already." She stood to see me out. "Are you sure I couldn't give you some money? I know your time is valuable."

"Not particularly. Besides, Eddie's a good friend. This was a favor."

"I understand. Thank you."

There are people who swear you can tell when a person is lying by watching the pupils of their eyes. The pupils are supposed to dilate when a lie is told. Maybe I should start wearing my glasses when I talk to people on a deal like this. Being farsighted, I need glasses to read, and apparently to study the pupils of someone's eyes, too. Because I had not been able to make anything out of Carol's eyes during our little conversation. Maybe I'd been trying a little too hard, staring into her eyes too much. Maybe that kind of eye contact had put her off, and that was why she was coming across as so spacey or preoccupied. But I'd always wondered about the eyeball lie-detector deal anyway. The worst lies I had been told were more matters of things being left out than of something untrue being said. And Carol hadn't talked about a couple of things I would have expected to be foremost in her mind. Eddie Cochran was just one of them.

A small ruckus in the kitchen brought me up short in the open door, and I followed Carol down the hall and back into the kitchen to see what was up.

Lois the housekeeper was standing in a mess. The bottom of a bag of groceries lying on the floor was leaking what looked like the yolks of a couple dozen eggs. She stood with her hands on her hips and her eyes closed. I think she was counting to ten. I also thought the reason the groceries were on the floor was because I'd left the platter of roast on the counter. From the physical evidence, I'd have guessed that when Lois put her first bag on the counter, the platter was in her way, and the whole works had gone tumbling. What was left of the standing rib roast was visible among the shards that were all that was left of the platter.

Carol made a big fuss over Lois, trying to calm her down. I started to help pick things up, but Lois, giving me a baleful look, waved me off. It was a few minutes before everything got squared away, and Lois was mopping the accident scene when I finally introduced myself and apologized.

"Don't worry. No problem," she said.

"And I don't blame you," I assured her. "My name's Jack Kyle. What's yours?"

"My name's Lois," she said.

Only she pronounced it "Rois." The L-sound in English is tough for most Orientals.

"Lois what?" I asked.

"Lois Li," she said, smiling and accepting my handshake as if to show that there were no hard feelings.

CHAPTER
11

The time I'd spent in Southeast Asia had not been exactly a research expedition, but I'd picked up a thing or two without having to try very hard. Among other things, I knew that Lee (it was usually spelled Li) was one of the most common names in that part of the world. First name or last name, I'd known a few hundred Lis in my two tours. It was like Smith or Jones. So there was no reason to believe that Carol's housekeeper had anything to do with Freddy's "Occidental" by the same name. I knew that. What I didn't like was that Carol hadn't mentioned Lois when I was grilling her about the other Li and the whole Asian angle. She'd seemed distracted, all right. And maybe she took Lois so much for granted that she simply hadn't made the connection. For all I knew, Carol didn't even know Lois's last name. The way people like her operate, there was probably a bookkeeper or business manager somewhere who wrote all the checks and kept up with the details.

It wasn't actually on my way back to the office, but from Highland Park to Baylor Medical Center was not a long trip, either. It could be a time-consuming one, depending on the traffic, but it was only a few miles. And the traffic wasn't terrible for an early Thursday afternoon. It was bad, but not terrible.

At least this time Eddie Cochran was in his room when I walked in. He was red-faced and cursing a streak, but he was there.

The lady putting up with his tantrum looked up when I pushed the door open and let myself in. She decided after a quick once-over that I wasn't going to cause her any trouble and went back to watching Eddie try to get out of his wheelchair and into his bed. She wore surgical greens and was bareheaded, so I wasn't sure if she was a nurse or a doctor. She had an air about her that made me think she was one or the other, not an orderly or anybody else used to being ordered around.

It wasn't immediately clear whether Eddie was cursing her or someone who'd already left the room. Finally, I decided he was just mad at the whole situation. But when I stepped forward to give him a hand, the lady in green signaled me to leave him alone, and I did.

With a final heroic effort and a wonderfully strung-together collection of oaths, Eddie at last rolled atop his bed and lay on his back, his chest rising and falling with the effort to catch his breath.

"Pretty good," I offered, meaning to give him some encouragement.

"You!" he snorted. "How long have you been lurking over there in the shadows?"

The room was lit up like an operating arena, and the only shadow in the place was under his bed.

"Oh," I laughed, "I missed some of the show, but I guess I got my money's worth."

"Well, just go . . ."

"Mister Cochran," the lady in green cooed menacingly. "I

thought we had an agreement about the *F*-word."

"Okay, okay."

Eddie's face was almost purple, just beginning to get its color back from all the effort he'd spent getting himself into the bed. He wasn't in any mood or condition for an argument.

"My name's Jack Kyle, ma'am. And I'd like to commend you on the civilizing influence you have over my friend here."

"Nell Farmer," she said in return. "Are you the one smuggled in the whiskey?"

"Me? Of course not. Tell her, Eddie."

"I told you, Farmer. I don't know where the hell the hooch came from."

"I know what you told me, all right."

There was a clear signal in the look she gave me, though, that put me on notice that she didn't believe Eddie Cochran any farther than she could throw him, or me, either, for that matter. But she looked like she could give either of us a pretty good heave.

"You settle down now, Mister Cochran. I'll look in on you after a bit."

When she was gone, I exchanged looks with Eddie, who just closed his eyes and shook his head to show me that he had been through a rough day.

"Who was that?" I asked.

"Felonious Farmer, local Nazi. She's supposed to be a physical therapist. Goddamn, I feel like hell!"

"Is that part of your therapy, having to drag yourself back into bed?"

"Not exactly. I'm trying to get them to let me the hell out of here, and they're trying to say I'm not ready to go yet."

"Oh."

"I swear, Jack. You don't know what it's like being cooped up in one of these antiseptic goddamned places."

"The hell I don't. And you know I do, because it was you

that came to get me the day I finally got out of Parkland after Arthur Crandall gutshot me."

"I forgot about that. Don't mind me, Jack. I'm just going a little stir-crazy."

"I know how you feel." I pulled up a chair where we could talk without being too loud, and I noticed his cast had been whittled down a bit. I could see more of his torso than the night before, and the leg cast stopped at about his ankle. "What's the story on the new cast?"

"That's part of me trying to get out of here. They want to see how I get along with a little less plaster before they talk about turning me loose."

"Fine. What's your hurry, anyway?"

"I just don't like being confined like this. Never have. And . . ."

"And you miss Carol."

"You're damned right I do. You've seen her, Jack, do you blame me?"

"No, but she'll wait. Won't she?"

"Screw you."

"Watch the language, pal. I'll get Miss Farmer back in here."

"I don't guess you've forgotten how you felt about Betty, Jack."

"Okay, I get the point. Don't get archaeological on me."

"And that's how I am about Carol. She's got problems, and—"

"Never mind about that, I'm in no mood for your personal problems. Speaking of which, the tapes have been delivered, and I imagine they're all up in smoke by now, if Carol hasn't forgotten where she put 'em or how to start a fire."

"Meaning what?"

"Is she always kind of . . . I don't know, distracted?"

"Not with me," he said.

"Hell, that's probably what it was. She must have been thinking of you the whole time I was there."

"It could happen."

"Of course it could."

"Okay, so enough bullshit. What's the deal on the tapes?"

We spent the next hour or so with me telling Eddie what I'd done and where I'd been. He flinched a little on the part about the housekeeper named Lois Li, too, just like I had. But all in all, he looked like he could live with the way I had handled things.

"I can't thank you enough for taking care of this deal for me," he said. "You know I wouldn't have asked you if I hadn't been laid up like this."

"Well, you should have, whether you were healthy or not. A man in your position can't afford to go around rousting punks like Freddy over a deal like this. The sleazy shit is more in my line."

"You may be right, but you and I both know I would have gone over there myself anyway."

"Then it's a good thing that bull stepped on your dick, or whatever happened."

"It wasn't no bull, pardner." Eddie smiled. "And my dick is about the only thing that doesn't hurt. It's just lonesome."

"Again with the personal problems."

"Hell, it wasn't supposed to be any big deal. We were just doing the wild-horse event."

"Sure, that sounds safe. What were you trying to do to the poor horse, anyway?"

"Just throw a saddle on him and ride him across the finish line. Buddy had him roped."

"Buddy?"

"Jenkins. You know him, works in Traffic. He was the roper."

"Shows he's no fool."

"Anyway, I got tangled in the rope, and then this goddamned

jughead rears up, and down we all go in a heap."

"What was the best that could have happened?"

"What do you mean?"

"If you and Buddy hadn't screwed it up and the jughead hadn't reared and all the rest of it. If you'd won the deal, what would you have gotten out of it?"

"Oh, you mean the prize. It was these big championship belt buckles. As big as your fist, engraved. 'Dallas Police Department Rodeo Champion.'"

"For Pete's sake, Eddie. They sell belt buckles in stores. If I'd known you wanted a belt buckle so damned bad . . ."

"That's not the point, and you know it. Besides, it was all for a good cause. We raised a ton of money for charity."

"And I'm glad. But I still think you're a dumb-ass."

"Well, I'm in no position to argue with you about that. When I think what I could be doing right now, I tell you what."

"No, don't tell me. I get the picture. Why don't you call the woman and see if she'll come to see you. Maybe I can sneak you a cold chisel and you can knock a hole in your body cast at a strategic point. . . ."

"You obviously have no idea of the love I feel for this woman," Eddie said, looking very stern. But then he grinned. "But that doesn't sound like a bad idea."

"You're suffering from more than broken bones, pal," I said, pushing myself to my feet. "If you need anything, give me a call."

"Oh, that reminds me," Eddie said, leaning off the bed to rummage through a drawer on his nightstand. "A guy came by to see me this morning."

There had been a bunch of guys by to see Eddie since he'd been laid up. There were flowers all over his room, and he had one wall plastered with get-well cards. The desk nurse had bitched at me when I had called the afternoon before about the parade of visitors trooping up and down the corridor. Eddie had lots of friends, cops and otherwise. The crowd he drew had been one reason I'd waited till after hours to pay him a visit the day before.

"Here it is," he said, fishing out a business card. "You need to give him a call."

"What about?" I asked, taking the card. "And who's William Scheiner?"

"He's a good guy, used to be with Dallas, years ago."

"I don't make the name."

"Like I said, he's been gone a long time. The last ten or fifteen years, he's been director of security for a freight company."

"And?"

"He wants to talk to you. Give him a call."

"Could this be business?" I asked.

"Better. It could be a job. Scheiner's going to be hanging it up in a few months. Got himself a condo on a golf course down by Kerrville somewhere. So he needs a replacement. He asked me to recommend somebody, and I gave him your name."

"Ah, Eddie. I don't know about that."

"You'd make thirty a year to start. Steady work, insurance, a pension plan, the works. You like it better where you are?"

"I'm doing okay."

"Like . . . Yeah, I know you are, Jack. But you've got a birthday coming up, how old are you going to be? Forty?"

"Thirty-nine."

"Sure you are."

"No, really. I'll be thirty-nine."

"If you say so. And I guess you're making a living, but how much longer do you want to live the life? This is a real job, Jack. There'd be some travel, but nothing too heavy. And most of the time, it'd be straight days, weekends off."

"Sounds pretty dull," I said, thinking to myself that it sounded pretty good.

"And I don't want to pry into your personal business or anything, but a job like this . . . It could give you a crack at getting your kid back, couldn't it?"

He was right about that. My ex-wife had legal problems, arising from her conviction for conspiring to murder her second husband, but that was another story. The thing was, Little Jack was staying in Paris with her folks for the time being. In other words, until she got straightened out or I got myself into a position to make a life for the kid.

"Yeah," I said. "That's something to think about, I guess."

"So call him. What can it hurt?"

"You don't have to do this for me, Eddie. The tape thing, that was a favor I probably owed you already. I don't want you to think . . ."

"I don't think. Scheiner asked me for the name of a good man. Somebody who was smart, tough, and honest, with plenty of experience. So sue me, I thought of you."

CHAPTER
12

B ack at my office, I mulled over the prospect of an honest job, while I busied myself with other things and put off calling William Scheiner of American Southwest Motorfreight. I made sure my case reports and expense vouchers had been delivered to the offices of Davidson and Associates, the P.I. firm I'd done the surveillance for. I took my notebook out of the pocket of the jacket I'd hung on the back of my chair and put my notes in order. Working in longhand, I laid out all my information as if I were going to have Della type up a report for a client, although of course that would not be necessary in this case.

I kept myself busy until almost five o'clock, and then finally I called the number on the card Eddie had given me. I figured Scheiner would be on his way out, going home for the day, and we'd set something up for the next day. That would get me off the hook by letting me call the same day but I'd still have the chance to sleep on it.

Mister Scheiner answered the telephone himself, but of course I had dialed the number identified on his card as "direct." He sounded friendly enough, said he'd heard some nice things about me and wanted to meet me. I apologized for calling so late, but he said not to give it a thought. How about dinner? he asked.

Naturally, I had no plans, but I told him I wouldn't dream of imposing. Not a problem, he assured me. It was his wife's night out with the girls, so he was at loose ends until she got home from dinner and a movie anyway. Where would I like to meet?

It was a little early for dinner, and I like to drop in on a friend of mine to have a couple of drinks when I'm not busy and I have a couple of bucks left over, so I suggested we meet at Red's bar down on Greenville Avenue and start with a couple of pops.

Scheiner didn't know about Red's, so I explained whose joint it was, and it turned out Scheiner knew Red Santee; they went way back. Either they broke in together or else maybe Scheiner helped break Red in. Or maybe they had worked together in Vice. I wasn't paying him much attention, because the youngsters today never pay any attention to my stories, so to hell with it and there you are.

"Boy, those were the days, back in the brown-boot army, I'm telling you."

I knew that was a cue for me to say something, so I just told Scheiner I'd meet him there and hung up the phone.

My disposable income at the moment came to three bucks and change. I dumped the contents out of a cracked ceramic coffee mug with a Dallas Police Association logo that I kept in my top desk drawer, and that effort rewarded me with another eighty or ninety cents' worth of loose change I'd dumped in the mug over the past few weeks. It added up to a couple of draft beers and the rest for a tip, if I didn't get the big woman Red had hired the month before. She was bad about throwing your tip at your head as you left if you were cheap enough to leave silver. At least I had smokes.

On my way out, I stopped by Della's desk for a word or two. It was a couple of minutes after five by then, and people were waiting for an elevator to get the hell out of there and go home. But Della was banging away at her typewriter, a big IBM, and from the stack of papers on her desk, I didn't figure she'd be leaving any time soon.

"Working a little overtime?" I asked.

"Yep. A little extra never hurts."

"So I take it dipshit is still out of town."

"One more night on the road, and then he's bringing it on home to me."

"What?"

"I heard it in a song. Maybe you know it, it's an old song. From the sixties, I think."

"Very funny."

"And his name is Bill."

"Whatever."

"You're going out?" she asked.

"Yeah, I have to meet a guy."

"Another case?"

"Not exactly."

"I thought for a minute there you might be trying to get solvent or something."

"Nah," I laughed. "Nothing like that. Listen, can you stop typing for a second?"

"Sure." And she did. "What's up?"

"That's what I'd like to know."

"What are you talking about?"

"That little business with you and Speed today."

"What business?"

"Don't cock your eyebrows so high when you're trying to

look innocent, will you? You're going to hurt yourself doing that."

"Well, cocked or decocked, I still don't know what you're talking about."

"The two of you were cooking up something, and it smelled like a fix-up. You wouldn't do that to me, would you?"

"I know how you feel about people trying to fix you up. Mind you, I think you're full of it. But I do know how you feel."

"Well, just keep that in mind, will you? The last thing in the world that I need right now is a blind date. And tell Speed that, too, will you?"

"Speed knows how you feel about it just as well as I do. But he does think, and I happen to agree with him, that you and one of Leslie's friends would make a great couple."

"Leslie Armitage? Why, she's a . . . a . . ."

"A retired hooker, I know. But you did fix Speed up with her, and they're very happy. I think Speed just feels like he owes you."

"I didn't fix them up, I ditched Speed on Leslie and a friend of hers one night at Red's because he was bending my ear and I had things on my mind. And they're not that happy—they fight all the time."

"The things you don't understand never cease to amaze me, Jack. Those two are perfect for each other. They're delirious."

"That's a damned good word for it. You just remember, if I ever want to be delirious, I'll drink myself into a stupor. No fix-ups, you got it?"

"I got it."

The elevator came about that time, and I wedged myself into it along with the rest of the people from my floor and a couple of guys riding down from upstairs. I looked back as the door closed. Della was definitely smirking.

The happy-hour crowd was thinning out by the time I got to Red's a little after six, and I found an old guy who turned out to be Bill Scheiner at the bar, deep in conversation with Red Santee, the proprietor. Handshakes all around, and then it was old war stories forever.

Finally, about a quarter to nine, I convinced Scheiner to leave Red's and go up the street to a pizza place. He said this and that about cholesterol and how his missus had him on a pretty tough diet, but in the end we went there and had all the pizza we could stand.

Scheiner seemed like a nice enough guy, and spoke highly of Eddie Cochran. He talked quite a bit, as a matter of fact, but that was just as well because I was not feeling particularly loquacious. Shorting myself on sleep the last couple of nights was beginning to take its toll on me, and it occurred to me that I couldn't handle all-nighters the way I could a few years ago, which led me to reflect upon my upcoming birthday. All of which brought me back to the notion of a real job, and I started paying attention to Bill Scheiner again.

The old songs on Red's jukebox had made Bill nostalgic, and there was quite a bit of "whatever happened to" to put up with. But that was tolerable. After all, he'd picked up the bar tab, and he was treating for the pizza and beer.

We were saying our good-byes on the sidewalk out in front of the place, Bill having told me a dozen times that the missus would give him what-for if he came dragging in late with beer on his breath, when he finally got down to talking about the job.

It was a good job, he wanted me to know. A responsible one. He'd saved American Southwest a lot more money than the salary they'd paid him over the years, and he took a lot of pride in that. He had plans for retirement, him and the missus in the Kerrville condo overlooking the fifteenth green. But he thought it was important to bring somebody on board to take his place. There were some people working for him who were good people, they were okay. But none of them had police experience, or connections, and he thought that was imperative. He didn't pronounce "imperative" right, but then he'd had a few, and I wasn't sober enough to correct him. Besides, I knew what he meant and I got the point.

He didn't have final say on it, he wanted me to understand that. His boss would be the one to make the decision, but Bill was sure his recommendation would carry a lot of weight. What he needed from me was a résumé. Could I get one to him tomorrow?

I told him I'd give it a shot, or words to that effect, wondering to myself how long it would take to put one together.

We needed to move on it right away, he said, because he'd been campaigning for months for a right-hand man, and the boss had finally okayed the position. Now there was a semi-rush on to fill the slot, and a decision would be made in the next week or so.

I told him I'd see him the next day with my résumé, and he suggested I try to stop by around lunchtime. He'd treat, and it would give me a chance to meet some of the people. If he could maybe get the boss to come along, too, that would be swell, he said.

Swell, I said, and we parted.

Driving back to my office, I was surprised at how I felt about the whole thing. I'd started out thinking, assuming, that the job was mine if I said the word. Now that I knew it was up in the air, damned if I didn't think I wanted it.

CHAPTER
13

A résumé was not something I'd had to worry about in my business, where things were pretty much word of mouth. It was like advertising; maybe it would be nice to draw in a little business, but until you got a little business, how were you going to pay for it? I knew P.I.'s who put up a hell of a front, with brochures and storyboards and audiovisual aids, the whole works. When they did a surveillance, the client ended up with an edited tape that looked like a PBS documentary, with narration and commentary dubbed in. Plus still photos in presentation albums, and specially designed charts and everything. They had collapsible easels and overhead projectors they'd take into the client's office to really put on a show. I'm sure it made the client feel like he was getting his money's worth, but then I worked considerably cheaper than those guys. I wasn't in their league, although I prided myself on doing a good job for the people who hired me. I just wasn't sufficiently capitalized for all the extras.

There wasn't much in my file cabinet, which was where my contracts and case files would go if I had any. There were a few things like that in there, but nowhere near enough to fill all four drawers. Of course, the bottom drawer was for my pillow and dirty laundry, but that still left a lot of room. So I had put in the drawers three or four large manila envelopes stuffed with papers and this and that that I had taken with me when I left the police department.

Figuring that training was an important thing to put in a résumé, I was digging through the contents of the envelopes looking for certificates until around midnight. It was really surprising how many things you accumulate in twelve years of police work, and there were things from all the in-service schools and college courses I'd attended when federal grants had been available. I was getting pretty impressed with myself and thinking that my résumé was going to look pretty good after all when my phone rang.

For a couple of seconds, I couldn't make out any of it. A lot of screaming, with the sound and volume of the voice coming and going every so often, like whoever it was was pacing back and forth, slinging the phone around.

"Slow down," I said. "Take it easy and—"

More hysterical racket, signifying nothing.

"Shut the hell up and take a deep breath," I said. The noise stopped. "Now who is this and what do you want?"

"Syd. This is Syd."

"Okay, Syd. What's the matter?"

"It's Liz. She's gone!"

"Gone from where? Where are you?"

"I'm in her room, and she's disappeared."

"Disappeared? Maybe she just left. Is her car still there?"

"Hang on, I'll check."

While she was gone, I wondered if Syd had a home of her own, or if she lived in Liz's room. I heard a door bang against a wall and footsteps, then Syd was back, huffing and puffing.

"It's not there!" she said, frantic.

"Okay, calm down, kid. That's good news."

"What?"

"Yeah, that means that Liz probably got in her car and went somewhere. If the car were still there, we'd have more to worry about."

"Oh."

"What kind of car does she drive?"

"A white Mustang convertible."

"Where did she go, Syd? Do you know?"

"She wasn't supposed to go anywhere. I was washing my hair and we were just going to stay in. I was going to sleep over."

It's been my experience that when people are upset they give you information in the reverse order of its importance, like Syd's shower and plans to stay in. This was in all probability not going to prove very helpful in finding out where Liz had gone.

"Where's her mom? Is Carol in the house?"

"No. She left around eight, said she'd be out late."

"Okay. So you're there alone, right?"

"Yes."

"Lois doesn't sleep in, does she?"

"No."

"Okay, now tell me what happened."

"I was in the shower, and when I came out—"

"Back it up a little for me, kid. Go back before you took the shower. Did Liz get any phone calls, have any visitors, say anything that might indicate where she was going?"

"She wasn't going anywhere. We were going to stay in."

"Okay, then. How about phone calls, visitors?"

"She got a phone call."

Finally. This was going to be the part that should have come first.

"Who was it from?" I asked.

"I'm not sure, but when she hung up, she kind of rolled her eyes around and said something about 'that goddamned Freddy.' Something like that."

"You're sure she said Freddy?"

"Positive."

"Tell me, Syd. Is this unusual for Liz, to take off like this on short notice? To leave without telling you where she's going, or even to let you know she's leaving?"

"Yes. She never goes anywhere without letting me know. And she wouldn't just up and leave like that, when we had plans."

I was almost curious enough to ask her what those plans were, but I thought I already had a pretty good idea. And I knew Syd wasn't exactly right about Liz never going anywhere without letting her know. Like the other night when they were out clubbing and Liz got bored and ditched little Syd and ended up needing a ride home.

"Okay, kid. I'll go run her down."

"I want to go with you."

"No. That would only take more time, for me to come by and pick you up. Besides, we need somebody there by the phone, to be like a command post. You can handle that, can't you?"

"Sure, I guess."

"Good. If anybody calls, just make sure you get a name and write down everything they say. I'll be checking in with you."

"You'll call me as soon as you find her?"

"I'll call as soon as I can."

"Okay."

As soon as she had hung up, I called Eddie's hospital room, but the call wouldn't go through. No incoming calls after midnight. That was too bad, because I had a hunch that Carol might be there with him.

I hustled out of the building and got the tired little Reliant to crank after a couple of tries. And all the way down the LBJ Freeway to Central and then south on Central to Meadow, I kept trying to figure out what kind of a bonehead play Freddy Barksdale was trying to make. Maybe I should have killed him when I had the chance.

CHAPTER
14

The people who lived in Freddy's apartments must have had their days and nights backward, because when I'd been there fairly early Thursday morning, the parking lot had been almost full of cars, like everyone was home. Now it was almost one o'clock Friday morning, and the lot was almost empty. Did they all work nights? I wondered. Or maybe they didn't work at all, just slept all day and partied all night. Hell of a deal if you can cover the overhead.

It hadn't taken long to solve the mystery of where little Liz had gone, because I spotted her white Mustang convertible nestled into a space right next to Freddy's blue Honda. And the lights were on in his apartment, number 118.

I left my car in the apartment parking lot across the street, not far from the pay phone I'd used sixteen or seventeen hours earlier to roust Freddy out of his place with the grocery bag. It stood to reason that I'd have to put Liz in her car and take her home, and I didn't want anybody taking it out on my Reliant if I could help it.

When I went across the street and Freddy's parking lot on

my way up to his apartment, I didn't duckwalk behind a hedge or anything, but I kept to the shadows where I could and didn't do anything to attract attention to myself.

Freddy's shades were drawn and his door was closed, so I couldn't see inside his place. But I could hear music playing, and someone singing. The singing didn't match the music very well, and I thought I knew why. I started to kick the door open, but thought to check it first, just in case. And it wasn't locked. I was surprised but relieved, because kicking doors isn't always as easy as they make it look on television.

When I stepped into the apartment, I was looking for Freddy and expecting trouble. Freddy I knew I could handle, but I didn't know about his mysterious Mister Lee, and it had occurred to me that some of Freddy's business associates might be there, too.

But they weren't, and for a while there was no sign of Freddy, either. There was just little Liz. She was the one doing the singing. And when I tried to look into her eyes, it was pretty obvious why she was having trouble keeping up with the song playing on Freddy's stereo. She was whacked, higher than a space shuttle in orbit. She was also naked.

She came at me as soon as she saw me, although the way she was having trouble getting her eyes to focus, or even to line up, I was sure she had no idea who I was. It didn't seem to matter.

"Gimme a hug," she mewed, wrapping her arms around my neck and pressing her remarkable body to mine. And she had a hell of a body, all peach-colored and creamy white, with coral nipples, and she was a natural blonde. She kissed me, running her tongue between my teeth and about halfway down my throat.

I peeled her off me, because I couldn't forget that she was just a kid and also because I didn't need an armful of her if there was going to be trouble. The quickest way to get rid of her without doing her any harm was to get control of one of her arms and turn her. I spun her around until she had her back to me and held her arms tight in front of her. She liked that. She wiggled her backside against me and giggled. Then I took a few steps across the room and gave her a push that plopped her down on the sofa, her face down in the cushions and her bottom in the air. She stayed that way, still giggling.

With her out of my way, I checked the bedroom quickly. Nobody there, not in the closet and not under the bed. Where was Freddy?

Retracing my steps to look in the kitchen and Freddy's cinematic pantry, I bumped into Liz again. She was standing pigeon-toed in the middle of the little front room, a drink in her hand, pouting.

"Where'd you go?" she said.

She reached for me, but I sidestepped her and went into the kitchen. That was when I noticed Freddy's phone was off the hook. I could hear a small, tinny voice rattling around in the earpiece. I put it to my ear and got a chill when I recognized the voice. Not the lady talking personally, but I certainly knew the type.

"If you can hear me, we have units on the way. Are you there?"

Whoever she was, her work number was 9-1-1.

I put the phone back down and opened the pantry door, pretty sure of what I'd find. Unfortunately, I was right.

Freddy Barksdale lay in a heap on the floor of the closet, his head jammed down onto his chest by one wall, his legs turned awkwardly beneath him, his left knee resting on the other wall. His camera lay on the other side of him, toward the far end of the narrow pantry, and the tripod lay on its side. Trying not to touch either wall with my fingers or palms, I worked my way over Freddy's corpse and bent down to look at the camera more closely. The hatch or door of the thing lay open, and I saw no sign of the videotape that belonged in it. I heard a siren that sounded like it was coming my way.

Freddy looked plenty dead, with the hilt of a knife planted about four inches below his left nipple and a little to his left, showing the upward track of the blade. From the way the hilt was turned, I figured a lefty had stabbed him from behind, but that was just a guess. There was no way of knowing what kind of grip the killer had used without dusting the thing for prints. I put the back of my hand to his throat and felt no pulse. He felt pretty warm, about normal, and his jaw was slack. Trying to hurry without screwing up the scene for the cops, I peeked under his shirt in the back and tugged down the waistband of his jeans a couple of inches, enough to see the light purplish discoloration I was looking for. Freddy's eyes were half-open, and I leaned in close enough to see that the corneas were clear, but his pupils looked flat and dull. He wasn't lying this time.

On my way out of the pantry, as I stepped gingerly over the pool of blood on the linoleum fake-tile floor, I saw a footprint in the blood. It was the crisscross waffling of some kind of sports shoe, but I didn't take time to look any closer.

A quick check of Freddy's kitchen drawers was enough to see that the knife in his chest would probably match the rest of the set I found there. It was a cheap set of steak knives, the kind you'd buy at a Tom Thumb.

"Gimme a hug," Liz mumbled, doing what looked like an impression of Boris Karloff as Frankenstein's monster, coming at me stiff-legged with her arms out in front of her. The siren was louder now, definitely coming toward us, and I noticed the blood on her hands.

I shoved her aside and ran through the little apartment. No sign of her clothes. Then I checked in the kitchen trash can, and I found them. They were blood-soaked, a black blouse and white miniskirt. Moving as fast as I could while at the same time trying to keep Liz off me, I wrapped the clothes in a sports section of the *Morning News* that I found in the trash as well. When I folded the clothes inside the paper, I heard the sound of metal, which turned out to be a set of Ford car keys. With the gory bundle under my arm, I grabbed Liz by her wrists and looked at her hands.

The blood was all in her palms, none on her fingers. With the sound of the siren growing louder by the second, I took the time to take a closer look at the blood on the floor of the pantry. This time I saw the pattern, the streaky arc on the floor beneath Freddy's legs.

I had her bloody rags in one hand and Liz in the other. She had started giggling again, because she'd spilled some of whatever she was drinking out of a plastic cup down her front, and she pointed to her nipples for my benefit, because they were standing up now, like a pair of toy soldiers, from the ice in the drink and the cool air of the apartment.

It was a nightmare, except in a dream I would never have conjured up anything that looked or sounded like Liz. I was about to make a horrible mistake, and I knew from the sound of the siren drifting up to us on the early morning air that I had an excellent chance of being caught at it, caught red-handed.

I shoved her toward the door and took off my jacket. I threw it over her shoulders and she shirked it off, so I picked it up to try again. She broke away from me and ran into the bedroom. Through the window in the front of the apartment by the door, I saw swirling red lights pass by outside, and heard the squad car's siren drifting, running down into silence. They'd overshot us. I had only a matter of seconds left, as long as it would take the officers to realize they'd gone past the address and turn around.

She was after something on the little nightstand, and she clenched her right hand into a fist as I grabbed her around the waist and carried her back to the front door.

I slapped her hard across the face to get her attention, and she stopped giggling. She fixed her big eyes on me, and I could tell she was trying to make them focus. She had no idea who I was or what I was doing to her. While she was still trying to figure it out, I force-fed her arms into my jacket and pushed her out the door. With my arm around her, and trying not to look like we were in a hurry in case anybody was watching, I got her into her car. The keys fit, and the little Mustang fired up with a rumble. The keys felt slippery in my fingers, and I knew they had blood on them, but there was no time to worry about that. I turned left out of the apartment parking lot, heading south toward Meadow, as the flashing red lights of the patrol unit appeared in my rearview mirror. I watched them gain on us for a couple of seconds, then they were gone, and I looked back over my shoulder and saw them turning into Freddy's parking lot. I shook my head in relief, then grabbed Liz by the nape of my jacket as she tried to climb over the side of the little convertible, for whatever reason.

CHAPTER
15

Before we'd gone far on Meadow, I pulled over to the curb and tried to get the top up on the Mustang. But I couldn't figure it out, and I knew I had to do something about Liz. She kept trying to stand up and jump out of the car, and she wouldn't keep my jacket on. There's hardly a better way to attract attention to yourself at one-thirty in the morning than to drive around North Dallas in a convertible with a naked girl trying to climb out of the damned thing. I wished to hell I had some handcuffs with me, then looked around the car for something to tie her down with. The best thing I could come up with was the seat belt. The Mustang had one of those three-point systems with the shoulder belt, and once I got Liz strapped down and buckled in, she was too dopey to figure out how to undo the thing, or if she knew where the buckle was, she couldn't operate it. I noticed her right hand was still clenched into a fist, and I tried to pry it open, but she made such a hell of a racket over it that I decided it could wait.

I was hoping Carol would be home by the time I got there, but when I pulled into the driveway, the house was dark.

When I turned off the headlights, Syd appeared like a phantom out of a shadowy hedge beside the little kitchen porch.

"Jeez," I growled. "You gave me a start."

"Is she okay? Is she all right?" was all Syd had to say. She ran to Liz's side of the car. "Liz, are you okay?"

"She's higher'n a kite and woefully underdressed," I advised her. "Is Carol home yet?"

"No. I haven't heard from anyone since I talked to you."

"How could you? I thought I told you to stay by the phone."

"And I did," Syd admonished me, holding up a portable phone in her right hand. "Just like you said."

"Let's get her inside," I said.

"Is she in trouble?"

"We all are. Give me a hand."

"No."

"What?"

"Not here. Let's take her to her granddad's place."

"The Doctor?" I asked.

"Yeah. That's where they all go when they're in trouble. He'll know what to do."

"Hell, I know what to do, I just don't want to do it. Where does he live?"

"It's not far. I'll show you."

"Getting into this car could get you into a hell of a lot of trouble, kid. I want you to know that. You can just tell me where Gramps lives, and—"

"No way. I'm going," she announced, clambering over the side of the car into the backseat.

What the hell. If we got busted, I knew I would buy the rap, given Liz's condition and the ways things worked in general. I could probably keep Syd out of anything really major. There might be a grilling, she'd have to give a statement, but she'd get over that. I was the one out on the limb here. So I told her she could go if she'd show me how to get the damned top up. Of course, she had it up in about two seconds, and off we went.

Along the way, I asked Syd to see if she could get whatever it was that Liz was holding in her right hand, and she did take a stab at it. But Liz was having none of it, so I told Syd just to keep an eye on it and not to let Liz put whatever it was in her mouth. I was pretty sure it was some of Freddy's high-tech peach-colored pills with the red ends.

Gramps's house was not what I had expected. For openers, it was down off Industrial, in a warehouse district. From the outside, the building Syd pointed out to me looked no different than everything else in its block, pretty bleak and gone to seed.

So it was with misgivings that I pulled the Mustang into the short drive in front of a corrugated overhead door and tapped the horn. About the time I noticed the closed-circuit television camera eyeballing us, the big door rose to reveal a dark chamber, and we drove in.

The door closed behind us, and some lights came on. Then a voice emanating from a speaker rigged up alongside another CCTV camera said hello. When I got out of the Mustang, the voice sounded concerned.

"Please identify yourself."

Before I could do that, Syd was out of the car and explaining things.

"He's a friend of ours. We have Liz in the car. She's in trouble, and we need your help, Doctor."

A door opened somewhere, and a man appeared on a set of steps that led up out of the garage or car trap or whatever it was that we were in. He was dark and slender, with Asian features, and he moved with the kind of economy you see in good lightweight fighters. He was casually dressed, with a short-sleeved shirt that was open at the neck and that hung loose down over his belt. His dark trousers were pleated and fashionably baggy. His shoes didn't make any noise as he walked down to the car.

"Hello," he said to me, before leaning into the window of the Mustang to take a look at Liz.

"Mister Li, I presume," said I, returning the little half of a bow he had made.

"Have we met?" he asked, looking up over the roof of the car at me.

"Not that I know of," I answered. I'd been guessing, but I thought he might be related to Carol's Lois. Of course, he might very well be the late Freddy Barksdale's "Occidental Mister Lee," too. If this guy was up to no good, my calling him by name didn't seem to have rattled him a hell of a lot. But then, a poker face is hereditary in some cultures.

Mr. Li unbuckled Liz and shot me a look that was quite a bit less than inscrutable when he realized how she wasn't dressed. I knew by that look that, as far as Mister Li was concerned, I had some serious explaining to do.

Pound for pound, Li wasn't much bigger than Liz, but he lifted her easily in his arms and carried her up the steps the way he had come. Syd followed him, and I tagged along after them, wondering how long it would be before somebody offered me a drink.

We trooped through a smallish door, made a sharp left turn, went up a slightly inclined and narrow hallway, and then through a second door that seemed to open on Mister Li's voice command.

Past the second door, I found myself in a surprisingly comfortable den or reception hall, or whatever. There didn't appear to be a ceiling, just open space that rose as far as I could see, until it became darkness above a series of suspended lights. There was no furniture to speak of, just a collection of pedestals of different sizes scattered around the big room. The floor was covered from wall to wall in white carpet that showed no stain or sign of where we'd walked, and the walls were all paneled in some kind of blond wood, with a finish that caught the light from the fixtures overhead, making shimmering points here and there on the walls.

Li laid Liz on one of the pedestals, and with the weight of her body, the pedestal, which looked as if it were made of hard plastic, yielded to form a cushion beneath her, and a light flickered to life inside the pedestal. It looked warm and comfortable.

Li covered her as modestly as he could with my jacket, but of course Liz wouldn't lie still. She wasn't as goofy as before; she seemed to be coming down now, and she turned on one hip and drew her arms up to her head as if to sleep. Li tugged my jacket down over her exposed bottom and turned to leave.

"If you would, Mister Li," I said, expecting my voice to echo in the big room, but it didn't. "See if you can get whatever that is out of her right hand."

Li looked at me, then at the girl. He tried to open her hand the way Syd and I had, but she frowned in her semi-sleep and tightened her fist. Then Mister Li placed a finger somewhere near her elbow, and this time when his other hand touched her right hand, Liz gently opened her fingers and he took whatever it was away from her. I made a note of that, because I didn't know if what he had done was accupressure or maybe something I hadn't even heard of, but I knew I didn't want Mister Li to get his hands on me.

"Pills?" I asked him.

He opened his hand to show me. They were pills, all right, but not what I had expected. Instead of the slickly manufactured peach-colored jobs, these looked more like what you usually buy on the street. They were a dirty-white color, and appeared to have crumbled a little from the warmth and pressure of Liz's hand. That was all I could tell about them from where I stood, and I was not interested in getting any closer to Mister Li to examine them until he understood that I was not the enemy. And I thought that might take some doing. I still had the little bundle of bloody clothes wrapped in newspaper under my arm, but no one seemed interested in that.

"What's going on. What's the matter with her?"

The voice came from nowhere in particular, and it wasn't until I tried to figure that out that I realized that there was music playing. Like the music I'd heard the day before at Carol's, this was so soft and low it was almost inaudible. It wasn't strings, though. It was an instrument I couldn't identify, but it had a rhythm and tone that I thought was pleasant, whatever it was.

The voice, on the other hand, entered the room at a quick march, and the man behind it. He was exceptionally tall, and as thin a figure as I'd ever seen. His thinness was accentuated by his clothes, which, like the music I'd only just become aware of, seemed alien. It was all I could do to keep from laughing at first, at this tall, gangly old man in some kind of skintight outfit that appeared to have no zippers, buttons, or seams in it, from the turtleneck collar all the way to his feet. If this outfit didn't have feet in it, like little kids' pajamas, then he was wearing some kind of soft-soled shoes that perfectly matched the light gray-blue of his costume. There was a shiny gold-colored band or collar around his neck that included some kind of eyepiece like a jeweler's loop on a thin jointed metal arm that held it up near his left eye but not in front of it. And he wore a bracelet on his left forearm that ran from his wrist almost to his elbow, full of buttons and switches.

This guy was dressed up for a costume ball, and my guess was he was going as Buck Rogers.

Before I could introduce myself, Li returned to announce that he'd prepared the something-or-other, and he picked Liz up again. Off he went with her through still another door that slid open in the wall for no apparent reason, and Buck Rogers lumbered along after him, having paid no attention to me or Syd. The door slid closed behind them, and I was left alone with the odd-looking kid with the bad hair.

"What the hell was all of that?" I asked.

"The Doctor takes a little getting used to, but he's okay."

"What's he dressed up for?"

"He does that. He's a genius, and he invents all kind of stuff. I guess he invented that outfit, too."

"And this furniture?" I wondered aloud, noting that the pedestal where Liz had lain had returned to its original hard-edged square plastic shape and the light inside it had gone out. "Is this his idea, too?"

"Neat, isn't it? It adapts to you, whoever sits or lies down on it."

"And the light?"

"It's got something to do with a thermostat, to regulate the temperature. If you're hot or cold, it can tell, and it brings you back to body normal."

"Terrific."

I teased the thing for a bit, touching it and moving, to watch the light go on and off. The damned seat, whatever it was, kept wiggling around, trying to figure out where and how I wanted to arrange myself on it. It might have been amusing if you had some free time, but I had serious business to tend to.

"I don't guess the old man keeps a bar around here anywhere, does he?"

"Shouldn't you wait until you're invited?"

"I'm sure he meant to tell me to make myself at home. Of course, he was distracted when he saw Liz. I can understand he'd want to see to her first, and I don't hold that against him. Where'd you say it was?"

"I didn't."

104

Syd looked pretty grumpy; her eyes had that squinty look I remembered from our meeting at the Art Bar, and her lips made a skinny incision under her nose again. Any relief she'd felt at my bringing Liz home was gone now, and she looked like she was wondering if maybe I hadn't had a hand in getting her into the condition she was in. The time element would have scotched that if she'd given it any thought, but I didn't think she was in the habit of thinking any too clearly where Liz was concerned.

"You mad at me, Syd?" I asked. She didn't say anything. "Or just men in general?"

"Small talk isn't really mandatory, Mister Kyle. Why don't we just sit down and wait for the word."

"The word?"

"The Doctor has stuff in his lab regular doctors never even heard of. He can tell just like that what's the matter with Liz."

"Hell, I already know that. She's high on those pills she washed down with cheap bourbon."

"Exactly right," came the Doctor's voice again, followed a moment later by the man, striding through the same door he'd left by. "She'll be good as new again in a couple of hours."

"Or however long it takes her to sleep it off."

"I'm Bobby Oppenheimer. How do you do?"

It only took a couple of his long strides to cross the room and offer me his hand. When we shook, I was surprised at his strength, and I noticed how his glasses magnified the pupils of his eyes. They were blue. They went from my face down to my newspaper-wrapped bundle, but they didn't stay there long.

"Jack Kyle," I said. "I would offer you a card, but they're in my jacket pocket."

"Right. I'll have Li fetch it for you." He punched some of the buttons on his bracelet. "I want to know everything."

"And I want a drink."

"Of course, please forgive me. Help yourself to my bar."

As if it had been listening, a panel in the wall behind me rose silently to expose a stainless-steel panel with two rows of spigots. There were tumblers arranged single file on a shelf to one side. As I moved in for a closer look, I saw that there was a drain across the bottom of the rig, to take care of any spillage.

"What'll you have, Mister Kyle?"

"Call me Jack. Scotch if you've got it."

"Certainly. How do you take it?"

"With a little ice, if it's no bother."

I drank Pinch when I could afford it, but I didn't insult the man by asking him what brand he stocked. I wasn't in a mood to be particular. He had the drink ready in a shake, and the first sip went down awfully smooth.

"Good stuff," I said. "Do you mind my asking what it is?"

"Can't remember the name. It's supposed to be as old as my grandchildren, though."

"I can believe it. Thanks."

"You're welcome. Now, sit down and tell me everything."

"First things first. Who's your lawyer?"

That took him a little bit by surprise, but he told me.

"Never heard of him," I said. "What is he, corporate?"

"Yes. Taxes, mostly."

"Call him, and tell him to come right over. Tell him to bring . . ."

Li entered the room at that point, carrying my jacket in both hands like he was taking trash to be burned. I took it from him and removed my notebook. I got one of my cards out of it and jotted down three names on the back.

"Tell him to bring one of these men with him."

"I take it they are criminal attorneys?"

"The best in town."

"You do realize, Mister Kyle, that it's a quarter past two in the morning."

"I do. Are you as rich as this layout looks?"

"I am rich."

"Then they'll come. Between you and me, Doctor, it's about keeping Liz out from under a murder rap."

He made the call.

CHAPTER
16

Within the hour, two lawyers were seated on the Doctor's seats, both of them ready to listen to my every word. The corporate type was in his late forties, clean as a pin in a starched shirt, albeit minus the power tie. He was fit and lean, and studied me with clear blue eyes and a notebook balanced on his lap. The other one, the criminal-defense specialist, was more my kind of people. He was paunchy and sallow, with bags under his eyes and tobacco stains on his fingers. His hair stood up on his head like a bad hat, and he was on his second cup of black coffee before I even got started. He had the look of a deal about him, the smell of a plea bargain hammered out in a jailhouse corridor. He would do.

I checked my notes as I talked, trying not to leave anything out while keeping to the pertinent points, the high spots. I'd made sure the handshakes had been made and the attorney-client thing worked out before I said anything. The funny part was, when the Doctor found out he'd agreed to hire the high-powered criminal lawyer to represent *me*, he almost spit out his teeth. But that was the deal. I was the one with the legal problems at the moment. If Liz got dragged into it later, he could hire her one then. I assured him that my guy would be happy to recommend somebody, probably a lawyer in his own firm, or somebody he had what lawyers call a "relationship" with. The criminal type backed me up on that. He'd seen the color of the old man's money.

When I got to the deal at Freddy's apartment, my second trip there, everybody leaned forward and listened close. The corporate lawyer looked like he was writing down everything I said, but the criminal guy just listened.

"And here," I said as I drew my little presentation to an end, "are the clothes I found there. As you can see, they're blood-soaked."

I offered them to the criminal attorney, who pointed to an unoccupied pedestal, so I put them down there.

"I found them," I said. "And I've had them in my possession ever since. Now, I release them to you. That's the chain of custody. So their evidentiary value is intact. A little tattered maybe, but at least we haven't destroyed any evidence."

"You still interfered with an investigation," the Doctor said.

"Probably. But if somebody accused me of that, I'd deny it. All I took from the scene was the clothes and Liz. The clothes are still available for forensic examination, and Liz was in no shape to give a statement anyway. Neither she nor I had any obligation to make a report, because it was obvious to me that someone had already done that. The phone was off the hook, and I heard the nine-one-one operator say there was a unit en route. There was nothing to be done for Freddy, because he was already dead. And yes, I am qualified to make that judgment, based on my training and experience as a police officer and in the military. As far as the bloodstain evidence goes, I'm prepared to testify, if my attorney advises me to, as to the blood I found on Liz's hands at the scene. I also have some opinion testimony I wouldn't mind giving about how the blood got on her hands, and on her clothes, too, for that matter, How does it sound, Counselor?"

"Like a lot of bullshit, but I think I can keep you out of prison with it."

"Music to my ears."

I had not said anything about the tape that Freddy had made of Liz, not specifically, and I hadn't gone into too much detail about my first visit to Freddy's apartment, only that it was business and that I hadn't hurt him enough to matter. What I wanted the lawyers to handle was strictly the thing tonight. As far as the good doctor was concerned, I'd leave it up to Liz and her mother to explain that part of it to him.

"But you're satisfied that the girl didn't do it?" the criminal lawyer asked.

"That's the way I see it," I said.

"And so she was just a witness, and not a very good one, from what I understand of her condition, or else . . . it's a frame job."

"Being as the killer called the cops, I'd say it's a frame."

"Do you know when the man was killed?"

"About half an hour before I found him."

"What do you base that on?" the Doctor asked.

"The body hadn't lost much heat, if any. Rigor mortis hadn't set in yet, because his jaw was slack and it usually starts there. His corneas were still clear. They turn milky a couple of hours after death. All of which means he was fresh. But postmortem lividity had begun, which tells me he'd been dead at least half an hour or so, and that he hadn't been moved."

From their reactions, Oppenheimer and the criminal lawyer understood what I'd said. I didn't care about anyone else.

"You don't think it took the cops half an hour to get there, do you?" my lawyer asked.

"Not if it was called in as a murder. That means whoever did it killed Freddy, then did something else for a good twenty minutes before calling the police. And then left just before I arrived. My guess is they were searching Freddy's apartment, but I'm not sure what they'd have been looking for."

"What is your opinion?" the Doctor asked, "about the blood?"

"A couple of things. First, the shoeprints I saw in the pantry looked like they could match the Air Jordans I saw those two Asian gangster types I mentioned wearing the other night at the Art Bar. The police can run down a match by brand and model. Second, the arc I told you about, the streak in the blood underneath Freddy's legs, it's my guess that's where whoever really killed the poor fool wiped Liz's clothes to get blood on them. Third, they got some blood on her hands, too, but only on the palms. There was none on her fingers. Probably made her grab her own clothes after they'd mopped up some blood with them. The stabber in a deal like this would have had a different pattern of blood on his hands."

"I see. Well, what do we do now?" the Doctor wanted to know.

"You people can do as you please," said the criminal lawyer, pushing himself to his feet. "Personally, I am going to take this possible alleged evidence my client has turned over to me and go put it under lock and key to preserve its integrity. When the young lady comes to, talk to her and see what she remembers, if anything. Then give me a call, and I'll advise you on whether she's going to be needing the benefit of counsel as well. If there's nothing else, Mister Kyle?"

"That's all I have."

"Then I'll bid you folks good day."

He took the bundle with him and made for the exit, the corporate attorney in his wake, fussing over his notes.

By my watch, it was a quarter to four, Friday morning, and I'd managed to put in another night without sleep. I yawned and stretched.

"Can I offer you anything, Mister Kyle?" The Doctor smiled. "Some breakfast?"

"No, thanks. I've got to be going. I'd appreciate it if you'd call my office after you've talked to Liz."

"Certainly."

"Come on, kid. Let's go." I said that to Syd, who'd been curled up in some kind of yoga position on a pedestal off to one side during our little meeting. She looked up at me with a frown. "I need you to drive me to my car, then bring the Mustang back here. Or take it over to Liz's house, whichever the Doctor prefers."

"Good heavens!" the Doctor exclaimed. "We still haven't heard from Carol, have we?"

He punched around on his bracelet a bit, then waited, watching the thing like he expected an answer. And I guess he did, because after a few seconds he looked up at me with a quizzical look. "Mister Li says she answered her home phone this time, sounds as if we woke her. She wants to know what's going on."

"You tell her, Doc," I said. "I've done all my explaining for one evening. Or morning, whatever it is."

"I'll speak with her," he said.

"I'm not leaving here until Liz is up and around," Syd put in, her lower lip pushed out like a bulldog's.

"Don't you have a home?" I asked her. "How about your mom and dad? Won't they be wondering where the hell you are?"

"I'm spending the night with Liz. No problem. And I'm not leaving."

"Well, I'm not going to drive Liz's Mustang back over to the murder scene and just park it there."

"Perhaps Li could go with you," the Doctor suggested.

"Terrific."

On the drive over to Freddy's apartment, I tried to get a conversation started with Mister Li.

"Made up your mind about me yet?" I asked.

"Not entirely."

"Good for you. You can't be too careful."

We drove on for a few blocks, with me hoping he'd say something, but he didn't.

"How long have you worked for Doctor Oppenheimer?"

"I imagine the Doctor would provide you with that information if he thought it was appropriate."

"Do you talk like that all the time, or are you just trying to fuck with me?"

"I'm sure I don't understand."

"Right. So tell me about Liz."

"What about her?"

"How long has she been dopey like this, doing stupid things and getting herself into trouble?"

"I'm sure I wouldn't know."

"Oh, wouldn't you? Well, how about a guy named Mister Li who deals drugs and trades in what they call 'keyhole porn'?"

"Li is a very common name."

"No shit. What part of Vietnam are your people from?"

He turned to look at me for the first time. I wasn't overly worried about pissing him off, because I didn't think he'd hurt me too bad while I was driving a car with him in it.

"You surprise me, Mister Kyle. Most . . . Caucasians . . . can't make such distinctions. I am usually taken for a Japanese or Korean, although of course there are considerable differences between the two."

"I wouldn't know about that," I said. "But I spent some time in Vietnam."

"Really?"

"Yeah, courtesy of Uncle Sam. The guy looks okay on a poster, Li, but I have to admit, he's a piss-poor travel agent."

Maybe he almost laughed; I couldn't tell for sure, and I was losing interest. I pulled the Mustang into the lot across the street from Freddy's place and slid out as Li moved over behind the wheel.

"Thanks for one thing, though."

"What?"

"I don't mind you stonewalling me, Li," I said. "But I'm glad you didn't give me any of that Charlie Chan shit. You know, all that 'tluth fry on the night bleeze rike butterfly in spling.' That kind of shit. I really hate that."

He didn't smile or say anything, but at least he nodded. Then he drove away, back the way we had come.

I fired up the old Reliant and headed toward downtown, wondering as I drove how early they let visitors in at Baylor, and whether they had free coffee in the lobby.

CHAPTER
17

It was almost five o'clock Friday morning when I parked my car at the Baylor Medical Center complex. I was down to pocket change, not counting my fifty-dollar emergency stash in the trunk of the Reliant, and the nearest place I could find to park that was free and not in a rush-hour tow-away zone was a pretty good hike from the hospital. I took my little away-from-home shaving kit out of the glove box, and off I went.

It started drizzling again not long after I started, and it didn't stop until I was inside the building. Naturally. I found a men's room and slipped off my jacket. I shaved and freshened up the best I could, wishing that I'd had a clean shirt in the car the way I usually did. Everything was at the cleaner's, except the shirt I was wearing and another one back at my office. By the time I was done, I was able to convince myself that I only looked depressed, which was appropriate for the hospital setting, and not quite so much like a homeless derelict. I didn't want to attract the attention of any of the hospital police, who were supposed to be on the lookout for derelicts, panhandlers, and deranged individuals. The eyedrops helped.

From what I could remember of my own days as a patient in hospitals here and there, breakfast was usually served around six-thirty or seven, and shift change was usually around that time, too. With any luck, I'd be on Eddie's floor at a time when all the nurses were wrapping up a night shift, and I knew from working deep nights for the city that you are not at your best in the last hour of your tour. Maybe I could waltz right in by them.

It almost worked. I was in the corridor outside the door to Eddie's room when a nurse challenged me. I smiled and explained that I was there on official business. Of course I knew the lieutenant was not to be bothered while he recuperated, but this was pretty important, it was something only he could answer, and it would only take a couple minutes. I promised. While I was telling her this, I had a clear mental image of Columbo, the rumpled little guy on television, the homicide detective. For whatever reason, I had found that people believed me when I talked like him. It was practically the only time that people did believe me. So it was no surprise when she said, Well all right, and let me go in to see Eddie. I thanked her profusely.

I had been right about breakfast; there were wheeled shelves of breakfast trays lined up down the hall. And I managed to locate a cup of coffee that was, if not free, at least unattended.

Eddie was lying with his back to me as I entered the room. This was good news, because it meant he had figured out a way to sleep on his side. His left foot wasn't hanging from the over-head framework anymore, either.

"Good morning," I whispered.

He turned enough to be able to see me.

"Same to you," he said. "Come around here where I can see you without turning over."

"How're you feeling?" I asked as I dragged a chair around to the far side of the bed.

"How thoughtful of you." Eddie smiled. "You didn't have to bring me coffee."

"Get your own damned coffee."

"That's no way to treat a fallen hero."

"Lying up here with a whole floor full of nurses waiting on you hand and foot. Sleep any damned time you want to."

"What time is it, anyway?" he asked.

"Twenty to six."

"You're up awful early."

"Ain't you the comedian." I made a face at him. "I haven't been to bed yet."

"Why not?"

"Let's see," I went on. "It's almost six A.M. Friday. I was up all night Tuesday night on a surveillance. Your friends kept me up until the wee hours Wednesday night, so I got all of about three hours' sleep. Now last night, they kept me up all night long. Do you see where I'm going with this, Eddie? What I'm telling you is, I am tired. I can't do this shit like we used to."

"I guess not. Hell, you're gonna be forty in a couple of days."

"Thirty-nine."

"That's pitiful, Jack. Be a man about it. Admit it's the big Four-oh."

"Check the records, goddammit. I'm going to be thirty-nine September the first."

"Okay, you're old and you're tired. And you can't get any sleep in the daytime because the only bed anybody'll let you into is that damned cot you keep stashed in your office. My heart bleeds for you. You should grow up and get a real job. Speaking of which, what did Scheiner say?"

"It looks pretty good. I'm supposed to have lunch with him today."

"I hope you can stay awake."

"So do I."

"So tell me. What kept you up last night?"

"This and that. Was Carol here with you?"

"Yeah, as a matter of fact. Why?"

"What time did she leave? How long was she here?"

"What the hell are you getting at, Jack? What's going on here?"

"There's been a killing. Nobody for you to lose sleep over. It was Freddy, the porno guy. Somebody took him out last night, or real early this morning."

"What does that have to do with Carol?"

"Probably nothing, if she was with you when Freddy got it."

"When was that?"

"I asked you first. All I'm saying is last night or early this morning."

"Look, Jack . . ."

"Eddie, I don't give a shit. Tell me anything, just don't change your story later. Because I might lie under oath to save your ass, but not hers."

"It was after midnight, fifteen or twenty minutes after," he said. He didn't look like he liked it, though. He looked like he wished she had left later, so he could alibi her for more time.

"You just asked me when I came in what time it was, Eddie. You're not wearing a watch, and I don't see any clocks in here."

"We had the TV on. David Letterman came on, and we watched the monologue, then she left."

"Okay."

If she went straight home, I thought, she would have been there when I brought Liz back and found Syd waiting outside the kitchen door by the driveway. But Syd said there had been no sign of her, and I hadn't seen her car.

"So, what does that do for her?" Eddie wanted to know.

"I think she's going to be okay," I told him.

I had arrived at Freddy's place shortly before 1:00 A.M., and Freddy was still pretty fresh but not exactly warm. If Carol left Eddie's room as late as a quarter past midnight, walked to her car, drove to Freddy's, and iced him without preamble, the way I figured the driving time, I would probably have walked in on her in the act. Plus, I couldn't see her doing all that and fleeing the scene to leave Liz behind to take the rap. It also didn't make any sense that she would have made the call to 911, and I wondered who had made that call. It would be interesting to know whether it was a man's voice or a woman's on the dispatcher's tape.

"Good. Now, tell me what you know about the killing," Eddie insisted. "How did you get involved?"

"You don't want to know the details."

"Like hell I don't."

"I'm telling you, you don't want to know. If I told you everything, you'd be obligated to report some of it, and knowing how you feel about Carol, you probably wouldn't do that. It's trouble you don't need, and it wouldn't help matters any."

"Why don't you let me be the judge of that?"

"And why don't you just trust me, for once?"

He didn't like it, and I didn't blame him. But for all the history he and I shared, the fact was that he was a police officer and I wasn't anymore. If I told him everything, that would make me his confidential informant, and he would have to report what I told him. It was better this way, and he would see that when all was said and done.

"Let me ask you one more thing," I said, after thinking about it for a couple of seconds.

"Go ahead. You're doing all the asking anyway."

"Where does Carol park her car? They have the big drive-way, but there's a garage, too. Does she usually park in the drive, or in the garage?"

"I don't know, Jack. I don't go over to her house."

"Why not?" I asked.

"Ah, you know, her kid's there all the time. It's . . . awkward."

"Is she a pretty heavy sleeper? Carol, I mean."

"When this is all over, you're going to explain to me why you're asking all these questions. You know that, don't you?"

"Absolutely."

"As a matter of fact, she has trouble sleeping. She takes pills to get to sleep."

"Okay. How does her phone work?"

"What do you mean?"

"Does she have an answering machine? How many rings before the machine picks up?"

"Yeah, she's got a machine, and she usually screens all her calls. I don't know how many times the phone rings and all that. I don't usually call her at home. There are too many extensions, somebody could be listening in."

"Okay." I rubbed my eyes and finished the hospital coffee. "I'll be checking in with you."

"You're damned right you will."

I stopped on my way out of the room.

"You look like you're feeling better," I said.

"I was doing okay until you showed up."

"One more thing, Eddie. Can you find out for me who's working the case? Without making a big thing about it?"

"Yeah. It'll be one of the night-crew guys. I'll check in on things in general, see who's working what. That shouldn't raise anybody's antennae. Call me this afternoon sometime."

"You got it."

Out in the hall, I bumped into the nurse who'd bought my

Columbo impression and let me into Eddie's room. She had her purse and an umbrella under her arm, and she was on her way to the elevator to go home. I told her again how much I appreciated her letting me have a few minutes with Lieutenant Cochran, and she assured me she was always happy to cooperate with the authorities.

CHAPTER
18

It was raining again when I slogged the half mile or so to my car, and so warm and muggy along with the rain that I had a hell of a time getting my defroster adjusted so it would keep my windshield clear without making the inside of the old car insufferable. I wound up having to roll my window halfway down to get some fresh air in. Falling asleep at the wheel was a problem I could do without.

Seven o'clock in the morning is a bad time to try to get anywhere in Dallas, especially if you're starting from East Dallas, as I was, and you want to end up in North Dallas, as I did. For some reason, rush hour these days was almost as bad outbound as inbound, and I found myself creeping north on Central in fits and starts as far as Mockingbird Lane.

There was plenty to think about as far as the murder of Freddy Barksdale was concerned, but for background noise I turned my car radio on. It was tuned to KRLD, the local talk-news-sports station. The Rangers had lost again.

Our local big-league baseball franchise, the Texas Rangers, used to be the Washington Senators, and moving to the so-called Sun Belt hadn't done a hell of a lot for their won-lost ratio. Nolan Ryan was their main draw, and there was something to be said for driving out to Arlington Stadium, about halfway between Dallas and Fort Worth, and watching a future Hall-of-Famer in action. He'd picked up his seventh no-hitter there that summer. But after actually being in contention as late as August one year, the local heroes had been playing .500 ball plus or minus a few games ever since, and were not seen by anybody as much of a threat in the tough American League West. Fans were up in arms again, dumping on manager Bobby Valentine and his pitching coach, who a caller pointed out had done books and videos on how to pitch, but whose staff had never finished a season with an E.R.A. under 4.00.

Most of the people I knew who cared about the subject, which consisted of armchair experts I ran into in local sports bars, didn't expect the Rangers to be contenders anyway. The Rangers' job was to give them something to talk about in the early summer weeks between the NBA play-offs and the start of NFL pre-season. Their other function was to bring the big-name teams to town, so Dallas fans could go out to see the stars of the American League in action. It wasn't too much to ask, and from that point of view the Rangers were having an okay season.

I was pretty thoroughly disgusted by the time I made it to Mockingbird, where the far-right lane had to exit, so I got the hell off Central there and turned west at the light, skirting the south edge of the Southern Methodist University campus, and worked my way slowly into the Park Cities. Mockingbird was pretty jammed, too, and I zigzagged north on Hillcrest and then west on University looking for a break in the action while the sports people on KRLD moved on to the promise of a new season for the Cowboys.

Before long, I found myself only a few blocks from Carol's house, and decided to change my plans. It had been my intention to make it back to my office, ask Della to type up a résumé based on the notes I'd made the night before, make a couple of phone calls, and take a nap before my lunch date with Bill Scheiner at American Southwest Motorfreight. But since I found myself in Carol's neighborhood, I decided to drop in on her and make it a personal visit.

Lois Li answered the doorbell this time, and let me wait in the entry hall while she went to fetch Carol. It was half past seven, and Doctor Oppenheimer's Mister Li had supposedly awakened Carol with a phone call around four that morning. I was a little surprised to find her at home, thinking she would have gone to her father's house to see about Liz.

When Carol appeared, dressed this time in a different dressing gown from the one she had been wearing the last time I saw her, I asked her about that, about why she wasn't at her daughter's side.

"You must think I never get dressed, Mister Kyle," she answered, tugging the lapels of her gown together and running a hand through her hair. "Won't you come in, and I'll have Lois make some coffee."

"No, thank you. I can't stay long."

Neither of us spoke for a moment, because I'd decided to wait until she answered my first question before I asked her another.

"Ah . . . the Doctor said she probably wouldn't wake up until later," she said finally. "I plan to go over there in a couple of hours, when the traffic isn't so beastly."

"I see. Do you mind if I look at your driveway?"

"I'm sorry? Oh, no, I don't suppose I do. Why. . . ?"

Since I knew my way to the kitchen already, I didn't wait for her to escort me. Lois was busy at the stove, making what smelled like a pretty hearty breakfast of bacon and eggs, and pancakes, too. It reminded me that I had not eaten since Bill Scheiner had treated me to pizza the evening before. A long time ago. Lois looked up as I passed behind her, but didn't say anything. From the kitchen door, I looked out at the driveway. There was one car there, a Toyota.

"That's your car, Lois?" I asked.

She looked at me, then at Carol, who'd followed me and stood in the doorway. Then Lois turned back toward me and nodded.

"Where's your car, Carol?"

"In the garage."

"Would you mind showing me?" I asked, opening the kitchen door.

"We can go this way," Carol said, indicating the hallway.

I followed her down the main hall and out through a service entrance into the garage, where her car, the same silver Jag I'd seen her in the first evening when I took her to her car from the Art Bar, was parked. She told me she always parked in the garage and almost always came in through the service hallway. When I asked, she assured me that she had done so the evening before. I asked her what time she got home, and she said it had been around one o'clock in the morning. She seemed surprised that I knew about her sleeping pills, but said that yes, she had taken a pill and gone right to bed. The phone finally woke her around four. It was Mister Li, calling for the Doctor to let her know about Liz. If there had been calls earlier, she hadn't heard them. By four, her sleeping pill had worn off, she supposed, and she hadn't been sleeping so soundly.

As she showed me to the front door, I told her I'd be in touch later that day, that I also wanted to talk to Liz about what she could remember from the night before. I told her I'd like to have a word with Syd, too, and I thought I saw something in her eyes at that, a bit of a reaction. But I didn't push it. There'd be time for that later. I thanked her for her time and jogged in the drizzle back to my car.

Driving away from Carol's tastefully decorated and well-tended house, I couldn't help noticing that, once again, Eddie Cochran's name hadn't come up. Of course, I hadn't asked her where she'd been the night before, but still, I'd expected her to say something about Eddie. If nothing more, I'd have thought she would ask me how I knew about her sleeping pills.

CHAPTER
19

After what seemed like an all-day trek, I finally made it to my office and walked into the foyer to see Della's smiling face at about quarter to eight.

"Good morning, gorgeous," I said to her.

"Morning," she answered. Then she looked up from the switchboard at me. "T-G-I-F, huh, Jack."

"You said it," I smiled. Like it mattered. Every day's a day at the office for me, but of course I do get to sleep in on the weekends. "Have you got time to do something for me this morning?"

"Sure. What is it?"

"I'll get my notes. How late were you here last night?"

I went into my office to round up all the stuff I'd scribbled down for my résumé.

"Until about ten," she said. "But I got it all done."

"Kind of a short turnaround for you, too, wasn't it?"

"I can handle it."

"Easy for you to say, kid. I must have just missed you."

"Oh?"

"Yeah. I got back from eating pizza with that guy I had to see a little before eleven."

"Get any sleep?"

"No, I had to go out again around midnight."

"Bummer. What've you got there?"

"This," I said, dumping the sheets I'd torn off a yellow legal pad on her desk, "is a bunch of crap. What I need you to do is to take this and make a résumé out of it."

"Okay. What's the deal?"

"Nothing, a guy just wants to see it."

"A client maybe?"

"A job maybe."

"A job? Jack, are you okay?"

"Sure I'm okay. What are you talking about?"

"I don't know, it's just . . . you and a job. I've never thought of you that way, that's all."

"I've had jobs."

"Name three."

"Well, uh . . ."

"The Marine Corps, that's one. The Dallas Police Department, that's two. In forty years."

"What, forty years? I'm only thirty-eight."

"Jack . . ."

"I'm thirty-eight, I swear to God. Soon to be thirty-nine, grant you. But there ain't no forty years involved here."

"Whatever. I just have this image of you . . . you know, the rugged individualist . . . hard-boiled private eye, with nothing but your trench coat and a battered old fedora . . . alone against the world. Fiercely independent, you know."

"Trench coat? Fedora?"

"I just can't see you punching a clock, holding down a day job somewhere."

"Neither can I—this is not that kind of job. So just take care of this for me, will you?"

"No problem."

"And, uh . . . I've got a couple of calls to make, then I'll be in conference until about eleven."

"Right."

"And, if my conference runs a little long, would you. . . ?"

"Give you a wake-up call?"

"Right."

"No problem."

"Thanks."

"Are you going to want to proof this résumé before your conference or after?"

"Neither. When it looks good to you, it's finished."

"Okay."

I stood in the doorway of my office for a couple of seconds looking at her as she shuffled stuff around on her desk to get started on my résumé. She was wearing the green dress that I was especially susceptible to, and she had her hair done up in back so that you could see the curve of her neck. I remembered that dipshit was due in that evening, and I thought how nice it would be to have his prospects for the weekend. But enough reverie, I had things to do, too.

Mister Li answered the phone at the Oppenheimer residence and put the old man on for me. He wished me a good morning, and I asked him how Liz was doing. She was resting comfortably, he assured me, and should be up and about in a couple of hours. I asked him if he would call my office and leave a note for me when she came around, and he said he'd be happy to. He figured I'd want to talk to Liz, and I assured him that was the case, and that I had a few follow-up questions for Syd, too. He promised both girls would be available to me later, and I thanked him for that.

Next, I got lucky and caught Speed before he got out of the house. As a matter of fact, from the sound of him, I caught him before he even got out of bed. Leslie answered the phone and demanded to know who the hell I was before she'd put him on. When I told her, she said long time no see and a lot of crap like that, and it was a couple of minutes before Speed came on. Speed was a human warehouse of information, due to the fact that he was constantly researching one thing or another for one of his free-lance jobs. His main thing was cameras, still and video, but he'd shown me a shoebox full of newspaper and magazine articles he'd written, too. So I used him from time to time as a research resource. I figured I'd overpaid him pretty handsomely for that little thing he'd done for me with the Liz videotapes, so I didn't mind asking him to do a little more. I wanted to know what he knew about Asian gangs.

"The triads, you mean?" he wanted to know. "Or tongs? Or the Yakuza? It's a fascinating subject, I promise you. And with Hong Kong going over to the mainland Chinese in '97, experts are predicting—"

I whistled into the phone to shut him up, and explained to him that I was interested in stuff a little closer to home. Like here in Dallas, Asian gangs, particularly Vietnamese. Did he think he could see what the score was on that kind of thing?

Sure, he said, and what was my time frame? Today, I told him, by noon would be good. Then I hung up without waiting for him to finish kvetching.

With all that taken care of, as far as I knew there was nothing more to do until lunch, so I put my feet on my desk, leaned back in my chair, and settled in for a nap to recharge my batteries. I wished I had a battered fedora to pull down over my eyes.

CHAPTER
20

I t was a good thing I'd forgotten to lock my office door, because when Della buzzed me on the intercom a few minutes after eleven, it didn't rouse me at all. She finally had to come in and shake me awake by my feet.

When I came to, I was half out of my swivel chair, one foot still on my desk, and I must have looked like a bear coming alive at half past April. Della was laughing at me, but she had a soft, cute laugh that I didn't mind too much.

"What time is it?" I asked.

"Ten after eleven. Your conference ran a little long."

"Yeah, right. Okay, thanks. I'm up now."

"Your résumé is on my desk when you're ready to look at it. I made you some copies."

"Great. Is there any coffee?"

"A fresh pot. I'll get you some."

"You're gorgeous, kid. Thanks."

There was a coatrack along the wall outside my office where I kept most of my wardrobe in a hanging suit bag. I fumbled around inside it until I came out with my last clean shirt and the striped tie. The paisley tie had fallen into the bottom of the bag somewhere.

Della set the coffee on my desk and watched me change shirts.

"A guy can't get a little privacy around here?" I protested. "Shut the door, will you?"

"Sure." Della smiled, stepping into my office and closing the door behind her. "Sorry."

"Yeah, that's better."

I got the tie about the way I wanted it and slipped my jacket back on. The only mirror I had was a round job hanging on the inside of my door, so I motioned Della to step to one side so I could check myself out. Not too bad, I thought.

"Nice tie," Della said.

"Thanks. Does it go all right with this jacket?"

"No."

"Why not?"

"The stripes in the tie clash with the wrinkles in the jacket."

"Oh. Yeah, I guess you're right."

"What about your navy blazer?"

"It's in the bag, on the coatrack."

She stepped outside, and I heard the bag and a clothes hanger rattling around against the wall. Then she came back in, holding the blazer out for me. I peeled off the gray jacket and slipped into the blazer.

"Well?" I asked.

"Much better. Dapper, even."

She was giggling.

"What is it?" I demanded. I had some time pressure to deal with, and I only owned two jackets. If this ensemble didn't make it, I had no options. What the hell? I thought, eyeing myself in the mirror . . . navy blazer, white shirt, gray slacks, what could be wrong with it?

"Nothing, Jack. You really look fine. Here, let me help you with that."

She came over and fixed my tie for me. There's a trick to starting your knot in the right place to make the length come out right, so the thing hangs just about to your waist and not too long or too short. And when you haven't worn a tie for as long as I hadn't, it was easy to get rusty. She retied the thing, standing close in front of me, and when she was through, not only was the tie the right length, but the knot was one of those nice smooth, round jobs I never could quite manage.

"Thanks," I said.

"You're welcome."

"Nice perfume, too. Or is that just you?"

"Must be me. Guess I'm looking forward to somebody getting back into town tonight."

"You slut."

"Why, Jack, how faw-wahd of yew," she drawled, giving me her impression of Scarlett O'Hara, of whom she knew only from TV reruns on cable. Then she laughed a throaty little laugh that sent a shiver up the back of my neck.

Enough fooling around, I had places to go and people to see, and hustled out of my office and onto the elevator, doubling back to grab the envelope with the résumés that Della held out to me. Time to go play with the grown-ups.

The grown-ups at American Southwest were a pleasant enough group who spent their days in a two-story brown brick office building that made the foot of an L, with the freight terminal itself playing the role of the vertical shaft of the L. The location was about what I'd expected, off Irving Boulevard just south of the Trinity River, on the Dallas side.

The receptionist in the lobby told me where to go, and I walked into Bill Scheiner's second-floor office just at the stroke of noon.

"Well, right on time, I see," Bill's voice welcomed me in

past the empty secretary's desk in his outer office.

As I found my way back toward the voice, he rose to meet me halfway.

"Estelle takes her lunch at eleven-thirty," he explained. "That way the office only shuts down for half an hour. I usually go from twelve to one, you know."

"I see."

"I spoke to John about going to lunch with us. . . ."

"John?"

"John Stewart, the general manager. He's my boss, the fellow I told you about last night."

"Right."

"Boy, we played the devil last night, didn't we?" He grinned and shook his head.

"We sure did," I agreed.

"I tell you, the missus was put out with me more than a little bit. And I don't blame her, you know. The least I could have done was call to let her know I'd be out late. So she wouldn't be worried, you see."

"Yeah, I guess you're right."

"Boy, that was really something. Haven't hung out like that in a while. Make yourself comfortable, Jack. I'll run down the hall and see what John has to say about lunch."

"Fine." I was thinking that if Scheiner thought last night was a big deal, he should make it a point to get out more often. But who was I to have an opinion? I seemed to remember his telling me that he and the missus had been together twenty-odd years. "Oh, I brought the résumé, and some copies."

He turned in the door. "Good," he said. "I'll be right back."

There wasn't an ashtray in sight, so I didn't dare light up, but I did make myself comfortable in' a chair in front of Scheiner's desk, and I took the opportunity to look over the résumé to see what Della had been able to put together.

She had managed to make me sound presentable, even about halfway impressive, at least at first glance. At the bottom, she'd typed "References Available upon Request." References, there was something I hadn't given any thought to. Since he'd suggested me in the first place, I figured Eddie Cochran would be one. I wondered if two would be enough and whom I'd find to be the second one, when Scheiner popped back in.

"John can't make it," he said, shaking his head. "Something's come up. Give me a sec to round up a couple of the people you'll be working with, and we'll be on our way."

I nodded and smiled. That could be good news, I told myself. Maybe the boss had decided to let Scheiner handle things after all. Of course, on the other hand, it could mean that Mister Stewart had his own ideas and didn't want to be bothered.

Scheiner was back in a couple of minutes with two men and a woman in tow, and off we went to lunch. He drove, and we ate at a little barbecue place a few blocks down on Irving Boulevard. The food was okay, and the people who worked for old man Scheiner seemed decent. One of the men had been with American Southwest since he got out of the army, and the lady had started out as a contract guard from a local service, then got hired on with the company. The other man was related to somebody. We all had a nice enough time, but I got the impression that Scheiner had told them I was going to be their new boss by the end of the year and everyone was on best behavior, more or less.

When Scheiner let us all out of his car back at the freight company, he offered to give me a tour of the place, but I begged off. I tried to give him the impression that I was pretty successful in my own way, or at least busy, and that I had things to do myself. If he was disappointed that I didn't hang around, he didn't show it, and sent me on my way with a hearty hand-shake and a big smile.

I stopped at the first pay phone I came to and checked in with Della. She said there'd been a call from a Doctor Oppenheimer, something to the effect that the ladies were ready to see me now. I thanked her and hung up without offering to explain what that meant.

CHAPTER
21

From American Southwest Motorfreight to Doctor Oppenheimer's little pied-à-terre was only a short hop down Irving Boulevard to Industrial and then a jog down a side street. I pulled into the short drive in front of the overhead door and the CCTV camera a couple of minutes after two o'clock. The sun was out again, and the sidewalks were steamy with the humidity.

The drill was about the same as the night before, or I should say, earlier that morning, as far as getting inside Oppenheimer's place went, except that this time a voice over the speaker in the garage just invited me in, and the door opened before I got there. There was no sign of Mister Li.

The good doctor greeted me in person when I stepped through the second door from the garage and once again stood upon the stain-resistant white carpet amid the funny pedestals and the shiny blond wood walls that concealed all his gadgets.

We exchanged pleasantries, including his offer of another round of his ancient and honorable scotch, which I did not hesitate to accept. If he thought it a bit early in the day, he was too good a host to bring it up.

He supposed that Liz and Syd would be finished with lunch and freshening up and asked me if I wanted to speak with both of them. I said I wanted them one at a time, Syd first. The Doctor didn't invite himself in on any of it, and I didn't concern myself about that one way or the other. The way he had the place wired, I figured he could listen in if he wanted to. Before he summoned Syd, I commented on his dress. He was wearing one of those Hawaiian print shirts over a pair of white pants and some snappy white oxfords, and I mentioned the way he'd been decked out before.

"Oh, that," he said, with a dismissive wave of his hand. "I was just trying out some things I've been working on. What did you think of it?"

"Nice," I said. "Distinctive, and yet obviously functional."

"You're very kind. We're bringing out a whole line, for men and women. I mean, of course, the hardware as well as the outfits."

"Now that sounds interesting," I said, with considerably more genuine enthusiasm, picturing Carol in one of the skin-tight pantsuits. Or Della, for that matter. "I hope it's the wave of the future."

"So do I, Mister Kyle. Ah, here she is."

Syd appeared through one of the Doctor's silently opening doors, and he excused himself.

"Let me know if you need anything," he said. "And, Mister Kyle, do help yourself to the scotch."

I promised him that I would, and then didn't waste any time getting down to business with Syd. At first she lied, denying that she'd seen Carol come home the night before. But she wasn't as tough or as smart as she wanted to believe, and before long I was hearing the real story.

She'd been upstairs, waiting by the phone, when she heard Carol's car pull in. She'd sneaked downstairs and out through the kitchen door without being seen by Carol, then waited outside with the portable phone until I showed up. When I asked her why she'd cut Carol out of the whole thing, she told me it was because she didn't trust her.

"You don't know these people," Syd whispered.

"Oh," I whispered back. Maybe Syd thought the house was wired for sound, too. "And you do?"

"I know Liz. She's the one I care about."

"Yeah, a little excessively, I think."

"Don't make fun of something you don't understand, Mister Kyle."

"Why don't you explain it to me?"

"You're making fun of me."

"No I'm not, I'm serious. What's the deal with you and Liz?"

"Why do you want to jerk me around?"

"I don't. Look, I think we can skip the basics. I understand about gayness, generally. What I want to know is, is that the case here? Are you gay, do you love Liz, is it a sexual relationship, or maybe it's not gay at all, some kind of sister bonding, or what?"

She looked at me hard but didn't answer.

"If it's sexual, does she feel the same way toward you?"

"Pretty personal questions."

"I'm in a pretty personal business, kid." I lit a cigarette, figuring the Doctor's room was rigged so that an ashtray would appear from somewhere at the smell of smoke. "And I only report to my clients, which doesn't include your mom and dad, if that's what you're worried about."

"You know about 'gayness,' do you?"

"A little," I told her. "I know some people are straight and some are gay, and I don't think it's an arbitrary choice people make. That's about all I know."

"It's more than a lot of people," she said. "I've . . . I've known I was . . . different . . . for a long time. I've always known."

"How old are you?" I asked.

"Eighteen."

"Okay."

"So, you want to know—do Liz and I have sex?"

"Yeah, for one thing."

"In a manner of speaking."

"Meaning what?"

"She submits to being adored, sometimes."

"Sounds one-sided."

"Less so than fantasy."

"Okay. What are you protecting her from?"

"What do you mean?"

"That's what you do, you try to protect her. That first night at the Art Bar, when I wanted Liz to show me Freddy's apartment, Carol had no objection, but you insisted on going along. You even sat between us at the table. Last night, you kept everything from Carol; you called me, and it was your idea to bring Liz here. But what are you shielding her from?"

The kid took a deep breath and let it out in a long sigh. Then she told me more than I had thought she would. She told me that Carol was an airhead, a conclusion I'd entertained independently. She also told me about Liz's dead brother, the genius Alan.

I was about to go into it with her when one of the doors opened and Liz sauntered in.

"Doctor said you want to see me?" she said, her eyes clear and open wide, her eyebrows high up her forehead.

Syd jumped at the chance to excuse herself, with something about calling her parents to let them know where she was. As Syd passed her going out, Liz eyed me evenly, and she didn't return the furtive little look Syd gave her. The door closed, and I drained my scotch.

To my surprise, no ashtray appeared, and my cigarette was making an ash. Maybe smokers didn't figure into the scheme of things in the home of the future. I left Liz standing in the doorway and returned to the Doctor's bar, which he had been nice enough to leave open for me. I selected a glass to serve as my ashtray and ran a splash of soda water into it to kill the butt. Then I freshened my scotch and checked my notes.

"I understand I owe you a debt of gratitude."

"Huh?"

"The Doctor explained what you did last night, and he told me I owe you a debt of gratitude."

"Oh."

"I mean, I know how much trouble you would get into if the police found out about what you did. I'd hate to see you get into any trouble."

"Don't worry about it. . . ."

"You could lose your license, couldn't you? Maybe even go to jail."

"I said, don't worry about it. Now . . ."

"I'd just hate to see you get into trouble like that."

"Then keep your mouth shut. I want to ask you some questions."

"You can ask me anything."

"Why did you go to Freddy's last night?"

"That wasn't very smart of me, was it? Sometimes I'm afraid I don't have very good judgment. I mean, I let my emotions get the best of me."

She had the fresh-scrubbed wholesome look you'd pay for if you were shooting a commercial for acne medicine, a real squeaky-clean ingenue you wouldn't have thought knew any more about porno tapes than the average Barbie doll. It was amazing what a little sleep could do, because she looked a lot different than she had in Freddy's apartment.

Her body language was something else. While she was talking, she managed to stretch like a cat, prowl barefoot across the impervious white carpet, and stretch herself out on her side

141

on one of her grandfather's pedestals, which accommodated itself to her shape the same way it had done the night before, when my jacket had not quite covered all her strategic assets. She was wearing another miniskirt, black this time, with a loose-fitting white sleeveless blouse that showed her midriff as she lounged in front of me.

"Is that about it?" I asked.

"About what?"

"You've shown me your stretch, your strut, your legs, and your tummy. Your smile, too, for good measure. And an excessive amount of concern for my well-being. If that's all, I'd like you to answer my question now. Why did you go to Freddy's last night?"

"He called me."

"And told you what?"

"He said you didn't get all the tapes, that he had another copy stashed. He threatened me with it."

"Threatened you how?"

"I don't understand what you mean."

"What did he threaten to do with the tape?"

"I . . . he didn't say."

"Try again."

"What's the matter with you?" she asked, looking hurt. "Why are you being rude to me? I haven't done anything to you. I mean, I know I got you in big trouble last night, and I can understand if you're afraid, or worried, but . . ."

She started to cry.

"You're awfully good, kid," I told her, trying to remember Bogart's line verbatim. "But take a tip. You go too fast. It's not convincing when you change moods so quick like that. You need to learn to pace yourself."

With that she sprang up off the pedestal and went stumbling and yammering across the room toward the door. Naturally, it opened before she got to it, and closed behind her.

I sipped my scotch and waited, but nothing in particular happened. Finally, I made an announcement.

"Doctor Oppenheimer," I said, raising my voice a little above conversational volume. "I'd like a word with you."

He appeared in about a ten-count, looking solicitous.

"Is everything all right?" he asked.

"About like you'd expect," I told him. "Did Liz come out your way?"

"I bumped into her," he said. "She seemed upset."

"And how do you feel about that?"

"Pardon?"

"About my upsetting her. Are you pissed at me for making her cry, or does she act that way so often you don't pay much attention to it anymore? Or are you just curious?"

He toyed with his hairless chin for a second with a long, skinny finger as if he really were trying to decide. Finally, he said, "Mostly curious, I suppose. I wonder what you said to upset her."

"I asked her why she went back to Freddy's apartment last night. She said he called her, said he had a copy of the tape that I hadn't found, and that he threatened her with it. When I asked her how he had threatened her about the tape, she turned on the tears and out she went."

"I see," said the Doctor.

"Any questions?" I asked.

"One. What's this about a tape?"

I looked at him, hoping it was some kind of loopy joke on his part. It wasn't.

"I thought you knew about the tape, Doctor."

"I'm afraid I don't. Unless I've forgotten. I'm pretty absent-minded when I'm working on something."

"Are you?"

"What?"

"Working on something?"

"Always."

"I see. You don't remember Carol saying anything to you about the videotape that Freddy made of Liz the other night?"

"No, I don't."

"Or Liz telling you about it?"

"I'm afraid not."

"And I don't suppose Syd's brought it up."

"No."

"But, Doctor, that was pretty much what all the fuss was about last night, when I brought Liz over here, and you hired the lawyer."

"I thought that was about Freddy's murder."

"It's all related. You do know who Freddy was, though, I take it."

"Only that he was murdered last night."

"Then why. . . ?"

"I understood that Liz was involved somehow, and you were trying to help her. That's all."

"I see. May I make a suggestion, Doctor?"

"Of course."

"I think you folks need to have an old-fashioned family sit-down. It's just you, Carol, and Liz, right?"

"And Alan."

"Alan's dead, Doctor. I mean, he is, isn't he? I was told he died last year on his eighteenth birthday."

"Yes, quite right. I'm afraid I didn't fully grasp your question. The three of us are the surviving family members."

"Well, let's just invite the survivors. That would be my advice. Anyway, the three of you people need to sit down and talk this over among yourselves, make sure everybody's on the same page."

"That sounds reasonable."

"You're damned right it does."

"But I'm afraid Carol doesn't like to come over here."

"Then you go over to her place."

"I'm afraid I really don't like to go out."

"Well, Doctor, you people are going to have to work something out, because you really need to talk. I mean, this is serious business. Do you understand?"

"Apparently. But couldn't you explain it? That would be simpler."

"I'd like to, but I'm not at liberty to divulge details. Look, call your daughter, the three of you get together and talk this thing out. Promise me you'll do that?"

"I suppose I'll have to."

"You need to. Look, I've got to run now, I have some people to see about this thing. I'll check back with you."

"Yes, all right. Thank you."

I left him looking puzzled, standing in the middle of his white carpet, stroking his hairless chin with his bony finger. As I made my way back to my car, I couldn't help wondering which of the three generations was the looniest.

CHAPTER
22

As is so often the case, my next move was to find a pay phone. I would not have been comfortable making a business call from the Doctor's place. Della had no word yet from Speed and his research into Asian gangs in Dallas. From his hospital bed, where I could pick up bits and pieces of his ongoing conflict with physical therapist Nell Farmer, Eddie Cochran did have a name for me: Augie Dann. He was the investigator handling Freddy Barksdale's murder.

"What kind of name is that?" I asked.

"What difference does it make?"

"I don't know. I was just wondering."

"Augie's a Choctaw Indian, from Oklahoma. His folks are from up around Atoka somewhere."

"That's not too far from Paris," I noted. "Across the river."

"Yeah, you guys are like neighbors, almost. Of course, he's a lot younger."

"I figured that."

"He's a pretty good little investigator, kind of closed-mouthed, low-profile. You know the type, a plodder."

"Will he talk to me?" I asked.

"I asked him to. I gave him a call at his house a little while ago."

"That won't raise him up, you think?"

"I ran a story by him, it's no big deal. He won't open up the books for you, but he'll help you if he can."

"What's my angle?"

"You're a P.I. working a case of your own, and there may be a connection. If you can help him any, it works that way, too."

"Okay."

"Jack, what time is it?"

"About five to three."

"Good, give him a call at the office. He's working three to eleven, he should stop in there first to stack his paper and make some calls before he goes out."

"Okay."

"And let me know what you find out."

"I'll tell you anything I can, you know that."

"Yeah. Hey, Jack?"

"What?"

"I been thinking about this deal since you were up here this morning. You and I both know you weren't expecting anything like this when you agreed to do me a favor. I mean, you're getting tied up in some pretty heavy shit on this, and I'll understand if you want to deal yourself out."

"I'm afraid it's too late for that, but I appreciate the thought."

"I hope you didn't do anything stupid last night, Jack."

"So do I."

I called the main number for Crimes Against Persons, and somebody located Investigator Augie Dann for me. By the time he finished giving me his official hello, I was thinking that if this guy moved as slow as he talked, he might still be working cases from last year. I told him who I was, and if that put a smile on his face, it didn't come across in his voice.

"I was expecting your call," was all that he said.

I told him I'd like to get together with him, at his convenience, to see if I had anything that would be of use to him on the Barksdale killing. I felt like a triple agent. What I was most interested in was if the cops had turned up anything that pointed toward Liz; I also wanted to make sure that nothing I'd done would keep them from finding the real killer. And, on a more personal level, it would be nice to know if I had been seen leaving the scene of the crime. So part of me felt legit, like I might be of some help to the guy; the other part of me felt like a spy.

Okay, he said, he wouldn't mind meeting with me. He rattled off an address. He wanted me to meet him at Freddy's apartment.

"What is this place?" I asked.

"Scene of the crime," he explained, sounding a little impatient with me.

"You're going back out there?"

"Yeah." A pause, like he was thinking. "We're going to canvass the area for witnesses."

"Oh, I see. I thought maybe y'all did that last night."

"We did. This'll be a follow-up."

"Makes sense. What time shall I meet you out there?"

"I'll be leaving here in a couple of minutes. Let's say about four o'clock."

"I'll be there."

From where I was, I knew I could get to Freddy's before Dann could hike over to the police garage, check out a pool car, and make the trip himself. Which meant I had some time to kill, and nothing productive to do with it. For lack of anything better, I checked in with Della again. To my surprise, she had something for me.

"Still no word from Speed," she said. "But you got a call from Mister Li."

"Which one?"

"How many are there, Jack?"

"Hundreds probably, but two that I'm interested in."

"He said he met you last night at the Doctor's."

"Okay."

"Does that help?"

"Narrows it right down," I said, thinking to myself that that was true only if Oppenheimer's Mr. Li didn't turn out to be the same "Mister Lee" that Freddy took his orders from. However that worked out, I was curious to know what Li had to say.

"He said to tell you that you've certainly stirred things up around there."

"Okay."

Della had to put me on hold to take a call for someone else, leaving me wondering about a couple of things.

"You still there?" she asked a minute later.

"Yeah. What else did Mister Li have to say?"

"That you and he need to have, quote, an old-fashioned sit-down, end quote. Said you'd know what that meant."

"Okay."

"That's it, plus a number where you can reach him to make arrangements. Got a pen?"

"Of course." People who make or take business calls without pen and paper handy piss me off worse than safe burglars. Della knew that. "Shoot."

She read off the number, and it sounded like a new one to me. I scanned my notes and didn't find it anywhere.

"He didn't say whose number this is, where it belongs, did he?"

"Sorry, Jack. End of message. He was polite, but not chatty."

"Okay. Listen, I'm going to be out meeting a guy for a while, and it may go past five o'clock. . . ."

"Which is the instant I'm out of here, Jack. I've got plans."

"You told me already. Dipshit's back in town. What I'd like you to do is if Speed calls before you leave, put a message on my machine so I can pick it up when I call in. Would you do that for me?"

"It depends. Hang on a second."

Another incoming call for someone else.

"Jack?"

"Yeah."

"Like I said, it depends."

"Well, if it depends on whether I'm going to let you help out on this case, I'd like to point out that you have better things to do this weekend. The private-eye racket is not a nine-to-five deal, kid, and I'm afraid you just have too full a personal life for it."

"Unlike you, Jack, who have no life at all."

"Exactly."

"You're probably right, but that's not what I had in mind."

"What then?"

"I was thinking it depends on what you have planned for Monday evening."

"Huh?"

"Monday evening. It's Labor Day."

"Why?"

"If you must know, there's someone."

"I knew it!"

"Definitely not a fix-up, Jack. This is *not* a blind date. Hang on."

Another interruption.

"Okay, I'm back."

"Yes," I said. "I have plans Monday evening."

"You do not."

"I certainly do."

"Well, let me just say this: If you can't take a few minutes to do me a favor and stop by Vincent's to say hello to someone . . ."

"Impossible," I lied. "I'm booked solid."

"Fine," she spat, and hung up.

I almost felt better about going to meet Augie Dann at the murder scene. That, I could handle. . . . Della as matchmaker . . . the mind boggled.

CHAPTER
23

I saw Augie Dann before I found a parking space in the parking lot at Freddy Barksdale's complex. Augie was a short, squat character. From a distance, he looked like a mailbox, the big kind you see downtown or outside a post office. There was a man on the balcony of the apartment building, talking to a lady in a T-shirt and shorts, with a basket of laundry under her arm. He figured to be a cop, too, because he was wearing a jacket and tie in the muggy August heat and humidity. But he had cotton-blond hair that lay in a humid forelock, and he was tall and thin. A Choctaw he wasn't.

I stepped out of my Reliant, grabbed my blue blazer off the hook over the rear window, and slipped it on. Naturally, I had ditched the striped tie as soon as I'd left the parking lot of American Southwest Motorfreight. With the jacket, I looked less like a non-cop, and there would be less to explain to the people we spoke with. That was assuming that Augie let me tag along.

Augie was talking to a lady standing just outside the apartment manager's office, an overfed matron with an expensive hairdo and too many rings on her fingers. Being careful not to interrupt by going too close, I waited at a discreet distance, and gathered from what I overheard that she was the manager.

"Of course, I wouldn't have given out any information over the phone like that . . ." she was explaining. ". . . but my assistant is pretty new in the business, and she just didn't think anything of it. Really, she thought she was doing Mister Barksdale a favor confirming the information. From what she told me, she thought he was trying to buy something on credit, you know. And . . ."

Augie nodded to the lady and turned around to look me over. "Can I help you?" he said.

"Jack Kyle. We spoke on the phone." I smiled.

"How you doing?" He offered me his hand, but he didn't smile.

"Fine," I lied, shaking hands with him.

"Mrs. Nagle is the apartment manager," he explained.

"Cynthia Nagle," she added, and we shook hands, too. "Are you a reporter?"

"No, ma'am . . ." I began.

"Mister Kyle may have some information for us," Augie cut in. "He's going to be with us for a bit."

"I see." Cynthia Nagle nodded, smiling for no particular reason. "Isn't it awful?"

"You were saying, ma'am, about your assistant?" Augie prompted her.

"Yes, well I'm afraid she gave this man who called Mister Barksdale's phone number. I'm not sure what harm that might have done, of course. She said he already knew Mister Barksdale lived here, even had his apartment number."

"When will this assistant be back, Mrs. Nagle?" Augie asked.

"Any minute now. She just ran to the bank for me. It's the end of the month, and we don't let any receipts pile up around here overnight, you know."

"I see." Augie was jotting something in his notebook. "We'll be in the area for a while. When she gets back, would you ask her to stay put until I get a chance to talk to her?"

"Certainly."

"You did say she thought she'd recognize the voice if she heard it again?"

"That's what she said. She told me it was an older man, kind of a mumbler, with a tired-sounding voice."

"Thank you. We'll be back before long."

"Well, if there's anything in the world that we can do to help you, Officer Dann . . ."

"Yes, ma'am."

She kept smiling and nodding as she backed into her office to escape the heat and humidity. When she was gone, Augie turned away from her door, and I moved to follow him. He led me into a stairwell that offered as much privacy as we were going to find, now that the occupants of Freddy's complex knew the cops were back on the scene.

"Lieutenant Cochran said I should level with you, Mister Kyle, but he didn't go into much detail."

"You don't look like you're happy to see me," I said, smiling to show him I knew about how he felt and that I didn't blame him.

"I like doing it by the book," he returned, eyeing me evenly. "I don't see anything wrong with that."

"I understand. If you'd rather I leave . . ."

"I'd rather you tell me what your part is in this."

Good question. That was the one I'd been trying to figure out my answer to all the way over there from Industrial Boulevard.

"I have a client, whose identity of course I can't divulge. In doing some work for that client, I may have come across information that would be of use to you."

"So tell me what that is," he said, flipping his notebook open to a clean page.

"What I had in mind," I began, trying to choose my words carefully, "was more like you'd tell me what you had so far, then I'd be in a position to see if anything I'd come up with would be of interest to you."

Augie closed his notebook.

"I don't think so."

"Lieutenant Cochran didn't think there'd be any problem."

"Cochran's a good man, and he's the only reason I'm talking to you at all," Augie explained. "But I'm not going to bring you in on this investigation, and then you tell me whatever you know if you think it's a good idea. You have to be reasonable, Mister Kyle."

"Yeah, I see what you mean."

"So, do you have something to tell me or not?"

"That depends," I said, checking my watch. It was twenty after four, and I wanted to see what Mister Li had to say, and I still wanted to check in with Speed on the Asian angle. "Are we talking about a conversation here and that's that, or are you going to want me to tag along downtown and go through all that statement business?"

"How do I know until I hear what you have to say?"

"Well, it's probably not anything that you haven't figured out for yourself anyway. So, let's just say I'm sorry I took up your time, and I'll see you around."

"Not so fast, Mister Kyle."

"What is it?"

"There's somebody I want you to meet."

"Who?"

"Come with me. You'll see."

The person he wanted me to meet was Mrs. Miller, in apartment 234. He led me up the stairs and along the balcony past the open door of an apartment in which his blond-haired partner was interviewing the lady with the laundry basket, all the way past the right-angle turn the balcony made into the other wing of the complex, the leg of the inverted L. At number 234, he rapped smartly on the door, and it opened to reveal a stylish wig and an ugly little dog. The wig belonged to a woman who'd never see fifty again, and so, too, did the dog, an ugly pug-nosed beast with a ribbon in his hair and toe polish on his claws.

"Mrs. Miller?"

"Why yes?"

"I'm Investigator August Dann, Dallas Police Department. We spoke on the phone earlier."

"Certainly, I remember?"

Mrs. Miller was one of those people who ends every sentence on an upswing, making it sound like a question whether it is or not.

"You told the officers out here last night . . . or actually, early this morning . . . that you saw someone in the parking lot. Is that correct?"

"Yes, it certainly is?"

I was beginning to have my doubts about Augie Dann. I was beginning to suspect that he was considerably nimbler of mind than his square body might lead one to suspect. At this late point in my first dealing with him, I finally realized that he was one of those most dangerous of people, especially of detectives: one who thinks fast and talks slow.

"Could you tell me what time that was?" he asked Mrs. Miller, who was unable to hide her delight at being the center of so much attention. True, it was only Augie and me, but I guessed that Mrs. Miller had replaced all the light bulbs in her apartment, and maybe some of the carpet, since she'd last had two men at her door.

"Pretty early?"

"I'll need you to be a little more specific, ma'am," Augie coaxed.

"I'd say . . . oh . . . Well, I had a beauty-shop appointment

156

at ten-thirty, and I dropped Benjy off on my way, and of course I wanted to stop off at the pet shop to buy him a little treat first? I'm afraid he doesn't like being groomed, so I always bribe him with a treat, you know? He's such a spoiled widdle baby, yes he is?"

She'd distracted herself with the reference to the ugly little dog on her arm, and now Augie and I stood watching while she tickled him under his slobbery chin and talked baby talk to him. The dog, whose pedigree I could only guess, put up with it for about an eight-count, and then snapped at the silly woman. She laughed, as if it were a game they played, and I figured out why there were flesh-toned Band-Aids on two of the fingers of her left hand. If she ever forgot to feed the little beast one night, she'd probably wake up missing some fingers.

"I'm not sure I follow you," Augie broke in on her. "What time are you saying that you saw someone in the parking lot?"

"I'd say it was about eight-fifteen, somewhere around there?"

"This morning?"

"Oh, no. No, yesterday morning. Thursday morning."

"I see."

I hoped Augie was disappointed enough not to follow up on that. Apparently, the message had been garbled in the relay, and he had been under the impression that Mrs. Miller had seen someone in the parking lot early this morning, Friday morning, around the time they figured Freddy had been murdered. I hoped he wouldn't pursue the matter of what she had seen the morning before, because I had a pretty good idea that what she had seen had been me and Freddy getting acquainted.

"Well . . ." he said, flipping his notebook closed.

The dog suddenly seemed to realize that his mistress was talking to someone, as if he'd been in a fog and just came to, and bared his fangs in a kind of idiot grin as he growled and snapped at Augie. To his credit, Augie saw that he was out of the little monster's range and reacted coolly. He didn't even flinch. But Mrs. Miller was chagrined, and lectured the dog soundly. Then she put him on the floor and stepped out onto the balcony with us, closing the door behind her. We stepped back to give her room, and she seemed to notice me for the first time.

"Hello," she said. "I didn't get your name?"

"Jack," I answered. "How do you do?"

We didn't shake hands because she didn't offer hers, and I'd been taught it was bad manners to offer your hand to a lady first. Besides, she was eyeing me very studiously, her brows knitted with the effort.

Maybe Augie noticed the way she was looking at me, or maybe he would have asked her some more questions anyway.

"This person you saw yesterday morning, Mrs. Miller," he began. "Can you describe him for me, and tell me what attracted your attention to him?"

"Well, it was that young man who lives downstairs," she said. "The skinny one with the funny little beard?"

"Yes, ma'am?"

"He was lying on the ground. He'd fallen down? And this other man seemed to be helping him up. Then they walked back that way, toward the young man's apartment. The other one seemed to be helping him, holding his arm, like this?"

She demonstrated, taking Augie's right forearm in her hands, in a clumsy and inaccurate imitation of the pain-compliance hold I'd actually used on Freddy that morning. But from the way Augie cut his eyes around at me, I could tell what he was thinking.

When she moved to show him what she had seen, I realized that what I'd first taken for a cheap costume necklace wasn't that at all. She was wearing a blouse with a bow at the neck, her shirttails hanging down over a pair of ski pants that did not by any means conceal her saddlebag hips. Threaded through the bow ran a kind of chain that I hoped meant what I thought it did.

"Could you describe this man for me?" Augie asked, his ballpoint poised over his notebook.

"Kind of average-looking, really?" she answered, still looking at me.

"About how tall?" Augie insisted.

"Oh, I don't know. . . . How tall are you, Jack?" she said.

"Six feet, give or take," I answered, smiling.

"And I'd say he was about your build, too," she added. "And the same color hair, dark like yours. He wore it that way, too. Pretty short, you know, but not real neat. Kind of windblown-looking?"

"Okay." Augie was getting all this down. "And how was he dressed?"

"A sport coat and slacks, no tie. The jacket was lighter-colored than the pants. I'm not positive, but I think they were both gray."

Augie looked at me as if he thought I might still be wearing the same clothes. But of course, thanks to Della's advice, I'd changed that morning into my navy blazer. I wished I hadn't taken off my tie after lunch with Scheiner and the gang down at America Southwest.

"Were you wearing your glasses, Mrs. Miller?" I asked, smiling, trying to sound helpful.

"My what? Oh, why . . . uh . . . I'm not sure . . ."

"You're nearsighted, aren't you?"

"How did you know?"

"Because you're not wearing them now."

At my first mention of the glasses, she'd begun looking for them, her hands playing across the front of her blouse. Now, she seemed confused.

"Yes, I am . . . nearsighted, I mean."

"Then you wouldn't have had them on when you first came

outside. Because you didn't need them then. You'd only wear them to drive, isn't that right?" I returned Augie's sharp look with a smile, as if I had an idea he wanted me to shut up but didn't want to say so in front of Mrs. Miller. "So did you put them on to see what was going on down there in the parking lot?"

"Yes, I suppose I did."

"But you're not sure?"

"I always carry them on a chain around my neck, you know? But . . . uh, I don't seem to . . ."

She fidgeted some more, frisking herself for the glasses.

"Mrs. Miller, if you're not sure you put on your glasses yesterday morning, can you be sure of what you saw, really? I mean, you don't think you could identify the man who was with Freddy if you saw him again, do you?"

It wasn't kosher, any of it. I'd gambled that the chain around her neck was for her glasses, and I'd gotten her rattled about not being able to put her hands on the glasses, then put such a leading question to her that it would never have been allowed in a courtroom. But this was no courtroom, and there was more than legal niceties at stake. The poor woman looked at me in helpless confusion. On the one hand, she'd described me to a T; from the look in her eyes, I thought she was even pretty sure I was the man she'd seen with Freddy. But if that was true, what was I doing here with Investigator Dann? Maybe she'd assumed that I was a cop, too. Augie hadn't given her any idea who I was, hadn't even introduced me by name. I figured he'd hoped she would come right out and finger me, put me face-to-face with the witness. That being the case, he'd overplayed his hand a bit. He should have spoken with her first, gotten her story straight, maybe even helped her locate her specs. But that was his problem.

"No . . . I don't suppose I could?" she answered finally.

"Thank you, Mrs. Miller." Augie nodded and smiled.

"Here's my card. If you remember anything else, give me a call, will you?"

"Certainly. Glad to be of help."

I nodded and smiled, too, but I didn't offer her any of my cards.

She was still addled, wondering what the hell had become of her glasses. So, before we left, Augie said, "Permit me, Mrs. Miller," and reached behind her. He pulled her glasses around in front of her. Somehow, they'd wound up dangling down her back, probably from her goofing around with her dog in her lonely apartment before we arrived, and that was why I had seen the links of the chain showing in the folds of her bow.

"Well, there they are!" she exclaimed, enormously relieved.

"Yes, ma'am." Augie nodded.

"I can't thank you enough," she burbled. "I would never have found them back there?"

"Thank you, ma'am," he told her, and off we went to see if his other witness, the assistant manager, would recognize my voice. He didn't say that was where we were headed, but he didn't have to.

CHAPTER
24

The drizzle had picked up its pace, threatening to bring our unnaturally sodden August to a record-breaking close. I'd heard on the radio that we already had our annual average of twenty-nine inches of rain for the year. We were ahead of schedule because ordinarily it doesn't rain at all in August in Dallas. The month ended Saturday, and if this Friday evening rain continued through the night, we'd have one of the wettest summers on record.

I thought about sharing that meteorological information with Augie Dann as we retraced our steps along the apartment balcony on our way back to the manager's office. But I guessed that he was in no mood to chat about the weather.

Instead, I said, "For the record, Augie, you'll have to admit that I'm pretty much an off-the-rack kind of guy."

"Meaning what?"

"Meaning I'm just pretty damned average. Average height, average build . . . dark brown hair and eyes. No facial hair, tattoos, or visible scars. You know, I'm generic."

"So?"

"So, just because Mrs. Miller's description might fit me, that doesn't necessarily mean it was me that she saw. If it fits me, it also fits thousands of other guys."

"Where were you yesterday morning between eight and nine o'clock?"

"Offhand, I don't remember at the moment."

"Offhand, maybe I could help you remember."

We were about halfway down the staircase on our way to the ground floor, and I didn't think anyone could see us. Maybe Augie was thinking about that, too, and wondering if he could sell the story that I slipped and fell down the stairs.

"Don't threaten me, man," I told him, shaking my head but not smiling. "You're too good an investigator for that."

"How would you know?"

"I thought that little trap you laid for me with Mrs. Miller was pretty slick."

"A little too slick, I'm afraid," he said.

"Look, Augie, I know you have no reason to believe me, except maybe that Eddie Cochran vouches for me, but the truth of the matter is that I had nothing to do with the murder of your man Freddy."

He stood more or less blocking my way and studied my face closely. Maybe he had also heard that you could tell when people lied by the pupils of their eyes. I had no idea what my pupils were doing, but the light wasn't that good in the stairwell because of the weather. I knew I wasn't exactly leveling with him when I said I had nothing to do with the murder, if you took into consideration that I had altered the crime scene pretty significantly by removing Liz. But I had already worked that out in my mind, rationalized it along the lines I'd covered with my attorney, and after all, one of the main reasons I had wanted to see Augie was to make sure he didn't get led off on a dead end in this thing. I was convinced that whoever killed Freddy set it up to implicate Liz just to confuse things, and the bottom line was that Augie and I were after the same thing. We both wanted to nail the real killer, and the less time he spent worrying about what Mrs. Miller saw or didn't see the morning before the murder and who called the manager's office to get Freddy's phone number, the sooner he'd get on the right track. All I had to do was convince Augie of that, without implicating Liz in the case. The ethics of it were a little scrambled. Even though I was working for Eddie, what I was really doing was acting in his place to protect Liz, and in a sense that made her my client. So, if you looked at it that way, I was obligated to keep her out of trouble by any legal means. The legality of my means so far might be open to interpretation, but I'd made the call under some time pressure, and now I had to stick with it.

"What do you have to do with this whole thing?" Augie asked.

"Fair question."

"How about a fair answer?"

"Freddy was in the keyhole-porn business. I guess you figured that out from his setup."

"So you've been inside his apartment?"

"Let's stick to what I know and leave how I know it until another time. Can you live with that?"

"Keep talking."

"His partner, who was the brains of the operation, was some guy who called himself Li."

"L-e-e?"

"L-i, I think, an Oriental type. Freddy would call him when he had video of some girl, and Li would take delivery of the tapes. He paid Freddy in cash sometimes, but sometimes in drugs."

"What kind of drugs?"

"Like this," I said, producing one of the two tablets I had

palmed from Freddy's stash the morning before. I handed it to Augie.

"What is it?" he asked.

"I don't know. Supposed to be some kind of designer drug. I've never seen it before."

"Where did you get this?" he asked. Another fair question.

"Can we let that slide for the time being?"

"I don't think so."

By quantity, most of my job is lying and loitering, as I may have mentioned before. But for criticality, the big thing is being quick on your feet, making tough decisions under varying degrees of pressure. And about two thirds of that is judging people. The call I had to make now was whether I could afford to tell Augie Dann how I knew what I knew, to admit to him that I was the man Mrs. Miller saw Thursday morning, that I had been inside Freddy's place, and why. About all I could hope to hold back was the identity of my client, and that was no sure bet. What swayed me was my read on Augie himself. He was sharper than he looked, but he remembered a little too much of the fine print in the manual for my taste.

"And I don't think I have anything else to say," I told him.

"Maybe you've already said too much."

"Anything's possible."

He looked past me for a moment, and I heard footsteps on the stairwell behind and above me. When I looked, I saw the lanky figure of Augie's partner clattering down the stairs. He stopped a couple of steps above me.

"Hi," he said. "I'm Investigator Wayne. No relation."

"Jack Kyle. No relation to whom?"

"The Duke." He smiled, then shrugged. "John Wayne. It's just a little joke, you know, kind of an icebreaker."

"I see."

Augie and I exchanged a look, and I thought both of us understood that our conversation had run its course because I was not inclined to tell him anything more with his partner as a witness.

"Yeah," Augie began, maybe a little annoyed at his partner's appearance on the stairwell. "I think you've said too much already."

"What does that mean?" I asked.

"That you've put yourself in the position of being a suspect in a murder."

"I don't think so."

"What would you say about material witness, then?"

"I wouldn't say anything. I'd let him do my talking for me," I answered, keeping my voice low and flat, not wanting to make a challenge of it. I handed Augie my lawyer's card, the high-dollar criminal attorney Doctor Oppenheimer had retained for me. He had won a few headline cases, and I thought I could see behind Augie's poker face that he was impressed. "His number's on the card. That one"—I pointed at one of the phone numbers embossed on the expensive-looking card—"is a digital pager, good twenty-four hours."

Investigator Wayne shuffled his feet on the wrought-iron and concrete stairway above me and cleared his throat. Maybe it was a signal to Augie to cue him in, but Augie paid him no mind. He stood looking from my lawyer's card to my face and back.

"I can't help wondering," he said, "why a low-rent operator like you would cough up the cash for a lawyer in his bracket. Unless, of course, you had something mighty important to hide."

I could have said any of several things to that, but I knew better. I'd invoked my attorney, and it was best to say no more. So I just raised my eyebrows and my hands, palms up, to let Augie know that he'd gotten all he was going to get out of me. For the time being, at least.

"And I suppose this means you wouldn't be interested in

stepping around to the manager's office with me, to have a word with her assistant."

I didn't say anything.

"Well, then, I guess there's no point in you hanging around here."

Still without saying anything, I nodded good-bye to Investigator Wayne and then had to turn sideways to wriggle past Augie and make my way down the stairs to the sidewalk. As I jogged across the parking lot in the blinding rain, I allowed myself a backward glance. Augie was walking toward the manager's office, and his partner was tagging along after him, talking and gesturing with both hands. He wanted to know what that had all been about, and I would have liked to hear Augie Dann explain it to him.

CHAPTER
25

The people of Dallas do not cope particularly well with inclement weather. This is especially true when it comes to rush-hour traffic, and it was five o'clock when I pulled out of the parking lot at Freddy's onto the two-lane residential street that would take me back to Meadow Lane. Knowing that Central Expressway was out of the question, I planned to go west on Meadow and eventually work my way back north on secondary streets to my office, where I could call Mister Li at the number he'd left for me and find out if Speed had come up with anything.

When it's drizzling or just beginning to rain in earnest is the most treacherous time for driving, because the film of water on the road mixes with the oils and goop of the surface, and if you drive at a normal speed your car will do what they call "hydroplaning." That means that your tires are not even in contact with the road, they're just gliding along on this sheet of oily water, and it plays hell with steering or braking. That was one reason why a rainy rush hour in Dallas always drove street cops crazy, the Traffic and Patrol types, anyway. There'd be more fender benders than the whole department could handle, which was partly why the cops nowadays didn't even bother with noninjury wrecks unless there was a hit-and-run or one of the cars was disabled and blocking traffic. Our rule of thumb used to be when it rained to get off the street, preferably somewhere that was paved and out of sight of the public. That way, the citizens you were sworn to serve and protect would not run over you or come to you with their problems, and you wouldn't get stuck.

Since my old Reliant's tires were carrying considerably less tread on them than I would have liked, I was really tiptoeing down the street, doing about twenty in a thirty-mile-per-hour zone. And I wasn't surprised when drivers passed me. One, a blond-haired kid in a Camaro, roared by me like I was parked, fishtailed back into our lane just in time to miss an oncoming bus, and looked up into his rearview mirror when he shot me the finger. A pretty typical North Dallas driver.

I tapped on and off my brakes to bring my old car to a safe and controlled stop at a Stop sign a couple of blocks north of Meadow and then sat there helplessly as cross traffic filled the intersection, and I watched in my rearview mirror as a lady driving a Toyota locked up her tires in a slow skid and rammed into the back of my car.

Cursing, I stepped out into the rain, tugging my jacket collar up around my neck, and slogged back to see how bad the damage was.

My car, an '85 with just over ninety thousand miles, already had its share of dents and dings, so I wasn't worried too much about the bodywork. There hadn't been much of a jolt to the impact, and the worst I expected to find was that she had busted a taillight. That I would have to get fixed. Body damage I could live with. All the insurance I had was the liability required by the state. I was relieved to see that she had swung enough to her right that her left front had hit me toward the middle of the rear of my car. Her left headlight was busted and her plastic left fender was crinkled pretty badly, but that wasn't my problem. My car looked okay, except that she'd put a new dent in the trunk lid near the lock and my rear bumper was crimped, making my license plate point down at the ground. It could have been worse.

So it was no big deal, but when I looked at the driver of the Toyota, I wasn't so sure. She sat slumped over the wheel of her car, not moving. I was already wet, and there was the chance that her insurance would pay off enough for my repairs, which I almost certainly would not waste getting my old car fixed, so I went back to see what her problem was.

"It's not that bad," I said, smiling, as I walked up to her open window. "Say, it's nothing to cry about."

There was no blood or broken glass, so she didn't figure to be hurt, really. But she wasn't wearing her seat belt, and the Toyota was too old a model to have a driver's side airbag, so you couldn't be too sure. Maybe she'd dinged a rib on the steering wheel. Terrific, I was thinking, as I leaned into her window to see if she was conscious. This is all I need, I was thinking.

The driver moved so quickly that I didn't react at all. I was leaning into the window, my left hand on the door, reaching in with my right hand to touch her on her shoulder, when in a flash the head resting on the steering wheel came to life and turned on me like a mad dog. The wig didn't turn as fast as the head, and I found myself looking into a pair of bugged-out eyes above a set of teeth that looked like fangs. I flashed for an instant on Mrs. Miller's ugly and ill-tempered little dog, but these teeth looked as big as tombstones, and the whole effect of this unexpected face was hideous and comical at the same time; because as it turned toward me, the wig atop it only made about a quarter of a turn, and wound up with the bangs over this ugly bastard's right ear and what should have been the left half of the downsweep of the pageboy hairdo running down this face. It was a stunning effect, and before I could react, he had my right hand in some kind of hold that jammed my whole hand back against my wrist. It hurt so bad I let out a roar like a big cat in a steel trap.

While all this was happening, which took maybe a couple of blinks of clock time, I heard a car door opening and saw a blur out of the corner of my right eye. That meant trouble, but I had to get my hand back from this crazy son of a bitch behind the wheel before I could do anything about it.

The pressure on my right wrist hurt so bad I almost went to my knees, but instead I jabbed hard with my left hand, fingers locked and extended, into the grinning idiot face. I got lucky, and my right hand came free. But there were two of them, and the one who came flying out of the backseat flew into the air and kicked me, driving the toe of his shoe into my ribs under my right arm. It's a good spot to shoot for, and it had the desired effect on me. I lurched to my left, dropped my right arm over my wounded ribs, and doubled over from the pain. That set me up nicely for the follow-up, something fancy I couldn't make out that paid off with the waffled sole of an Air Jordan flush in my face, with a lot of force behind it. I went down hard on my back, banging my head on the street beside the Toyota's left front tire, and tasted blood in my mouth. My nose was busted, and I had some crazy lights dangling around my eyes.

Before I could roll away or try to get up, one of them fell on my chest, straddling me, and I took three or four quick, sharp punches to the face, with a swipe down across my windpipe for good measure.

After that, it all got murky for me, because I was choking on my own blood and trying to get my vision to clear, while also fighting to breathe. The weight left my chest, and I thought I rolled to my right, away from the car toward the middle of the street. But I must have been mixed up, because I banged my face on a tire, and then somebody kicked at the back of my head. He didn't get a clean shot, skimming his foot off the pavement first the way a golfer might get under a long iron off the fairway. But it was good enough, and I was in the dark for a while.

I came to faceup in the rain, with blood in my throat and what sounded like a busy signal throbbing in my head. When I tried to roll over onto my side, I got an eye open and finally figured out that I was in the ditch at the side of the road, my head lower than my feet, and I scrambled around until I could get myself up into a squat. That hurt like hell, and I rested in that position until I felt up to standing. It took a few minutes, and I was pretty shaky when I did it, but a quick inventory made me hopeful that nothing was broken. Well, almost nothing. My right wrist hurt like hell and felt swollen. There are a lot of little bones in your wrist, and I wouldn't have bet all mine were in their original configurations. I did finally find a way of turning my body so that I could breathe without so much pain in my ribs that it didn't seem worth the effort. I stood rocking to and fro at the side of the road and watched the cars driving by. Here and there I spied a face in a car window, mouth open, staring at me until the car was gone into the rain. Nobody stopped to offer me a hand, and I didn't blame them. My clothes were soaked through, and I had an idea what I must have looked like.

People who won't take the chance of stopping to see what's going on will call the police, though, and I didn't want to waste any time explaining things. There were things to do, and I knew that as soon as I got myself to a dry place and got as much of the hurting stopped as I could manage, I was going to be pissed off more than a little. It wasn't much of a mystery to me who had left me in this condition, and as far as I was concerned, they'd made the same mistake as the Japs at Pearl Harbor. They'd sandbagged me and fucked me up pretty bad, but they hadn't killed me. Now, they had Hiroshima to look forward to, if I had anything to say about it.

It was wanting to get the hell out of there before some well-meaning police officer showed up to waste my time making out an aggravated-assault report that motivated me to put up with the pain involved in climbing back into my car. There I found out, as cars stacked up behind me and horns honked while all the southbound drivers worked their way around me into the intersection, that the shits hadn't been satisfied with beating the hell out of me. They'd also taken my car keys. Maybe they'd just tossed them into the hedge that bordered the apartments on the corner, to mess with me some more. But I figured the odds were they'd taken my keys so they could get into my office if the notion struck them, or my home, whatever the keys led them to. Of course, I kept only car keys on the ring, in case I ever leave the old Reliant in a parking lot that has attendants. My office key I kept separate, and they hadn't found it. Losing the car keys was not a problem, because I kept a spare set in one of those magnetized gizmos stuck to the undercarriage of my car, just in case. It hurt a hell of a lot bending over and reaching underneath the car to retrieve them, but I was glad I made a habit of keeping extras like that. It was no particular private-eye deal, I was just bad about losing my keys.

The old car cranked all right, and I pulled it around the corner to get out of everybody's way. That was when I realized that my trunk lid was open. It bounced and banged around behind me as I poked slowly down the side street to clear the area before any cops showed up. I drove for five or six blocks before I spotted the back of a school that faced onto Meadow and pulled into the teachers' parking lot. It was empty except for a pickup that may have belonged to a custodian, somebody getting ready for the start of school next week.

There I scrambled out of my car and limped around to the back to assess the damage. When I lifted the trunk, I got a little madder.

They'd made a point of leaving my fifty dollars. The two twenties and the ten lay crumpled atop my spare tire. That was all there was. My bag was gone.

It wasn't much, just a cheap cotton bag with vinyl trim. I kept my stuff in it, a pair of binoculars, a pawnshop 35-mm camera, a microcassette tape recorder, and some blank notebooks. My Mapsco had been in the bag, too. Total replacement cost was probably a couple of hundred bucks. But it was a couple hundred bucks I didn't have, plus the principle of the thing. My personal arrangements being what they are, I felt attached to my old Reliant the way normal people are to their homes. You might say I practically lived out of the car, and thinking that way, I remembered the wardrobe that was missing, too. I kept all kinds of clothes in the trunk, cowboy boots and jeans, a couple of different coats, some hats, stuff I used to change my appearance when I was on surveillance. Some of the stuff I kept on hangers I could put up on a broom handle across the backseat. That way I could sit back there and hide while I was on a stakeout. All that crap was gone, even the broom handle.

When I picked up the money, I saw that they had left me a message. There was something on each of the three bills, and when I arranged them in order, they spelled out in black Magic Marker, block print: MIND YOU OWN BIDNES.

CHAPTER
26

My office building was quiet and dark except for the security lights outside and in the lobby. It was a quarter to seven and still raining when I hobbled onto the elevator, on Friday of Labor Day weekend. There was not much to worry about as far as being interrupted went.

First, I checked around my floor to make sure there were no visitors lurking. I'd taken all the precautions I knew on my way back to lose anybody who might have been tailing me, or at least to make them show themselves, with negative results.

When I felt as safe as I was going to, I went into my office to get my key to the supply closet and Della's cabinet. She'd had a copy made for me, and this would be the first time I'd actually used it. I knew that she kept a first-aid kit in there from the time she'd taken a course at the Red Cross. I remembered coming in once with a cut on my face from the pinkie ring my ex-wife's second husband used to wear. Della'd gone overboard on the lifesaving drill, and I'd ended up with a bandage big enough to cover a gunshot wound. But that was a different story.

Since the wet and bloody rag I was wearing had been my last clean shirt, I took the first-aid supplies I found in Della's cabinet with me back into my office and chose the least wrinkled of my dirty shirts out of my file-cabinet drawer. I found some clean underwear in there, too, and retrieved my khaki slacks from the suit bag hanging outside my office. All this crap I dumped into Della's swivel chair because it had wheels on it, and I pushed the whole works down the hall and into the men's room. When I turned the light on and saw my reflection in the mirror over the sink, it almost scared me. I needed a drink.

Back in my office, I ignored the remnants of a quart bottle I'd been nursing for a week or so and went straight for the unopened fifth I'd been saving for my birthday. It was Johnnie Walker Red, and pretty damned good scotch for the price.

While I was there, I checked my phone machine, and got some pretty good news. Speed had checked in, with a message to call him at the crib. And Doctor Oppenheimer's Mister Li had called again, leaving the same number as before. I was glad to hear from both of them, but the breathy message from Liz saying she owed me an apology and wanted to see me—that I could have done without. Eddie was also on the tape, wanting me to check in with him. He sounded anxious, and I could understand that. So I had things to do, but the first order of business was to patch myself up.

When I looked into the men's room mirror the second time, I saw blood on the fingers of my left hand, the ones I'd shoved into the driver's face. Good deal, I thought. Maybe I poked his eye out. I downed a sizable slug of the scotch, and I wasn't disappointed with the warm burn it sent down my spine. Then I peeled off my wet and bloody clothes and stepped under a hot shower, thankful that our building manager had finally installed the damned thing to accommodate all my suitemates who jogged or otherwise worked out on their lunch hours. Of course, that hadn't been done until we lost a few occupants to an office building on the other side of LBJ that featured a spa in the building, complete with showers and hot tubs. I was just grateful for the torrent of hot water after the evening I'd been through, knowing that the night was far from over.

I stepped out of the shower once for another dose of scotch, and convinced myself that the guy in the mirror looked a little better than before. The nose was worse than I had thought, but it had been broken before. You might say that a deviated septum was an occupational hazard.

Back under the steaming shower, I told myself that I was lucky the two kung fu masters who'd jumped me hadn't known about my bad back. The last bruiser who worked me over had been told about that little problem that I had, and he had made it a point to pay my lower back special attention. This time it was mostly just my head.

Finally, I had to quit the shower and get down to business. I toweled off and moved in close to the mirror for a better look. I worked with an extra towel, applying pressure this way and that until I had the nosebleed pretty well under control. When I got the thing cleaned up, I realized for the first time that all the damage wasn't internal. There was a gash across the bridge of my nose that was accounting for a lot of the bleeding. Della had splurged for the heavy-duty first-aid kit, and I found enough gauze and tape to do the job on my nose. Then I took a look at my wrist.

It was swollen and reddish, which made me think something inside there probably was broken. Since I couldn't afford medical insurance and didn't have a couple of days to sit around the county clinic at Parkland Hospital waiting for my number to be called, I'd have to take care of it myself. Working clumsily with my left hand, I finally got the damned thing wrapped with an elastic bandage and then put tape over that. The result was not pretty, but I could use my hand without making a face, and that was progress.

After poking around at it for a while and fiddling with another roll of elastic bandage, I decided there wasn't much I could do about the ribs and closed the big first-aid kit.

By that time, the men's room was too steamy to get dressed in, so I loaded Della's chair up again and pushed it back to the foyer. There I toweled off again and slipped into my fresh clothes. I hung the wet stuff up over the window in my office and found a glass and some ice in the little office fridge. I poured myself a drink and settled in behind my desk to make some calls.

Mister Li himself answered at the number he'd left with Della, and said he thought I was owed an explanation. I assured him I wouldn't mind hearing one, and then we started trying to figure out a place to meet. I suggested my office, but he wasn't enthusiastic. After squabbling back and forth, I told him I could vouch for my phone if he could vouch for his, and we might as well cut up our business that way and save us both from driving anywhere in the rain. He said he'd call me back, which told me he was none too sure of the phone he was talking on and had probably gone to find a better one.

Next, I called Speed, and he said he had a source for me on Asian gangs in Dallas. It turned out to be a man I knew, an ex-cop who had gone back to graduate school and worked for the state now as a social worker. Speed gave me his number, and I jotted it down. Speed noticed something in my tone of voice and asked a lot of questions. I let him know I'd picked up another ass-whipping along the way, and he wanted to know if there was anything he could do.

"You wouldn't happen to know where I could put my hands on a gun, would you?"

"Christ, Jack. I'da thought you'd be the source on guns."

"Ordinarily, I wouldn't have any trouble finding one," I explained to him. "But I'm low on cash, and the few people I know who might have a loaner are out-of-pocket." I reminded him of the time and the holiday. He said he'd be right over, and hung up before I could tell him any different.

Next, I called Eddie at the hospital. I'd save Liz for last.

At first, Eddie sounded sore that he hadn't heard from me sooner, but when I caught him up on all that had transpired, he mellowed. He even showed a little concern for my health. He said he blamed himself for getting me involved. I said I blamed him, too, and poured myself another drink.

But as sorry as he was that I'd been waylaid, he was troubled about my run-in with Augie Dann. He didn't like it that I might be more involved in a murder than he'd suspected, that I'd had him vouch for me to Augie without knowing the whole story. I explained to him again that there was just some stuff he didn't want to know about this deal, due to his professional obligations. I thought to myself that he might hear some of it from his girlfriend, Carol, or loopy Liz, but that the least I could do was not to put him in that bind. He didn't sound like I had convinced him, but he did finally let the matter drop. He asked me if there was anything he could do, and I told him that I might need a little help with expenses when everything was said and done. He said not to worry about that, and to watch myself. I lied and said I had everything under control, not to worry.

Liz answered at her mother's house, the main number, and said that Carol had gone to see Eddie again. She wasn't due back until after ten o'clock. According to my watch, it was twenty after seven, and I was expecting Speed to show up at my place inside of half an hour. Allowing for whatever conversation Mister Li and I were in for, I estimated that I could get away by eight or a little after, and I could be at her house by eight-thirty. I asked her if what she had to say could be taken care of over the phone, knowing how she would answer. She didn't disappoint me, insisting that she had to see me in person. She offered to try to find my office, but I didn't want her out in the rain in her Mustang. I told her I'd be over around nine, to give myself a little elbow room, and she sounded like she appreciated it.

When I got off the phone, the adrenaline or whatever had kicked in to get me that far must have run down, because I suddenly felt dizzy and light-headed, and I hurt all over.

I still knew there'd be hell to pay before this deal was over, but I wasn't as sure as I had been who was going to be settling up and who was going to be doing the collecting.

CHAPTER
27

Speed was so pumped for whatever kind of trouble he'd dealt himself in on that he didn't even use the elevator to get to my floor. He crept up the stairs instead, just to be doubly careful, and I only heard his crepe-soled shoes squeak a couple of times as he duckwalked across the hall into the foyer outside my office.

"That you, Speed?" I called out from the office fridge, where I'd gone to get more ice.

"Jesus Christ!" he squealed, simultaneously demonstrating a flat-footed vertical leap that belonged in the NBA. He came down with eyes round as saucers, and I almost expected him to do that cartoon thing where his legs would turn into wheels and he'd run in place for a few frames before he finally got traction and screamed off-camera in a blur, "Jack . . . Jesus, man."

"Take it easy," I told him, trying not to laugh because of my sore ribs. "Nobody home but us chickens."

He looked at me like I'd done it to him on purpose, and leaned on Della's desk to catch his breath. I noticed he had his right hand stuffed down inside a paper sack, holding something.

"Jack, you oughten to do shit like that. I might have a heart attack or something."

"Sorry, Speed-o. I didn't mean to startle you. What you got in the sack?"

"Hang on a sec," he shushed me, then tiptoed back to the stairwell exit door. He rapped on it a couple of times, and I saw it open. He stuck his head through the door, then reappeared with Leslie Armitage by his side.

"Les," I said, making myself smile. "Long time no see."

They walked over toward me, Speed looking a little sheepish.

"I told her this was not a coed deal, Jack. But . . ."

"I know how it is," I finished his thought for him. "And I appreciate both of you coming over."

"Well, you might as well know, Jack, that I'm along strictly to look out for my Speedy. You can take care of yourself, but you and I both know Speed's not cut out for the heavy stuff."

"Sweetie pie . . ." Speed waved a hand at her to hush. "Jack's my friend, and if he needs our help, then . . ."

"Actually, Speed, all I need is a gun. Is that one there, in the sack, by any chance?"

"It's mine," Leslie announced.

"Then I appreciate the loan of it," I told her, and I meant every word of it. "I'll do my best to get it back to you when this thing's over."

"Meaning what, exactly?" she demanded.

"Lighten up, sweetie pie," Speed put in. "He just means if he has to use this baby on anybody, the cops'll want to keep it for a while, for ballistics. Right, Jack?"

"That's one way it could go."

"What's another?" Leslie had been conned before.

"Well, there are a couple of possibilities," I said. "For one, the bad guys might win this one, and then I don't guess you'd get the piece back. If you don't want to risk it . . ."

"Nah, it's not that," Speed was quick to assure me. "You're more than welcome to it. Keep it as long as you like."

"It does have a little sentimental value," Leslie said.

"It was given to her, Jack. It was a gift from a joh . . . custo . . . an old friend, a long time ago."

"That's right," she said.

"Well, like I said, if you don't want to risk something happening to it . . ."

"Not another word, Jack. The gun is yours," Speed said, slapping the sack and its contents into my palm for emphasis.

"For as long as you need it," Leslie added, in case I had misunderstood the gesture.

"I appreciate it, both of you. Is there anything you'd like me to sign?"

Speed laughed the notion off as ridiculous, but I could see that Leslie didn't think that was so bad an idea. The thing was, Speed trusted me, and Leslie, deep down, didn't trust anybody. Whoring can do that to a person. Besides, it might have been a whole different deal if I'd been asking the loan of one of Speed's cameras. A gun he'd feel better without anyway, but he always said his cameras were his eyes. I didn't know how Leslie felt about cameras, but I understood that a loaded gun could give a person a certain feeling of security, even without the sentimental value.

The phone rang in my office, and I thanked Speed and Leslie again, profusely, explaining to them very briefly that I had to take the call and that they had more than fulfilled any obligation either of them had to me by delivering the gun. That sounded like a hell of an exit line to Leslie, and she was more than ready to leave before things got out of hand. Speed would have liked to hang around for the action, or at least to have stayed awhile and talked about it in more detail; but as was often the case, Leslie got her way, and the two of them headed, squabbling, toward the stairwell. I waved as they disappeared, hoping it hadn't been an oversight on my part not to make sure they'd brought bullets, too.

I'd made it to my desk and had Mister Li on the line when Leslie popped back into sight, fishing something out of her shoulder bag.

"You may need these, too," she said, dropping a scarf onto my desk with the telltale rattle and clunk that told me there were bullets wrapped up in it.

"Thanks," I said, shielding the mouthpiece.

"Jack, if you don't mind my saying so . . ."

"Hang on a second, please," I told Mister Li over the phone. "What, Les?"

"Did it ever occur to you that you're not really, you know, properly equipped for the line of work you're in?"

"Almost daily," I assured her. "At least once a week."

"Good luck anyway." She smiled and blew me a kiss.

"Thanks again," I stage-whispered after her as she clicked across the hallway in her high heels.

Since I'd already put Mister Li on hold, I thought I'd go ahead and see what they'd brought me. I opened the paper sack and pulled out an old Smith & Wesson Model 10, a K-frame .38 with a two-inch barrel, one of the old workhorse revolvers of cops and gangsters alike for years. That part was fine, but the look of the thing! It was nickel-plated, with whorehouse pearl handles that featured on each side a big red valentine heart with Leslie's name spelled out in rhinestones.

"If anybody sees me with this thing," I mumbled aloud, "I'll have to kill 'em."

CHAPTER
28

"Mister Li, sorry to keep you waiting."

But he had no time this evening for amenities. Without any lead-in, he told me that he felt I had not been properly served by my friend Eddie Cochran or by any of the members of Carol's family.

I wasn't very clear on who knew what about whom in this whole deal, but Eddie had given me the impression that he and Carol, for reasons of their own, were not exactly flaunting their romance around Liz or anybody else in her family. If Li knew about Eddie and Carol, it was news to me, so I made it a point not to say anything that would confirm what he'd just said, in case it was only a suspicion on his part. I did say that I appreciated his concern and asked him for some details.

"I am not at liberty to divulge these matters."

"Then why are we having this conversation?"

"Be patient with me, Mister Kyle," he said. "You understand, I believe, the requirements of confidentiality in certain matters. This is true of your profession as well as of mine, is it not?"

"Probably," I admitted. "But of course I don't know what your profession is."

"I am a scientist."

"I see," I said, angry at myself. I'd assumed he was Oppenheimer's houseboy, or whatever the right word for it is. "You're under some ethical restraint, then?"

"It's very complicated. However, I do not feel I am remiss in suggesting to you that there is a great deal more to the situation you face than meets the eye."

"I see," I said, thinking here was a real scoop.

"As a professional in your own right, having been employed to serve the interests of the family, you are, I feel, entitled to certain information."

"I think we've already established that, Li. The problem is that you don't think you can tell me."

"The Oppenheimer Dilemma," he said.

"I beg your pardon?"

"I'm afraid I cannot tell you any more."

"And I'm afraid that's not nearly enough. Not by a long shot. What's the Oppenheimer Dilemma?"

"Ah, that's the question. When you have the answer to that, you no longer will be playing Pin the Tail on the Asshole. Do you understand?"

"I believe I do." I knew from trying to pick up Spanish for my fishing trips that it is the idioms that are the hardest part to master. "Is there anything more you can tell me?"

"I'm afraid not."

"Not even anything about a couple of rowdy youngsters who wear gang jackets and Air Jordan tennis shoes? I may be mistaken, but I believe they're into the martial arts, though, not basketball."

"I'm afraid I don't understand."

"Or about a Mister Li who traffics in designer drugs and keyhole pornography?"

"Li is a very common name, Mister Kyle."

"I know that. Christ, everybody knows that. Tell me something I don't know."

"The Oppenheimer Dilemma, Mister Kyle. That is the thing."

"Terrific."

CHAPTER
29

I got to the Highland Park house that Liz and Carol called home a little early, around a quarter to nine. And I did not feel a bit paranoid about the way I chose to approach the place.

Leaving my car parked on the street and far enough to one side that it wouldn't be seen by anyone looking out the front windows of the house, I eased the door closed and worked my way around the house, through the backyard, around by the driveway and the kitchen door, and back to the front, where I rang the bell. By the time I heard footsteps coming toward me down the entry hall, I was satisfied that there were no surprises lurking in the shrubbery. And I'd managed to peek into enough of the windows to think that the inside of the house didn't hide any threats either, at least on the ground floor.

She swung the door open with a smile on her face, but Liz's expression changed when she got a look at me.

"You look awful!" she said.

"Is it the jacket?" I'd had to go back to my wrinkled gray one to cover the gun butt sticking out of the back of my waist. The blue blazer looked hopeless, with all the rain and blood, and I only had the two jackets. "It doesn't really go with these pants, I know."

"Your face! What happened to you?"

"Why don't you let me in and we can talk about it."

"Oh, I'm sorry. Please, come in."

She showed me into the den or whatever they called it, the room where I'd had coffee with her mother what seemed a long time ago, and made such a fuss about me that I figured she'd never seen a broken nose before. She demanded to know everything, and I told her enough to get her off the subject. She was very solicitous, and offered to fix me a drink.

"No, thanks, kid. I've already had a few."

"I don't blame you."

"The first one was medicinal, the others were to get my nerve up."

"What for?"

"I wish I knew, whatever comes next."

"I think you're going to have a couple of black eyes, too."

"It wouldn't surprise me." I smiled to show her it was no big deal. "If it wouldn't be a bother, I could use a bite to eat, though. I didn't stop on my way over. You sounded like you might need whatever time we have before your mom gets home."

"Sure, let's see what's in the fridge."

That I wasn't worried about. In fact, it was thinking about that big industrial-strength refrigerator that Lois Li kept overstocked that had started my stomach growling in the first place.

As I followed her into the kitchen and took a seat at the table to watch her put together a generous sandwich, I marveled again at the kid's knack for showing a new side of herself. In the few days I'd known her, I'd seen her four times, and you'd almost have thought she was four different people. The blasé, tough-talking party girl one time. Then the loopy dopehead who kept trying to climb out of her convertible and run naked down the street. At Oppenheimer's, she'd come on like some kind of Lolita, the wide-eyed seductress. Now, she was somebody else entirely.

She was wearing jeans with a baggy SMU sweatshirt, and a pair of white sneakers. She had her hair brushed back, and she wasn't wearing any makeup. Miss Schoolgirl. And she'd already shown more concern for me than I'd seen her show for anybody in the short time I'd known her.

With a pretty smile, she put the sandwich in front of me on a plate and asked what I'd like to drink. I opted for a soft drink, and she picked one out of a shelf on the door of the fridge. Then she settled cross-legged into a chair around the corner of the table from me and watched me eat.

"It's good," I assured her. "You're a hell of a cook."

She laughed, and it looked good on her.

"See if that fills you up. If it doesn't, I'll make you another."

I told her one would be plenty, being that I had my hands on more food than I'd normally eat in a week. Then I asked her what was on her mind.

Her smile faded, and she looked away from me for a bit. When she turned back, she looked into my eyes, and I thought she was going to cry.

"I don't know who else I can talk to," she said.

"You make it sound like nobody cares about you."

"Mister Kyle, I . . ." She stopped and put a finger in her mouth.

"What about your mom? Or Granddad Oppenheimer, or Syd for that matter?"

"It's not easy for me to explain this," she said, talking around her hand and not looking me in the eye anymore. "Some of it, I'm not clear about myself."

"Take your time," I told her. "Start anywhere."

Instead of saying anything, she got up and left the room. I

had finished my sandwich and the soft drink by the time she came back. She was carrying a book. She put it on the table in front of me, taking away my plate and drink can at the same time. I heard her rattling the plate into the stainless-steel sink as I opened the book.

It was a hardback job, taller and narrower than most books, with the kind of design on the cover that you see on the journals sold in stationery shops. There had been a tag or label of some kind on the front of it at one time; I could see where it had been peeled off. The first page had a heading, the dates "March–May, 1982," and "Laboratory Notes." It was all in a slanted scrawl, the letters skinny and tall across the lined pages. I thumbed through it, and every page was the same, most of it done in symbols and the illegible handwriting. The symbols looked to me like some of the stuff I'd come across in my brief and indifferent college career. I thought it had something to do with mathematics, logic theory, chemistry, or maybe some of all three. When I looked up from the pages at Liz, it was with the hope that she was going to explain it to me.

At first she didn't say anything.

"What is this?" I asked.

"It belonged to the Doctor."

"Your grandfather?"

She nodded. "He used to keep a lot of books like that. Now, it's all on computer, of course."

"It's some kind of diary, isn't it?"

"It's a journal of his experiments. One of them, anyway. I'm sure of that. Pretty sure."

"Okay, what's the point?"

"See, this is the weird part. You're a friend of Eddie's, aren't you?"

Now that was a tricky little question. I had no idea how much she knew about Eddie and her mom. I didn't want to give anything away that would cause any of them a problem, especially Eddie. But if she knew about the two of them and I tried to con her, she might decide I wasn't trustworthy, and then I would never hear whatever it was she was trying so hard to get out. Was this some kind of test? I wondered.

"Yes," I said. Safe enough.

"Obviously, he trusts you."

"We trust each other."

"So that's one point in your favor," she said. "And you're an outsider, that's another."

She was thinking, working her way around to every finger and thumb, gnawing on her cuticles, and I kept quiet and waited.

"I guess if you were going to take advantage of me, you'd have done it last night. I was pretty vulnerable, to say the least. You didn't, did you?"

She stopped chewing on her fingers and looked me in the eye again.

"No. Don't you remember what happened?"

"Not really. I woke up this morning hoping it was a nightmare."

"Tell me what you do remember." I figured if she couldn't tell me whatever secret she was playing Hamlet over, I might as well get her version of Freddy's killing. It had to be done sooner or later anyway. "Have you heard from the lawyer your grandfather hired for me?"

"He left a message on my machine, but I didn't call him back. Should I?"

"I think so. He probably wants a statement from you about last night. Freddy called you?"

"Yes. He said he still had a copy of the tape, one you'd missed. I told you that."

"Yes, you did."

"He threatened me, said if I didn't come over there, he'd

make sure the tape went where it would do the most harm. And that he'd make more copies. He said he'd make a movie star out of me. I believed him."

"You should have called me," I said.

"I wasn't thinking, I guess. So, anyway, I went over there."

"You didn't have any trouble finding his place?"

"Not after I'd gone back there with you that night. And he gave me directions, just in case."

"What happened."

"He said he'd give me the last copy of the tape if I'd . . ."

She ducked her head again and started on her fingers.

"If you'd have sex with him again."

She nodded.

"Then what?"

"I didn't want to do it, but . . . I guess I knew when he called what he had in mind. He wanted to be rough, and I . . . I told him I couldn't do it, not straight. He said he had some pills."

"The ones you grabbed when I was there later, the ones you wouldn't let go of?"

"I don't know about any of that. They were just these little tablets. Some of his designer crap, I don't know."

"Were they all white, like the ones you had when I took you out of there?"

"Uh, yeah. Yeah, they were just these little white pills, kind of off-white, you know? Just regular pills, like you see around the clubs all the time."

"Have you ever seen any that are peach-colored, with red on the ends?"

"No, I don't remember any like that. Why?"

"It doesn't matter. So what happened after you took his pills?"

"He was drinking. He'd already been drinking when I got

there. So I had a drink to wash down a couple of the pills, I don't know. I'm not sure how many pills . . ."

"Then what?"

"He took my clothes off, I think."

"You're not sure?"

"He started to, and then . . . yeah, he took my clothes off. I'm pretty sure about that. I don't remember the rest of it. I don't remember anything until I woke up at the Doctor's and then you were there and I was a real shit. I'm sorry about the way I acted to you."

"Are you?"

"You don't understand. I mean, I don't even understand, you know? I felt like a . . . I don't know, like a real slut. Have you ever done something, gotten out of control like that and done shit, and then the next day you couldn't remember? I mean, Syd told me. She told me about the condition I was in when you brought me home. How I was acting. God, I felt like such a . . . I don't know."

"You've had a pretty rough time."

"Yeah, and whose fault is that? I asked for it. You know, I'm not really like that. Partying and clubbing, doping . . . it's just that . . . I don't know anymore, like . . . who I am. Okay, Liz, that sounds pretty stupid, pretty trite, I guess."

It came as no surprise to me when she started crying, and I didn't do anything about it, just let her do it until she was ready to talk some more.

Liz got up from the table and went out into the hall. She came back in a minute or so with a tissue. I'd heard her blowing her nose while she was out of my sight. While there was a break in the action, I asked her if she'd mind if I smoked, and she got me an ashtray. Then she settled down and started talking about her dead brother, Alan.

They had been pretty normal, she'd always thought, no closer than most of her friends were with their big brothers, all the usual stuff. And she hadn't thought his death had hit her all that hard. In fact, she'd felt guilty because she hadn't really felt the way she thought she was supposed to about it. There hadn't been any of the deep grief or depression she'd expected. Her mom had taken it pretty hard, in her own way. In other words, she'd become even more spacey, distracted. The two of them would sit at the dinner table for hours sometimes, neither of them eating, neither of them saying a word. Liz was afraid to admit that she wasn't grieving, and she had no idea what her mother wasn't saying.

But Alan's death really had affected Liz, more than she'd realized. She knew that now. Because a few months after Alan died was when she changed. That was when she started doing all the crazy, stupid things that weren't like her. She understood that now, it was her brother's death, the whole thing of facing death itself for the first time, that made her behave that way. But it was more than that, too.

"What else was there?" I asked.

"Something Alan said not long before he died. He showed me that book. He's the one who took it from the Doctor's house. Alan was a genius, you know. He worked on stuff with the Doctor, far-out stuff I didn't understand even when he tried to explain it to me. But Alan stumbled onto something at the Doctor's. Something that scared him to death. I've forgotten what he called it. He had a fancy name for it."

Not wanting to prompt her, I didn't say anything.

"But . . . here's the weird part, Mister Kyle. Alan told me that what that book was about was . . . us. Alan and me."

"What do you mean?"

"We were the experiment in that book."

"Did he say what kind of experiment it was?"

"If he did, I didn't understand any of it. But it scared Alan to death."

"That's the second time you've said that. Do you mean it literally?"

"I'm not sure."

"Alan died of some kind of rare congenital heart condition, I was told."

"So was I," she said.

"And I was told that you've been examined, and that you don't have that condition. Is that true?"

"There's nothing wrong with my heart. My head, maybe," she said, and laughed a little so I would know she meant that as a joke, with a tear working its way down her cheek. "Oh, speaking of my mind, I remember now what Alan called the Doctor's experiment."

"What was that?"

"The Oppenheimer Dilemma."

CHAPTER
30

Carol got home about half-past ten and found me and the kid having our heart-to-heart at the kitchen table. There were a lot of looks swapped back and forth between us, all of which I took to mean that Carol was upset about my being there alone with Liz, for whatever reason, and also that Liz didn't want me to say anything to Carol about what Alan had told her. The kind of undercurrents you'd expect in your average dysfunctional family.

The three of us made small talk for a few minutes, most of it about how Eddie was doing. Carol told me that he'd negotiated himself into an even smaller cast, and that he was getting up and about in a wheelchair several times a day now. He and Miss Farmer were still going at each other like Jack Nicholson and Nurse Ratched in *One Flew Over the Cuckoo's Nest*. All of that was safe enough to talk about in mixed company and pretty good news all around, for me in particular. Because the sooner Eddie got on his feet, the sooner he could relieve me as the shepherd of this squirrelly little bunch.

Neither of them seemed disappointed when I said it was time

for me to be going, and Carol offered to walk me to the door Liz said good night and disappeared up the staircase, at least until she was out of sight. It wouldn't have surprised me if she stopped about halfway up in hopes of overhearing whatever her mother and I had to say.

Carol wanted to know what Liz and I had been talking about, and she may have looked relieved when I told her I'd just stopped by to get Liz's version of what went on at Freddy's apartment. Or maybe Carol was just tired, and I was reading too much into things.

She thanked me for all that I had done and said that she was glad that her father had hired an attorney to keep me out of jail if it turned out that I'd been too smart for my own good. She didn't object when I offered the opinion that her father didn't seem to have too sure a grasp of things. He had been there in the room when I'd gone over everything with the two lawyers, but the last time we'd talked, he hadn't seemed to understand it all. Of course, we hadn't talked that night about Liz's porn debut. I asked her if they'd had the family sit-down I'd recommended to the Doctor, and she said he'd called her and they'd made plans to get together the next morning. She said she wasn't looking forward to it, and I asked her where they'd planned to have their meeting. She said it was to be at the Doctor's, "of course." That was added with such a bitter tone that I didn't ask her why she didn't like to go to her father's house. All I did then was say good night and leave.

It may have just been that I was tired and all my wounds were stiffening, but as I trod gingerly to my waiting Reliant, I had the feeling that both of the women in the house were watching me.

After driving away from the house, I worked my way over to Preston Road and turned toward downtown. There was no hurry, because I hadn't decided where I wanted to go. Preston would turn into Oak Lawn, and from there I could just as easily make my way to Oppenheimer's or over to Deep Ellum. There were some pretty good reasons to go both of those places.

Deep Ellum was the only place I knew to look for my Asian chums, the kung fu twosome with the Air Jordans. Tonight would be a good time for round two, I figured, because I didn't think they'd expect me to be up and about quite so soon. And the element of surprise might mean everything the next time the three of us bumped into each other. With any luck, one of them was one-eyed now, so maybe I'd come up on his blind side.

Then there was this business about the Oppenheimer Dilemma. Basically, I thought I knew what a dilemma was without looking the word up in a dictionary, but I couldn't make any sense out of that as far as what kind of an experiment the old man might be running on his two grandkids. There were two of them, of course, and a dilemma required two options. But it required two bad options, and that was puzzling. It was also a little puzzling that two different characters in this little show had dropped the phrase on me within a couple of hours. Things didn't normally work that way. This thing had all the earmarks of a clue, and I was accustomed to digging those things up on my own.

By the time I pulled up to the intersection of Oak Lawn and Wycliffe, I'd made my decision. I turned left onto Wycliffe and started giving myself a little pep talk, psyching myself up for a rematch with the martial artists. From the way I was feeling, I figured that if I didn't take a stab at evening the score with them that night, I might not be up to it later. Before long, I hoped to get a little shut-eye, and if everything that was hurting me now got cold and stiff after a night's sleep, I wasn't going to be in any condition for payback the next day. Besides, I didn't think I was ready for any kind of showdown with old man Oppenheimer, because not only did I not have any answers yet, I also didn't know what questions to ask. For that,

I would need a little time to think. And some coffee, a pot or two of strong black coffee.

It was almost midnight when I pulled into the parking lot of a convenience store at Carroll and Columbia to pick up a fresh pack of cigarettes and use the pay phone. For about the dozenth time since my run-in with the Asians, I jammed my hand down inside my empty jacket pocket, looking for the notebook that wasn't there. They'd taken it while I was knocked out, along with my bag and its contents, and of all the crap they'd made off with, it was the notebook that I missed the most. It had all my phone numbers, among other things, and being without it was about like waking up to find someone's sneaked in while you were asleep and given you a lobotomy. It meant I was having to try to actually remember stuff, and that was a pain in the ass.

One name and number I did have was the expert on Asian gangs that Speed had come up with, the ex-cop social worker. Of course, all I had was his office number, and that wouldn't be any use to me until at least Tuesday, when everybody came back to work after the long Labor Day weekend. But maybe, since this guy was not a cop anymore, since he was nowadays a social worker and it stood to reason nobody was likely to be particularly interested in harassing him or his family, he might have a home number that was listed. Of course, since I was trying to use a pay phone in East Dallas, there was no phone book attached to the shelf on the wall of the convenience store. There was only the cable that had been used to secure the book. Why people insisted on stealing phone books was a mystery to me, but maybe it was a matter of principle. I dialed Information, and sure enough, the phone company had one of those robotic taped messages that told me the man's home number, in the jerky, nonhuman voice that must have cost millions of R&D dollars to engineer. Even more amazing, the guy was at home. He said he remembered me from our days together on the DPD.

"The reason I'm calling," I explained, "is that I understand you're the local expert on our Asian gangs."

"I don't know about that, but I'll do what I can. What do you need to know?"

Actually, I had a pretty long list of questions, some of them coming to me as I stood there with the phone cradled on my shoulder, writing down what he told me on a sheet of Della's typing paper I'd folded longways. I was fresh out of notebooks.

He had some names for me when I asked about the little gangsters with the team jackets and Air Jordans. Yes, he told me, they were Vietnamese, and they were pretty heavy into drug trafficking. They'd move anything that had a price on it, and lately they'd gone from selling heroin and cocaine more into designer drugs. There was plenty of demand for the stuff, particularly among the trendy club set, neo-punk, post-yuppie types who favored Deep Ellum for its cutting-edge yet freewheeling milieu. He actually used words like that, but I was writing pretty fast trying to get it all down, and there is a chance I've misquoted him a time or two. But I was getting the gist of it.

In particular, I made sure I got the names right that applied to my kung fu friends. My man was pretty sure from the way I described them and the job that they'd done on me that they were part of a local Vietnamese gang who called themselves the Tiger Boys. They all sported some kind of tiger tattoos; it was part of their initiation deal. And aside from drug dealing, they were supposed to be pretty heavy into strong-arm stuff, shakedowns and their own version of the protection rackets. For that, they specialized in victimizing Vietnamese immigrants, of which there were several thousand in Dallas and its suburbs. The Metroplex had attracted more than our share of refugees from Southeast Asia in the aftermath of Vietnam, and nobody knew for sure how many Vietnamese, Laotians, and Cambodians had settled in the area. A lot of them hadn't picked up the language, and also hadn't made it out of their homelands with much more than the clothes on their backs. Understandably, they didn't trust the authorities, and were not inclined to take their problems to the police. Not even when those problems included assholes like the Tiger Boys, who could make their lives a living hell. It was not a pretty picture, and I found myself wondering for maybe the thousandth time if Vietnam would ever be over.

The social worker told me that the Tiger Boys drew most of their members from a couple of extended families, and odds were that my two playmates were either named Li or Thieu. He also told me that the DPD was working on the problem. They'd hired some Southeast Asians to work as community service officers, and a handful were in the academy to become commissioned police officers. They had opened some community centers that specialized in working with the Asians in their neighborhoods and enclaves, and he was optimistic that things were going to get better for these people. But it would take time. He gave me some names of police-department people who were working in the program, and asked me to keep him posted on any developments. I thanked him for the primer and apologized a couple of times for calling him at home.

With a fresh pack of cigarettes and a small cup of coffee, I stood beside my car in front of the convenience store and surveyed the area for a couple of minutes. The intersection of Carroll and Columbia was pretty much the hub of the part of the city that these days we called East Dallas. At one time decades ago, East Dallas was a city to itself, but like most of the dozen or so little settlements of the early days, it had been annexed into Dallas proper as the "Big D" sprawled into the late twentieth century. Across Carroll I saw the closed and heavily secured front of a pawnshop owned and operated by a friend of mine, another ex-cop. The building had been many things in its career, including at one time a boardinghouse for East Dallas denizens down on their luck. We'd had to pull a few of them, kicking and screaming, out of some of the second-floor rooms one night because the building was on fire. I knew, although it wasn't apparent from the street, that another old friend, a retired auto-theft detective whose real calling was painting and sculpture, was in the process of converting the shambles of the second floor into a studio. I knew that if my need for a handgun had been a little more timely, I could almost certainly have gotten what I needed from one of those guys, either the pawn-broker or the artist. Then I wouldn't have to worry about get-ting caught packing Leslie Armitage's gaudy whorehouse special. But that couldn't be helped.

Although I thought of myself as having no friends, or at least precious few of them, it occurred to me that this might not be the case. Everywhere I went in this town, I found memories. And connected with many of them, I knew there were people I'd shared those memories with. Maybe I should make the time for a social call once in a while, to renew a few of those connec-tions. It seemed that I only ran into friends these days when they or I needed something.

When I tossed my empty plastic coffee cup into the trash can beside the front doors of the convenience stores, I noticed the two clerks inside had their heads together and were watching me. That made sense. I knew I didn't look very reputable, with my nose bandaged and the dark circles under my eyes like the charcoal daubs of an outfielder against the high sun of a day game, and I didn't blame them for keeping an eye on me. Rob-bery was a fact of life for these guys, and neither of them had come to America to die for a handful of ones out of their cash register. I wondered where they had come from, because I hadn't been able to place their accents, and I also wondered how my native country looked to them.

All of which—my conversation with the social worker and my ruminations about old friends and the rest of it—had me in a more or less philosophical frame of mind by the time I drove out of the parking lot and pointed the old Reliant down Columbia, heading toward downtown and Deep Ellum. It was the first hour of Saturday morning, the last day of August and the day before my birthday. I was feeling a little older than I liked to admit, and was surprised to find that I wasn't so sure anymore that I wanted to find my two Tiger Boys, or what I'd do if I did.

As I drove around, I couldn't help remembering things, things that had nothing in particular to do with the business at hand. That's how it is with cops, practically every street corner or liquor store has a story that goes with it. Sometimes it's something you got into personally, sometimes just a part of the local lore. I remembered once I pulled over a tourist, a guy who obviously didn't belong in the East Dallas combat zone where I found him. It was good advice I gave him about getting out of the neighborhood, but he didn't take it. He wound up spending a long weekend at Parkland after somebody found him robbed and beaten in an alley later.

Like most natives, I seldom visited the tourist attractions of my own hometown. In fact, it always puzzled me to find that we had tourists, people who elected to spend their vacations in the city where I had lived and worked for twenty years. What was there to see here? I always wondered.

For one thing, I had never made the obligatory tourist excursion downtown to the Kennedy Museum. People who had been there assured me it was a tasteful and informative experience, but I had no desire to check the view of the triple underpass from that particular window of the old Texas School Depository.

The view from the revolving restaurant bar atop Reunion Tower was nice, and I'd been there a few times. But I'd only been to the West End, for example, a couple of times, and then on business. It had reminded me of the French Quarter, without the really good jazz or the pornography. The seafood was no match, either.

Deep Ellum was something like that, too. It had that kind of feel to it, a little stretch of blocks on the east end of downtown, the opposite of the West End as much in attitude as in geography.

There was some car traffic, but mostly the streets were for walking, and wandering gaggles of tourists and local party-goers bumped and jostled along the sidewalks and spilled over into the streets themselves. Finding a place to park was a chore, too. The rain had let up, but from the look of the sky, what you could see of it beyond the garish lights and street noise, the respite was only temporary. The crowds were swarming, at half-past midnight.

Cover charges came with the territory in a setup like this, but I talked my way past most of them as I ducked into and out of the Art Bar, Club Dada, and the Blind Lemon Bar, all three places sharing space and interlocking doorways in a big old building that had been many things in its life. There was live music, and people who looked happy and relieved to be taking a break from the everyday on a holiday weekend, but no sign of my Tiger Boys. By half-past one, I was tired of elbowing my way among hordes of young people and people working too hard to be young again, all of them in baggy clothes all black or black-and-white, T-shirts with the names of bands I'd never heard of, and all the dopey hats and chopped purple hairdos. Relieved in a way that I hadn't forced myself to decide how to settle my score, I pushed myself, feeling my wounds and fatigue, back through the throng to my car and headed for my office and a few hours' sleep.

CHAPTER
31

Saturday morning was my second-best chance of the week to sleep in, because the cleanup crew didn't usually show up until around ten o'clock in the morning. Sundays were best, because it was rare that anyone came onto our floor all day. But this Saturday I had things to do, and I was up and busy by a couple of minutes after nine. My face was still stinging from the cheap but inoffensive after-shave I'd splashed on after scraping my face clean with a disposable plastic razor. Due to all the bandaging on my face and wrist and my not wanting to have to redo it all, I'd opted to skip another shower, but all in all I felt reasonably fresh, under the circumstances.

My third cup of coffee was steaming on my desk, and I'd transcribed my scribbled field notes onto a clean sheet of typing paper, to which I'd added everything I'd learned about the case so far. I did that sometimes, because I'd found that writing things down helped me think. My method was to kind of free-wheel, jotting down unrelated and often insignificant stuff as it popped into my head. When all that dried up, I'd go back over it and draw circles and arrows to connect things that seemed to be related. Then I'd start over on a clean page, putting everything down again, more organized. It may not be scientific, but I'd found that it worked for me, and I'd often been surprised at the connections that evolved, links I hadn't seen before, from doing it that way.

Satisfied that I'd exhausted my little exercise for the time being, I checked my phone messages. Speed had called, to see if I was all right, and wanted me to call him back for an update. I'd do that later.

Liz had called to tell me out loud what she'd tried to signal to me the evening before, namely that she didn't want me to tell her mom what she'd told me about Alan and Doctor Oppenheimer. Eddie had called at some unspecified time to say that he expected to be released from the hospital, maybe as early as Monday morning. He didn't forget to ask me to call him as soon as I could, to bring him up-to-date on whatever I'd found out. It surprised me a little that there was no message from Carol.

After I'd run through my messages, as I was about to make my first call of the day, my phone rang and I found Syd on the line.

"Good morning," I told her.

"Oh, you're live."

"More or less."

"I'm so used to getting your machine."

"You haven't been leaving messages."

"I don't like talking to machines."

"Neither do I. What's up?"

"You tell me, Mister Kyle."

"Give me a hint."

"I know you went to see Liz last night. What did she tell you?"

"How do you know that?"

"She told me not to come over, that she had plans. I got it out of her."

"But not what it was about, huh?"

"Not exactly. So?"

"So I think you should ask Liz. If she wants, she can tell you. That doesn't mean it's a deep, dark secret, kid. I just don't like to repeat things."

"Professional ethics?"

"I guess you could call it that. I just don't like doing it. Why don't you call Liz, or drop by to see her?"

"She has plans again this morning. Do you know what that's all about, or is that another professionial secret?"

"I dunno."

"You're not much help."

"Guess not."

"I care about Liz. You know that."

"What's your point?"

"I'm the only one who has her best interests at heart, Mister Kyle. If you know anything . . ."

"We're going to start repeating ourselves here, kid. I believe you think a lot of Liz, and I don't even have a problem with the way you express your feelings for her. I think you're both a little young for some of the things you're doing, but, hey, I'm an old fart. I can't help that."

"You're patronizing me."

"Not on purpose. Don't you think Carol has Liz's best interests at heart?"

"Who knows with her? They're not going over to the Doctor's place, are they? Carol's not going over there, is she?"

"Would that be a bad idea?"

"Carol doesn't go there."

"Then why the question?"

"Liz said something about a meeting, with her family."

"Sounds pretty harmless."

"If you mean that, you're dumber than you look, Mister Kyle."

"That's a possibility. What can you tell me about the Tiger Boys?"

"What? What do you know about them?"

"More than I'd like to. What can you tell me?"

"They're local color, poseurs. We run into them in the clubs sometimes. What've they got to do with anything?"

"Good question. What did they want with Liz that first night? One of 'em put his hand on Liz as we were leaving the Art Bar. What was that about?"

"Who knows? He's probably got a crush on her."

"You kids ever buy dope from them?"

"No, of course not."

"They ever give you any?"

"No . . . not me, anyway. I'm not their type."

"But Liz is."

"I've never seen her do anything like that, not with them."

"But you're not always there. Like the night she gave you the slip and ended up at Freddy's apartment."

"Nobody's perfect."

"How about a guy named Li?"

"Mister Li, the Doctor's pal?"

"Maybe. Do you know another one, one that's tied in one way or another with the Tiger Boys? Or with Freddy Barksdale, or both?"

"No."

That was her shortest answer yet, and the kind of break in a pattern that I paid attention to. I repeated the question, and she told me that Li was a common name among Southeast Asians. No shit, I thought, but I didn't say that. What I did was ask her if she knew anything about peach-colored designer drugs, to which she gave me another monosyllabic answer in the negative. I made note of that.

"You were there, at Liz's, when she got the call from Freddy the other night, weren't you? The night she went back over to his place and I wound up bringing her home? I just want to get the details straight."

"Yes. Kind of."

"What does that mean?"

"I was there, but not exactly in the room with her when she got the call. I'd gone down to the kitchen for something to snack on. When I got back up to her room, she was hanging up the phone."

"She told you it was Freddy who had called."

"That's right, like I told you that night when I called you. She kind of rolled her eyes and said, 'That damned Freddy,' something like that."

"But you didn't hear the phone ring?"

"No, I was downstairs in the kitchen."

"There's an extension down there. You would have heard it ring."

"I . . . I don't know, it came in on Liz's line."

"Carol's line is the only one that doesn't ring through on the extensions. Liz is very sensitive about that. It's one reason she doesn't like to talk on her phone. It's one reason she wanted to see me in person last night."

"I don't know what you're getting at, Mister Kyle. Maybe I just didn't notice the ring, maybe the bell on the kitchen phone was turned down or something. What difference does it make?"

"How would I know? Just thought I'd ask."

"I thought your job was to protect Liz."

"Actually, what I'm doing doesn't qualify as a job, since I'm not getting paid. But what I was supposed to do was get the tapes of Liz back from Freddy."

"And you did that."

"Yep."

"So now you're out of it. Your part's over. Why don't you leave us all alone?"

"Of course, according to Liz, Freddy claimed I didn't get all the tapes. He's supposed to have told her that he had one more. You're not forgetting that little matter of a murder, are you?"

"What's that got to do with it?"

"Quite a bit, since Liz was on the scene."

"You took care of that."

"Yeah, and that means I dealt myself in on the deal."

"Freddy? You're stirring everything up on account of Freddy? He was a creep, he was slime."

"Murder's murder, kid. You can't dabble in it. It'll always come back to haunt you. Sooner or later, my part in the thing will come home to roost. Too many people know about it already. And when that pigeon comes home, I plan to have some answers ready."

"You're covering your own ass, then."

"Among other things."

"You have no idea what you're stirring up."

"You could explain it to me," I said.

"That's the point, that's why I'm even talking to you. I don't know exactly what's going on, but I do know it's something evil and it goes a long way back. And I know it could destroy Liz if you don't leave things alone."

"Or maybe if I do. Did you ever think of that?"

"For all our sakes, Mister Kyle, I hope the hell you're right."

That left me with something to think about, a couple of things, as a matter of fact. Some of the pieces were coming together, and I couldn't argue with Syd's notion that whatever it was, it was plenty dark and went a long way back.

Syd's call hadn't been part of my plan for my Saturday morning, but it hadn't been exactly a distraction, either. It had given me more bits of information to jot down in the margins of my notes, and I found myself drawing a couple of new circles and arrows.

When I was done with my doodling, I called the police. The number I dialed was the Crimes Against Persons main line, and I told the clerk who answered that I wanted to talk to an investigator. Rounding up one of those at half-past nine on the Saturday morning of Labor Day weekend took a couple of minutes.

The name he gave when he answered didn't ring a bell, but times change, and since I'd been gone from the department, a lot of people had been promoted or transferred, and more than a few had retired. So I didn't know him and he didn't know me, and that meant that what I wanted to get done would take a lot of explaining. Fortunately, I had plenty of coffee and a few cigarettes left.

First, I wanted him to write up an offense report on an aggravated robbery. After he explained that I was supposed to call Communications to have a patrol officer come out or to dictate my report to somebody else if it was a cold crime, I assured him there were some special circumstances and tossed Augie Dann's name around a bit. It was important that Augie get a copy of the report, and I made that clear. If Augie had enough pull to get the weekend off, more power to him, but I knew he'd want to know what I had to say about this. The investigator decided to humor me, and started asking all the questions. He got the date, time, and location, and I told him all about the two Tiger Boys and how they waylaid me with the old fender-bender trick.

When we got down to the suspects, I gave him their heights and weights, and told him they were Vietnamese. I also told him everything the ex-cop social worker had told me, and gave the investigator his number for follow-up, along with a suggestion that the Southeast Asian storefront operation probably would be a good source of information also. When he asked about scars or marks, I told him I thought the one who had played the role of the lady driver probably had a bad eye, the right eye more than likely. He asked me to explain, and I did, describing the blood that I had found on the fingertips of my left hand, and how that had done my heart good, giving me hope that maybe I'd gouged the little bastard's eye out. The investigator didn't say anything.

"Why didn't you report this when it happened?" he asked.

"I wanted to kill them myself, but I had trouble locating them last night."

"I see."

"They hang out in Deep Ellum, I understand. The Art Bar, I believe."

"Okay."

"Now, here's something I'd like you to include in the narrative, okay?"

"Shoot."

"These two guys murdered a man by the name of Freddy Barksdale. Augie Dann is working the case."

"What makes you think so?"

"A footprint in the victim's blood is going to match one of their Air Jordans. Also, I'm hoping the Crime Scene Search people lifted some latents. And I'm willing to bet that they'll match."

"Are you an officer?"

"No, but I used to be."

"Where?"

"DPD, same as you."

"I don't make the name."

"I wasn't very memorable."

"You a friend of Augie's?"

"Not yet."

"How do you know about the bloody footprints at the scene?"

"I was there, after the fact. The guy was dead and patrol was

en route, so I didn't stick around. Augie'll be happy to hear I
told you that, so don't forget to mention it when you talk to
him."

"Okay. Anything else?"

"That's about it."

"Where can we reach you if we need . . ."

"Tell Augie I'll be in touch. I owe him a statement, but there
are a couple of details I have to take care of first. You got that?"

"I got it. One other thing, though."

"What's that?"

"Are you sure you know what you're doing?"

"That's a damned good question. When do you expect to
speak with Augie?"

"I was thinking I'd probably call him at home right now."

"I'd appreciate that. I'll be checking back as the day pro-
gresses. Oh, there is one more thing."

"Yes?"

"You needn't bother sending anybody around to my office. I
won't be in for the rest of the day."

"If you say so."

Augie would send somebody by anyway, and so would I if
I'd been in his place. This was some pretty dicey stuff I'd just
laid on the guy who caught the phone, and I hoped Augie
would follow up on the robbery beef. Kicking my ass and taking
my stuff constituted aggravated robbery, just as if they'd gone
into a convenience store with a couple of guns, as far as the
Penal Code was concerned. It didn't matter that I'd waited
awhile to phone in the report. If I'd still had my camera, I'd
have taken pictures of myself as proof of the damage they'd
done. But the offense report was enough to book the Tiger
Boys if Augie could get them I.D.'d and located, which I
thought was pretty likely given the background sources available to him. Then they could be printed and processed. They
might even have to give up some blood and hair samples, de-

pending on what kind of physical evidence CSS had come up with in Freddy's apartment. Once he'd gotten that far with them, I figured it was even money that one of them would roll over on the other. The ethnic family deal was supposed to discourage snitching, but a murder rap is thicker than blood sometimes. If Augie could show that they took anything from Freddy's apartment in the process, they'd qualify for the death penalty, and I hoped that might give him the leverage he'd need to break one of them down.

For myself, I had plenty to do, and I didn't want to be dawdling around my place when whoever Augie sent to look for me showed up. So I finished my cup of coffee, turned out the fire under the coffeepot, and cleared the area.

CHAPTER
32

Miss Farmer, the physical therapist, answered the phone in Eddie's room, and told me that he was out in the halls somewhere practicing with his wheelchair. He'd be back in a minute, she assured me.

"I hear he may be getting out Monday," I said.

"He's got his heart set on it, but I'm not so sure. He was banged up pretty bad, whether he'll admit it or not."

"Yeah, he's a little over the hill for that cowboy stuff."

"Not to hear him tell it. Oh, here he comes now."

She left the phone on the bedside table and went after Eddie. From what I could hear over the phone, Eddie hadn't come back into the room; he'd just happened to be passing by. I don't know what he thought Miss Farmer wanted with him, but from the way her voice trailed off into the distance, I got the impression she was chasing him down the hall. It was a minute or two before the noise that the two of them made came back my way, and then Eddie was on the line.

"Did you get my message?" he asked.

"Yeah, you're getting out Monday. That's great."

"You're damned right. How's it going?"

"Depends on how you look at it."

"What the hell does that mean?"

"It means I've just about got it figured out, but I don't think you're going to like it."

"I'm listening."

"It would take too long to explain. I'm sending you something in the mail. Watch for it. I think you'll see where I'm going with this deal."

"Why don't you deliver it yourself, Jack?"

"Because then I'd wind up in the clutches of Augie Dann, and I'm afraid that would cramp my style."

"What are you talking about? You think Augie's got somebody watching this place?"

"If not now, pretty damned soon, more than likely. I can't chance it."

"Why?"

It only took a couple of minutes to explain my phone call to Crimes Against Persons, the aggravated-robbery report, and the message I'd left for Augie. The deep, dark stuff I didn't go into. Eddie could read my notes and figure that out for himself as far as I'd gotten. When I'd told him all I was going to tell him, I asked him if he'd do me a favor.

"What?"

"Don't try to call Carol."

"Why the hell not?"

"Because if I'm right, all this crap is about to come to a head, and you'll only be putting shit in the game."

"I don't—"

"Eddie, you brought me into this thing. You're going to have to trust me. I don't know any other way."

"Jack."

"Yeah?"

"If you hurt her, I'll kill you."

"Well, you may just have to do that, Eddie. Because, one way or another, I can't see how this deal can play out that she won't be hurt. It's a real nest of snakes, partner. All I can promise you is that I'll do the best I can."

"You'd damned well better."

"Yeah. Good luck to you, too."

Lois Li answered the phone at Carol's house, and she said that Carol and Liz had both left early to go over to Doctor Oppenheimer's house. She didn't expect them back until late that evening.

So far, so good.

Next, I called Mister Li at the number he'd left for me earlier, and I got lucky again. He was in. I told him I was on my way to Oppenheimer's, and that I wanted to see him there.

"I'm not sure that's a good idea, Mister Kyle."

"Neither am I, but that's the way it's going to be."

"I see. And you think it's important for me to be there?"

"It's imperative, because I want you to do a thing or two for me."

"Oh?"

"Yeah. For openers, I want you to be the one who lets me in."

"All right, but why?"

"Because unless I miss my guess, part of the hardware built into the Doctor's entryway there, along with the TV cameras and the intercom, is some kind of metal detector. I want you to make sure it doesn't go off when I come in."

"Why do you suppose such a thing?"

"Because if I were Oppenheimer, I'd have one."

"You won't have a problem."

"I'd better not, Mister Li. Because if I do and anybody gets hurt, you're damned sure going to get hurt, too. Understand?"

"The threat is unnecessary."

"Then I won't mind apologizing for it later. But I mean for

you to understand that this is damned serious business."

"I understand. When will you be arriving?"

"Don't worry about that. You just go over there now, if you're not there already, and keep your eyes open."

"Very well."

That took care of all the phone calls I needed to make and exhausted my supply of quarters at the same time. I went inside the 7-Eleven at Preston and Royal and bought a pack of cigarettes. The clerk asked if I didn't want the special three-pack deal, but I declined. My cash flow was running dry for real since I'd had to dip into my office checking account. I couldn't even spend my fifty-dollar emergency fund, because the Tiger Boys had written their little warning on the two twenties and the ten, and that made them evidence. If nothing else worked, maybe Augie could rap one of them out on a handwriting match. It was a long shot, and I hadn't bothered to mention it to the investigator who took my report. Besides, I had an itchy feeling that the way my Saturday was shaping up I might not need more than one pack of cigarettes. That was a day's supply, and I figured it might very well do me.

Hunches played a pretty big part in my business, and they usually fell into two categories. One is judging people. It's part of being quick on your feet, making judgment calls under time pressure, like I said before. The other has to do with timing. And I had a hunch that time was running out on this deal. All the pieces and players were there, and I had a pretty good feeling for the outline of the thing. The details were kind of up in the air, but if I waited for all the pieces to fall into place, I'd be a historian, not a private eye. Every investigator develops a way of working. Mine had gotten me through a lot of tight places, and I still had my license, even an occasional client. It might not be the best way to do things, but it was my way. Mainly, it consisted of assuming the worst and then pushing until something broke. Elegant it wasn't, but like I said, it more often than not got the job done.

The notes I had scrambled and rescrambled that morning in my office went into a stamped envelope I'd lifted from Della's desk drawer. Eddie's home address went on the outside of it, and I dropped it into the mailbox at the corner of Forest Lane and Preston Road. Allowing for the holiday, it wouldn't get to Eddie's place until Wednesday, long after he'd been released from the hospital. And long after I'd made my play, for better or worse.

CHAPTER
33

It was almost eleven o'clock in the morning when I pulled up in front of Oppenheimer's place on Industrial. Mister Li was as good as his word. He showed me in through the double door and the ramped passageway, and nothing that I could see or hear gave any indication that I had Leslie's revolver tucked into the small of my back. Of course, there didn't have to be a lot of bells and whistles there at the spot. I knew that the gizmo might be set up to enunciate a signal remotely, somewhere else in the big house. But I couldn't cover everything, and I'd already made up my mind to take my chances.

As Mister Li and I entered the big room with the pedestals and the blond wood walls, I thought I'd take the opportunity to get something settled, something small that I'd been wondering about.

"What relation is Lois Li to you, Mister Li?"

"She is my aunt, Mister Kyle. My mother's sister."

"I see. Your family is here in Dallas?"

"There is only Lois and me. The rest of us didn't make it." He said that in a very quiet voice, an even, factual tone that neither invited nor discouraged further inquiry. I had some idea what his words might mean, what might have become of the rest of his family. But I didn't pursue it. Another time, maybe.

"I'm sorry," was all I said.

Mister Li smiled tightly and made a small bow as a way of acknowledging my sentiments.

"I've only just arrived myself," he explained.

"Where is everybody?"

"I'll go and see."

"There's no hurry."

"That wasn't the impression you gave me on the telephone, Mister Kyle."

"Yeah, but we're all here now. The rest of it may take a little time."

"I see."

"Tell me, what exactly is your role here? You said you were a scientist, I believe."

"A biochemist, like Doctor Oppenheimer."

"Really? What does a biochemist do?"

He showed a touch of confusion in the way he reacted to my questions, and I thought that was pretty understandable. He'd picked up on my feeling that it was time to settle this thing once and for all, that today was the day to get everything out into the open. I guessed that I'd made that pretty clear, to him and to Eddie. But that was what I'd call the strategic part of it. What came next, now that all the players were assembled, would be the tactical part, putting the pieces together. And, for that matter, we were still a player short. But I had it in mind to take care of that in due time, too.

"Doctor Oppenheimer and I are involved in research on the brain."

"I see." That had been general enough, but Mister Li didn't seem inclined to go into any more detail. He probably assumed that I wouldn't understand anyway, and I figured he was right about that. "A fascinating subject."

"We find it so."

"But you're not Doctor Li?"

"Merely a doctoral candidate."

"Oh, I see. Then you're Oppenheimer's lab assistant, something like that?"

"Our working relationship is rather involved. . . ."

"Mister Kyle! Good to see you again."

Oppenheimer was back in one of his Buck Rogers outfits, and that suited the hell out of me. It was a different color this time, though, what I thought fashion designers and interior decorators liked to call mauve. It was a better color for him.

"Good morning, Doctor."

"I wasn't expecting you," he said, extending his long and bony hand. "Was I?"

"No," I assured him, shaking his hand and wincing a bit when he overdid it and my busted wrist hurt. "I've arrived unannounced."

"No problem. We've just had brunch. Are you hungry?"

"No, thank you."

"Mister Li, would you like something?"

"I'm fine, Doctor."

"Come to think of it, Li, I don't believe I was expecting you today, either. Did we have something planned?"

"No, Doctor Oppenheimer. I just wanted to go over a few things on my own. Nothing important."

"I see. Well, whatever. And what can I do for you, Mister Kyle?"

"There's no particular rush about that. How did the family meeting go?"

"Eh? Oh, very nicely, thank you. Good idea, to get everyone together, sit down and talk things over. That was your suggestion, wasn't it?"

223

"I believe so," I said.

"Capital idea. Really."

"How do things stand now?" I asked.

"I've no idea, particularly. Women confuse me, and I'm afraid my mind wanders. We all seem to be getting on, though, and that's something."

"Did they tell you about the videotapes?"

"Tapes? Yes, they did, in fact. Curious business, isn't it? Still, I don't suppose we should be surprised that there's a market for that sort of thing."

"You weren't . . . upset with Liz over it?"

"Upset?" Oppenheimer put his fingers to his chin in a move I'd seen before. It was what he did when you asked him how he felt about something, like he had to stop and think it over, or maybe tune in to something inside, trying to calibrate what he felt. "No, I don't think so, particularly. Upset with her for getting involved, you mean? I don't think that's the main point, is it? Unfortunate, probably very upsetting to her, I could see that, of course."

"I wonder if you'd consider a hypothetical question for me, Doctor."

"I imagine so." He smiled. "We do rather a good deal of hypothesizing, don't we, Mister Li?"

Oppenheimer and Li exchanged smiles.

"What would you have done if someone had delivered that videotape to you? If you hadn't known about it—if it just showed up in your life and there was little Liz. What would your reaction have been?"

"I'm not . . . sure. In what context?"

"In the context that whoever this was who showed up with the video threatened to circulate it unless you did something or gave them something valuable. Would you have been inclined to go along with that kind of deal?"

"Extortion of some kind, you mean," he said.

"Yeah, something along that line."

"I suppose so. I wouldn't want the poor girl on video all over the country, mail-order catalogs and computer bulletin boards, all that sort of arrangement. You can see, can't you, it would be awful for her."

"Yes, it would."

"It might depend on what they wanted, though. I'd have to consider that."

"I suppose so."

"Some kind of toxic virus, I mean. If they wanted me to infect the water supply of a city or something. Then, I think the complexion changes."

"Could you do that?"

"What?"

"Poison the water supply."

"Probably. It's not in my line, you understand. I just meant it as a 'what if.' An illustration. If they wanted money or something, of course I'd give it to them."

"Would the amount matter?"

"I suppose it would. I couldn't give them more than I have, could I?"

"How much do you have?"

"I'm not sure. Millions. Right, Li?"

"Yes."

"How would you know if you had all the copies of the tape, Doctor? How could you be sure they hadn't held one out on you?"

That entertained him for a couple of minutes. I'd noticed that about the old man—when he had something to think about, he didn't mind ignoring whoever was in the room to consider it. And it wasn't particularly rude of him, because it was so obvious that his immersion in whatever it was was genuine, part of the way he was put together. Finally, he came up with an answer.

"I don't know of a way. Do you, Mister Kyle?"

"No, sir. I was just curious."

"Oh. Oh, yes, of course. That was the problem you faced when you retrieved the tapes from Freddy What's-his-name. I see, your interest is certainly understandable."

"I'm relieved that you don't know a way, either. I was afraid I'd overlooked something."

"No, I must say, from what I've been told, you did a first-rate job. He's dead, I understand."

"Freddy? Yes, sir. Murdered."

"Right, right. And that brings us back around to the other night when you brought Liz over here and we had all that business with the lawyers, doesn't it?"

"Yes, it does."

"Then I suppose I'm fully informed now?"

"Pretty much."

"Good. Are you sure you won't eat something?"

"No, thank you."

CHAPTER
34

" Where are Carol and Liz?" I asked.

"Oh, they're around here somewhere," Oppenheimer said, waving a hand.

"I'd like to speak to them," I said.

"I see. Both of them?"

"Yes. Carol first, if you don't mind."

"Why? I mean, why her first?"

"I have my reasons."

"I see." Oppenheimer drifted off into thought for a moment. Then, "Do you mind if I ask you a question, Mister Kyle?"

"Not particularly."

"What exactly is it you're doing here? I mean, what are you after? You got the tapes back, you kept Liz out of the murder, I hired you a lawyer. . . . What else is there?"

"Liz isn't really out of it until the killer's caught. She was there when it happened, as near as I can tell. There's no way to know that she's safe until it's settled."

I thought about telling him about what Liz had said, that Freddy'd told her he had held out on me, that he had another copy of the tape. But I didn't think it was important any more.

"I can see your point there," he said. "But then shouldn't you be out looking for the killer or something?"

"The police are handling that part of it. I need to get to the bottom of a couple of things."

"What things, for heaven's sake?" Oppenheimer was beginning to whine a bit, as if I was finally becoming an inconvenience. Or a bore.

"Everything Liz's gotten into so far happened for a reason," I explained. "Why she was picked, why she did what she did, why she went back to Freddy's. Until I get a handle on the reasons behind all that, this won't be over for any of us."

"Well, all right. Come with me."

Oppenheimer pivoted on the heel of his funny-looking shoe and strode off into the wall. Of course, the wall opened for him to expose a doorway, and I followed him. Mister Li tagged along, too.

We made a couple of turns and went up a short stairway through another automatic door into what looked like the bridge set from the TV show *Star Trek*. There was a bank of monitors along one wall and a couple of captain's chairs, separated by a horseshoe-shaped console chock-full of buttons, switches, and dials. Some of the square buttons were lit up yellow, some were red, and some were dark. Along the wall opposite the monitors, I saw what looked like half a dozen computers built into the wall itself. There were colored screens displaying elaborate patterns that could have been anything or nothing, for all the hell I knew.

"Here we are," Oppenheimer said, indicating with a long finger where I should stand to be out of the way.

"Excuse me," Mister Li said as he edged by me into one of the chairs. Oppenheimer remained standing.

"I would remind you, Mister Kyle, that every family has its share of secrets."

"Okay."

"And I don't think it's unreasonable to expect that you will respect our confidence . . . our confidentiality, that is."

"Whatever."

Oppenheimer pressed a switch here and there, and the TV screens in the wall all came alive, one after the other. Most of them were stuff of no interest to me, crap I didn't even understand. But I did understand one of the pictures. It was Carol and Liz sitting at a table somewhere, in a bright and sunny room. There was fresh fruit in a bowl at the center of the table, and what looked like the remains of brunch on plates in front of them. They were talking, but there was no audio on the TV.

"By the way," he said, "this also isn't real time. . . ."

I was about to ask him what that meant, when I saw the good doctor himself walk into the happy family scene on the screen.

"This was taped earlier, you mean?"

"Yes."

"Where are they now?"

"Show him," Oppenheimer said to Mister Li, who operated some of the machinery on the console.

While the après-meal scene we'd been watching continued on the first screen, another screen next to that one popped into life, and I saw Carol in a completely different setup. I knew it was Carol and not Liz, because the two women's bodies bore little family resemblance. Liz was prematurely curvaceous, even voluptuous, while her mom was more svelte and angular. I was watching Carol, all right, but I had no idea what was being done to her.

"Have you ever heard of 'virtual reality,' Mister Kyle?"

"I don't think so."

"Very interesting. What we're doing here, of course, is considerably more advanced than anything you'd have seen in any of the magazines." Oppenheimer turned his back on the TV screen to face me, so he could explain "virtual reality" better.

But I couldn't take my eyes off the screen. Carol lay on what looked like a gynecologist's examining table, her feet up in stirrups, and she was wearing some kind of mask over her face, a crazy contraption with cables running out of the dark bug's-eye goggles that covered her eyes. On her hands, she wore some kind of odd, oversized gloves, with more cables streaming out of them down onto the floor and disappearing behind her somewhere.

There was still no sound with the picture, but I could see that she was panting like a racehorse, her chest rising and falling desperately, then her whole body clenching like a fist as she seemed to squeeze her whole torso down into her hips somehow. And beneath the lower rim of the mask, I could see her lips. They were drawn back over her teeth in a twisted, gaping grimace. She was screaming.

CHAPTER
35

"It's also known as 'artificial reality,' or 'cyberspace,'" Doctor Oppenheimer explained patiently. "CAD graphics . . . that's computer-assisted design graphics . . . are fed into the sensory inputs to duplicate the desired actual experience. Subjectively, I assure you, it feels very real indeed to the subject of the exercise. My version—excuse me, Mister Li, *our* version—is superior to any of the others I've seen or read about in the literature, because of the special feedback features. Unlike the rather simple approach computer programmers have taken, after all, we approach the concept from our exhaustive concentration on the human brain, you see. . . ."

"What the hell are you doing to her?" I demanded. Out of the corner of my eye, I saw Li wiping his lips with the back of his hand, like he might be afraid he was going to be sick. But I didn't know if he was upset because of what they were doing, or only because I was being permitted to watch. "You're killing her!"

"What? Oh, hardly, Mister Kyle. It's perfectly safe. Perfectly normal, as a matter of fact."

"Bullshit."

As I watched her on the screen, with no idea where she was in the big house, Carol suddenly exploded in a big sigh that I couldn't hear, and then went limp, her arms tumbling down from her sides to dangle loosely off the table. She turned her head to one side, toward the camera, and I could see her gulping air in desperately. Her face was glistening with a sheen of sweat from the exertion of whatever she'd been put through.

"I assure you, Mister Kyle, she is in no danger. What you're watching is simply—"

"I want you to stop whatever the hell it is, right now. Where is she?"

"Watch, Mister Kyle. Just watch."

Carol was holding something close to her, nestling something tight against her bosom, rocking softly from side to side. I saw her mouth work, but she wasn't screaming anymore. She was saying something, and there was an exhausted smile on her lips. I looked closely to see what she was holding, but there was nothing there. She was holding nothing in her arms.

"Okay, explain it to me, Doctor."

"We have just watched Carol give birth."

"And the baby?"

"It was Liz this time. See? She's holding Liz in her arms. She's cooing over baby Liz. Isn't it remarkable?"

"What's the point?"

"You're not impressed with the system? I can assure you, you're the first layman to have such a demonstration. There are people who would pay a fortune to be in your shoes. Isn't that right, Mister Li?"

Li nodded, but I didn't think his heart was in any of this.

"What's the point?" I asked again.

"A form of therapy. For some time now, Carol has been entertaining the delusion that she has no children, that neither Alan nor Liz are actually hers. By helping her relive their birth in this way, we help her connect with the intense memories that she's trying to repress."

"Why would she repress having her own kids?"

"A form of grieving. I'm afraid that Alan was her favorite. She's taken his death very hard. I've been concerned about her emotional stability."

"That doesn't look to me like it would do her emotions any good," I said. Carol seemed comfortable enough now, even happy. She looked up, from one side to the other, as if people were talking to her, standing over her.

"As I began to explain, Mister Li and I come at this from our years of work with the human brain, its structure and electrochemical processes. When we build a 'virtually real' experience, it's much more than a computer game with 3-D effects. That's what I meant about our sensory inputs, the feedback systems built in. Right now, I guarantee that Carol is experiencing the very same elevation in neurochemicals and adrenaline, as if she'd actually just given birth. That's happening inside her body because we've designed our system to stimulate the brain centers appropriately with the experience she's supposed to be having. Of course, we're not limited to childbirth."

"Oh, no?"

"Hardly." Oppenheimer and Li shared a laugh at my expense, Oppenheimer with considerable more relish than his associate, I thought. "The industrial application of a system like this is in training. Think about delicate heart or brain surgery, for example. Before a doctor ever made his first incision on a living patient, he could have performed the entire procedure in hyperrealistic detail over a thousand times, using our system. The same for astronauts and jet pilots—the possibilities are endless. So you see, we're hardly mad scientists hatching sadistic plots against damsels in distress here, Mister Kyle."

"I'd like to hear what Carol thinks of the drill."

"She doesn't."

"What does that mean?"

"It means that she won't remember any of what you saw just now."

"Then how does she learn anything from it?"

"Don't confuse the two applications. Training is the future, industrial application of the technology. What you've seen here today is a strictly therapeutic use. We've reinforced deep memories in her brain here today. Subjectively, from inside Carol's head, all that's happened is that she's remembered giving birth to Liz. A very vivid memory, to be sure. Perhaps a very lifelike dream."

"A dream?"

"Yes. She's taking a nap now."

"Was that her idea?"

"Not really, no. I gave her something at brunch to make her drowsy. And we'll return her to a guest room before she awakens. So it will all have been a dream, you see. A dream based on a memory. Therefore, the memory will have been reinforced, and that will thwart her subconscious effort to repress the fact that she really did give birth to two children, Alan and Elizabeth."

I didn't know why it hadn't hit me before, but it all came clear to me then, at least a big part of it. The whys and hows were yet to come, but all of a sudden I had the basic thrust of the thing.

"Are you a real doctor?" I asked. "I mean, like an M.D. as opposed to a Ph.D., no offense."

"Both, actually. I'm a full-fledged physician, a psychiatrist. And I also hold a doctorate in biochemistry."

"Jesus," I said, shaking my head. "You must have a tub of brains like a load of wash."

"Thank you." Doctor Oppenheimer smiled graciously. "I think."

"Oh, it's a compliment, all right."

"Then you don't think our little exercise here this morning was so terrible after all?"

"Maybe not." I smiled back at him. "But is it kosher to treat somebody like that and they don't even know about it?"

"That's a fair enough question, Mister Kyle. And I suppose the classroom answer is it wouldn't be ethical. But I'd also add that it's like a private investigator spiriting a witness away from the scene of a murder. How do you like that answer?"

"Not much, but I get your point."

"Not that I disagree with what you did. Every profession has rules, and journeymen must learn and follow them. But mastery comes with knowing when to make exceptions, don't you agree?"

"I've heard that theory."

"So I hope that you don't think—"

"Are you Carol's doctor, then?" I asked.

"Yes, as a matter of fact."

"Is this kind of thing the reason that she doesn't like to come over here?"

"I assure you that she has no recall of our little sessions."

"So why doesn't she like it here?"

"She associates this place with poor Alan. He spent most of his time here. We worked very closely together, Alan and I. And Mister Li, of course."

"Were you his doctor, too?"

"I treat all my family members, Mister Kyle. There's nothing unethical about that, certainly."

"Probably not. Did you sign Alan's death certificate?"

"Yes."

"What exactly did he die of? I've heard, but I'm not clear on it."

"Congenital heart failure was what I put on the certificate."

"But actually, he died of . . . what, Doctor?"

"Is this really necessary? Is all this part of your job, this thing about What's-his-name's murder?"

"Yes, as a matter of fact. I wasn't sure until today, but now I see that it is a part of all of that."

"It's important?"

"A matter of life and death, I'd say."

"Very well, then. Alan committed suicide."

The weird thing was, it didn't surprise me. Having the Doctor spill it like that wasn't what I'd expected, but it made sense in a way, if you thought about it. I mean, I couldn't really prove it, even that he'd said it. But there it was, and I knew that what I had been thinking was on the right track. It wasn't good news by a long stretch, but at least it meant that the thing was coming to a head, one way or the other.

"How did he do that?" I asked.

"Overdose. I don't like talking about it."

"I'm sorry you have to, but there it is. An overdose of what?"

"You wouldn't know if I told you. It was something Alan had been tinkering with, a chemical he'd concocted for reasons of his own."

"It doesn't have a name?"

"Not really. You see, by altering a detail of the molecular structure, you change the nature of the material. We deal with things here all the time that haven't yet been named, unless we choose to publish, and give the things names ourselves. That's only worth the trouble if you've come up with something that has promising applications. The drug he made and took stopped his heart, basically. It mimicked a heart failure similar to what might have been caused by the defect I cited on the death certificate. I lied to protect Carol."

"Another of those exceptions that you and I know when to make because we're masters of our professions," I said.

"Exactly."

"So, getting back to Carol," I said. "What happens next? You just leave her lying there?"

"Of course not. I'll return her to her guest room, and she'll awaken refreshed from her nap, having had the dream you saw a moment ago."

"You schlep her around yourself?"

"Everything in this house is automated, Mister Kyle. Including the table she's lying on. If I wanted, I could program it from here to take her into the guest room, put her into the bed, and tuck her in. But actually, I do like to go along with her when she's moved. It's a peculiarly charming thing, you know, to watch your child sleeping. Even at that age. If you'll excuse me?"

"Where's Liz during all this?" I asked. "The real-time Liz."

"She's puttering about in her room, I expect. I keep a room for her here. She likes to visit, stay over. And I enjoy having her, especially since Alan . . . Take a look, Mister Li."

Li punched up some things and some lights flickered, and there was little Liz on another of the TV screens, lounging on a bed in a room that looked about right for her. There were posters on the wall of rock stars I'd never heard of, a stereo with speakers like footlockers, the usual stuff. Liz was talking on the phone. Without any prompting from me, one of the two men in the room with me did something that brought her voice alive. We could hear both sides of the conversation, and I could tell by the second voice that Liz was talking to Syd. Liz wanted her to come over, but Syd sounded reluctant at first. Liz assured her that everything was okay.

"We had the big summit conference already," she said. "It was no big deal."

"The Doctor wasn't pissed?"

"With me? Of course not. He understood. I was the victim, after all. So come on over, already."

"You're sure I won't be intruding? On the family thing, you know?"

"No way. I'll be looking for you."

"Okay. Bye."

"Do you have every room in this house wired, Doctor?"

"Of course. You aren't surprised, are you, Mister Kyle? I got the impression that you understood that the first time you were here."

"I suspected. Why did you do it?"

"Why not, it's my house. Saves repeating things. If you'll please keep Mister Kyle company, Mister Li, I'll go and tend to Carol."

When he had left, I turned to Mister Li, who gave me a sheepish smile.

"Tell me," I said. "What's a nice guy like you doing in a place like this?"

CHAPTER
36

Mister Li explained that he handled the business end of things for Doctor Oppenheimer, the vast majority of which involved Asian organizations and investors, mostly Japanese, but more Koreans over the past year or so.

"Americans are still great inventors and discoverers," he told me. "The best in the world, probably for a little while longer. But there's no capital for manufacturing here, no R and D support."

"Why not?" I asked, as if it mattered.

"American businesses can't be bothered with anything that won't show up on their next quarterly report. The Japanese don't mind waiting for a big payoff."

"It's that simple?" I asked.

"More or less."

"The Doctor plays fast and loose with these people, his family, don't you think?"

Li shrugged, either because he had no opinion or he didn't want his opinion recorded.

"He is a genius, Mister Kyle. In some circles, he is a legend in his own time."

"Okay. But his family life is a piece of shit. Is there such a thing as a safe phone I can use?"

"I wouldn't think so."

"Can you show me the one most likely?"

Li dug a phone out of a drawer behind the chair he was sitting in and found a clear space on the console for it. He shrugged again, to let me know he wasn't guaranteeing anything. The risk of my call being monitored was one I was willing to take, as a matter of fact. For one thing, I knew that it wasn't the being taped that got you in trouble, it was when somebody found the time to sit down and listen to what had been recorded. I figured the Doctor had better things to do. Besides, the time was fast approaching when there were going to be precious few secrets left, anyway. Although he offered, I didn't even ask Li to leave the room.

The investigator in Crimes Against Persons sounded glad to hear from me, or at least relieved. He said he'd relayed my message to Augie Dann, and that Dann had left instructions that if I called again he was to give me Augie's home number. I thanked the investigator and called Augie at home.

"Augie Dann," was all he said when he answered.

"Jack Kyle. How's your Saturday shaping up?"

"Where are you?"

"Later. What are you doing about the information I put in that report?"

"You know, I'm kinda used to asking the questions."

"Humor me. This thing'll be over soon, one way or the other. Have you got a line on the Tiger Boys yet?"

"We're working on it. I expect results before the day is over."

"Sounds like a press release."

"Which is all you're entitled to."

"Cut me some slack, Augie. Like it or not, we're on the same side on this thing."

I waited while he mulled that over.

"Okay," he said finally. "It's not for publication, but we picked one of 'em up this morning."

"Good work. Is his name Li, by any chance?"

"As a matter of fact."

"He wouldn't be the one with the sneakers, would he?"

"He would."

Sometimes you catch a break. I felt I was due.

"Did you make them on the prints at the murder scene?"

"That's confidential."

"Of course it is, and I won't tell a fucking soul. This is important."

"We ran 'em through the lab, but it came up negative."

"They didn't match the stain?" I asked. I wanted to be sure.

"That's right. Maybe the other guy . . ."

"He wasn't wearing sneakers," I interrupted. "There's one more thing."

"You're kidding, Kyle."

"It's about the murder scene."

"I hear that you . . ."

"We're working on it. I expect results before the day is over."

"Sounds like a press release," I said. "Can you be trusted?"

"I ain't the one making all the dopey moves."

"Fair enough. I need to know about the murder scene on the Barksdale killing."

"I hear that you were there. Maybe you know more about it than I do."

"Yeah, I was there," I said. "And you can quote me on that one. I told your boy that I owe you a statement on that one, and I'll do that, when I finish up a little angle

I'm working on right now. What about the search of the scene? How far did your troops go looking, and what did they find?"

"If you weren't a friend of Eddie Cochran's, Kyle, I'd hang up on your ass right now. As it is, what you're asking is none of your business. We looked all over, and we found this and that. What are you getting at?"

So I told him what I was after. I needed to know if a particular item had been found. If not, I wanted to know how thoroughly Freddy's place was tossed. Did they check the dumpster in the parking lot? Did they pull up the carpet looking for stash holes, get into the attic? How hard did they look? Without being much more specific than he'd been the first time, Augie promised me they had been thorough, twice. Patrol and the forensics people had gone over everything the night of the murder, and Augie and his people had done it all over again the next day, after I left. And they hadn't found the particular item I was interested in.

"Okay, then listen to this," I said. "You can forget about the Tiger Boys on the Freddy Barksdale murder."

"What?"

"Yeah. They're good as gold on my aggravated robbery, and that's plenty to drag 'em down for. If you want, go ahead and check their prints and body fluids. But you ain't going to make them on the killing. I'll go this far . . . they may have been in Freddy's apartment at some time, but they weren't in on the killing."

"We'll see about all the rest of it, hotshot. But there weren't any prints on the knife."

"Doesn't surprise me a bit, Augie."

"What the hell are you trying to pull on this deal, man?"

"It's a long story. Maybe we can sit down here pretty soon and play Twenty Questions. The thing is, the way I see it, the Tiger Boys tie in with Freddy only on the drug angle."

"That's not what you told the investigator a couple of hours ago."

"I know. It's coming together pretty quick now."

"Where are you, Jack?"

"You coming in to work today, Augie?"

"Answer my question first."

"I'll make you a deal."

"I'm listening."

"You come to work at three, right?"

"Right."

"I'll tell you where I am, if you'll give me your word you won't show up here before three. How's that?"

"I don't get the point. You're not wanted for anything. Why would I show up there?"

"Because the killer is either here now or soon will be. Along with some other folks. By three, I think I'll have the whole deal wrapped up."

"That's my job. If you know something, you give it to me, and I'll work the damned case."

"I'd love to, but it's not going to be that easy. You'll understand when it's all over."

"It's noon now, Jack. Let's make it one o'clock, and I'll meet you there, wherever there is."

"Split the difference. Say two o'clock and bring along a little backup when you come. These people are squirrelly, and the place ain't easy to get into."

"It's bullshit, Jack. If you know something . . ."

"You're right, Augie. I'd feel the same way if I were in your shoes. So do we have a deal?"

"Why not? It's your ass."

"Two o'clock?"

"All right, two o'clock. Now where the hell are you?"

I gave him the address and a couple of tips on getting into

the place in a hurry if he had to. Then there wasn't anything else to say, and I hung up.

Mister Li was busy with one of the control panels, and acted like he hadn't heard a word. When he realized I was watching him, he looked up at me with an innocent expression.

"You're off the phone?"

"Yeah, Mister Sincerity, I'm off the goddamned phone."

CHAPTER
37

Finding myself alone in the control room or whatever it was with Mister Li was a bonus I hadn't expected. Or, rather, I'd expected that I'd have to finagle myself some time with him without any interruptions. It was important to what I had in mind for me to get a couple of things straight with him, so I didn't waste any time.

"You and I have about three things to talk about," I told him. "And I don't have time for any bullshit."

"All right."

"First, convince me that you're for real here."

"I'm not sure I understand."

"Sell me on your motive, Mister Li. Why did you call and tip me off about this Oppenheimer Dilemma thing? You went along with me on the metal detector this morning, and now you sit here during the Doctor's little demonstration looking like you're about to lose your breakfast. You've been pretty helpful so far, without really burning anybody. Why is that?"

"Family," he began, then looked down at his hands and swallowed hard, "is important to me. Perhaps you can understand—you were in Vietnam, weren't you?"

I nodded. "A couple of tours. Marines."

"We were a large family when the troubles began for us. My parents lived with me and my wife. We had three children, a boy and two girls. My wife's sister, Lois, lived nearby with her husband and two kids. Our family was our world in those days. Now, there is only Lois and myself."

"The connection here being that you don't care for the way the Doctor treats his family, is that it?"

"He's a brilliant mind, Mister Kyle. But, as you said, he treats his family like shit."

"And you're talking about a lot more than the dream machine, aren't you? How much do you know about his experiment on the two kids?"

"Only what Alan told me shortly before his death. He had suspicions, but he hadn't pieced it all together. He was very angry, and if his suspicions were true, he had every right to be."

"You liked Alan?"

"He was not so much to like, Mister Kyle, as he was to . . . He had enormous potential."

"Profit potential, you mean. In the technology business."

"Profit is the engine that drives progress."

"Sounds like a bumper sticker."

"The point is that I don't mind if the industrialists make money out of science that saves lives or makes peace unavoidable. That is my personal view."

"Hard to argue with. How is the business end of all this set up?"

"What do you mean?"

"When the old man dies, who gets his millions?"

"His family, naturally. There were trust funds for Alan and Liz, administered by the doctor's lawyers until each of them turned twenty-one, then they'd take charge. Carol inherits the bulk of the estate, his patents and royalties. A fabulous amount.

I know this because I was asked to sign as a witness when the lawyers drew up the paper."

"Did Liz's take double when Alan died?"

"I believe so. She'd be sole beneficiary of the trusts."

"And how would you come out?"

"While I am not remembered in the will, Mister Kyle, I have participated in the rewards of the Doctor's work. He has not been selfish with the credit or rewards that our work together has brought. And I have made excellent contacts among corporate clients. My prospects are good, whether he lives or dies. Perhaps that is why . . ."

His voice trailed off, and he rested his chin in the palm of his hand, looking a little like Doctor Oppenheimer trying to decide how he felt about something.

"Why what?" I prompted him.

"Perhaps that is why I decided to help you, in the hope that you would somehow put an end to this whole thing. Perhaps if I were not so well off, my morals would not be so offended. It's something to think about, isn't it?"

"Probably, but not right now. Right now, I have another question for you."

"You ask a lot of questions."

"It's my job. I don't know any other way to get answers. Question number two: How can I be sure you're not the Mister Li that Freddy said he was in business with, in the pornography business?"

"I've no idea how to prove a negative, Mister Kyle. But can you suggest a motive?"

"According to you, I don't guess it would be the money. Maybe the porn thing's a turn-on for you. We haven't talked about your sex life."

"And we shan't, Mister Kyle. But as for a turn-on . . . well, let me show you something."

He fired up one of the machines, and things started humming, as another set of patterns and colors replaced the inert darkness of the screen where we'd watched Carol giving birth.

"What're you doing?" I asked.

"Who's your favorite movie star?"

"What's that got to do with—"

"How about Marilyn Monroe?"

"Okay."

"Watch this, please."

So I watched, as a shapely nude appeared on the screen, a saucy spring in her step as she strutted away from me, then stopped. A couple of cross hairs played over the image, then a kind of a wash as a wave of some kind ran from top to bottom, and she turned to greet us with a wink and a smile. It was Marilyn Monroe. She held out her arms toward us, and I couldn't help admiring the body she was so unashamed of. Then Doctor Oppenheimer walked into the picture as if coming from behind whatever camera was taking these pictures, and Marilyn laughed and put her hands around his neck. They kissed, and she peeled off his white lab smock to reveal a powerful young body, the muscles across his back rippling as he bent to take her in his arms. She threw back her head and sighed loudly as he lifted her off her feet and carried her to a round bed where he tossed her down among scattered pillows and lowered himself onto her, showering her throat and breasts with kisses. Then it all stopped in a freeze frame.

"How's that, Mister Kyle?"

"Fine." It had been exactly like watching real people, the Doctor and Marilyn Monroe. It had not been like any computer animation I'd ever seen. "The point?"

"The point is that with this equipment I can create any scene. Literally, any combination of characters and action that I can imagine. Would you like to see that same bit with Lauren Bacall and Bogart? Mary Pickford and Rin Tin Tin?"

"So, if your tastes ran to this sort of thing, for fun or profit, you wouldn't have to resort to Freddy's brand of cinema verité for your product, right?"

"Exactly. We could whip up whatever scenario our customers demanded, from whips and chains to historical gothic, just with the data we have already stored in memory here or that we can ad-lib to taste. What would be the point of risking all that business with some amateur with a home video?"

"Okay." I mulled that over. "You present me with some interesting possibilities, Mister Li. But we'll come back to that. It's time for question number three."

But before I could get into that, a signal on his control panel caught his eye.

"Someone's at the door," he said.

Punch, punch went some more of the buttons and switches, and we saw Syd standing outside the door, looking up into the camera mounted overhead. Oppenheimer's voice from somewhere, asking for someone to see who was at the door, was answered by Liz's from somewhere else saying she'd get it. We watched Liz show Syd in, and then went back to our conversation.

"How much longer do we have here before Oppenheimer comes back?" I asked.

"Let's see," Mister Li answered, his right hand flying over his controls. "There he is."

The Doctor was sitting at the side of a bed in a room somewhere in the big house, watching Carol sleep on the bed. She looked peaceful enough. Then we saw Liz and Syd in animated conversation, Syd looking serious, Liz apparently reassuring her about something. All this was without audio, and I didn't mind.

"Okay," I said. "Here's the third question, and it's a multiparter."

"Shoot."

Watching Carol giving birth in the "cyberspace" mask and

gloves had given me plenty to think about, and part of my mind had been at work on that ever since, piecing things together. There was a good bit of guesswork, and that was one thing I needed from Li, his opinion of some of the possibilities I'd come up with. For one thing, I hadn't been convinced that what I'd seen with Carol had been exactly what the Doctor'd said it was, and I ran a theory by Li that he didn't like but had to admit was a possibility. Then I needed to know about that memory thing he'd mentioned, about what was done with the hundreds of hours of tapes they'd accumulated as all those cameras recorded everything that went on in the house. Their control center, Mister Li explained, was about like a human brain. Everything the cameras saw was remembered, but, unlike with the brain, all those memories could be retrieved on demand, by time or content, without all the random mixing and matching that went on with real brains. Could the Doctor defeat the system if he wanted? In other words, if he didn't want us to spy on him as he sat watching Carol taking her nap, did he have a button he could punch to shut off the system in that room? Probably, Mister Li admitted. But the Doctor thought of the house and the system he'd built as his own mind, he said. He'd never seen the Doctor override the system before. He didn't think Oppenheimer entertained any notion of privacy within the walls of his home. Overriding the system in any of its components would be like shutting down part of your brain, he explained. If there was something the Doctor didn't want to see again, he simply chose not to retrieve it, to recall it. There were two more parts to my third question for Mister Li. First, did anyone else besides him and the Doctor know how to operate the system? He thought not, although Alan had been learning it before he died. None of the rest of them had ever shown any interest or aptitude for it. They simply accepted that it was there. Liz seemed oblivious to it, and Carol tried to avoid it by staying away. The last part of my question had to do with a kind of audiovisual aid I had in mind, something built out of stored memory as much as possible, with created pieces thrown in where necessary, the kind of self-driven deal that would be hard to stop once it got started.

When he'd heard what I had in mind, Mister Li put his chin in his hand again and closed his eyes. He was really thinking this time.

CHAPTER
38

It was straight-up one o'clock when the Doctor joined us in the big room with the pedestals. He came in through one of the automatic doors that appeared and then disappeared in the blond wood wall, and Carol was on his arm. I thought Carol looked a little wobbly on her feet, and she had a slightly baffled look on her face. But, of course, by that time, I'd figured things out enough to understand why. As a matter of fact, I thought she'd held up pretty well, considering.

Liz and Syd were already there, having come down from Liz's room at the request of Mister Li, who'd spoken to them through the intercom system that wasn't really a part of the Doctor's house/brain/mind setup, just an everyday intercom like you'd find in a normal home. Neither of the girls looked happy to see me again, although of course Liz in her yellow outfit didn't have to look happy to be a welcome part of our little ensemble. She really was striking, and that wasn't lost on poor Syd, who sat close to her like the protective and possessive lover that she was.

"Would anyone like some lunch?" the Doctor offered as he entered and walked Carol over to a pedestal, where she settled into a semireclining position, resting her weight on one hip, supporting herself with a braced arm. "It wouldn't be any trouble to have DUS put something together."

Nobody showed any particular interest in eating, and I didn't even bother quizzing him about DUS, which by that time I already knew stood for his Domestic Utility System, a little subsystem that acted like the gizmos I used to see in the newsreels back in the fifties, the "home of the future" stuff where robots served coffee and a computer stashed away in the attic turned on the lights when it got dark and the heat when it got cold. It automatically changed channels on the TV, which was just a flat sheet of something ultramodern hanging on the wall like a wallpaper remnant. In the newsreels, the robot that served the meals usually had some kind of cute head on it, and more often than not was decked out in an apron. The Doctor's real version, of course, was nothing like that, but it got the job done and eliminated any need he might have had for keeping domestics on staff.

"Who called this meeting?" Liz asked, smiling. "I thought we'd already had the summit conference."

"And I'm not sure I should be here," Syd put in. "I don't want to intrude on family matters."

"If no one's hungry, is anyone thirsty, then?" the Doctor offered. He didn't entertain often, and he seemed determined to be hospitable. "Mister Kyle, help yourself to the scotch."

I heard the bar slide open behind me as if it had read my mind, but for a change I wasn't thirsty.

"No, thanks," I said.

"It's officially afternoon, Mister Kyle." The Doctor smiled. "And a man who works your hours shouldn't be expected to stand on ceremony in any case. You needn't wait for the cocktail hour here, you know."

"Thanks, but I'm fine."

"Well, I'm going to have something. Carol, will you join me, dear?"

Carol hadn't been paying any of us much attention. She'd been leaning on her hand, looking distracted. At the sound of her name, she looked up at her father.

"I'm playing bartender. What would you like?"

"I . . . whatever you're having."

"Well, I'm going to attempt a gin rickey," the old man said over his shoulder, still smiling. "I know you don't care for them. Shall I make you one of your—"

"She'll pass," I said.

"I beg your pardon?" The Doctor stopped tinkering with the stuff on the bar and turned to look at me. "What did you say, Mister Kyle?"

"I said Carol'll pass on the drink. One Mickey a day is enough."

"What . . ." Oppenheimer sputtered.

But he didn't finish his thought, and Carol wasn't paying him any attention anyway. Nobody was. That was because, all around the room, TV screens of different sizes had begun to appear along the walls. Nobody said anything, and the room was so quiet we all could hear the faint hum of little motors peeling away the wood paneling that covered the screens. They were everywhere. Mister Li had been listening, and he'd not missed his cue.

"I'm the one who called this meeting," I said, to answer Liz's question, but also to get everyone's attention and get the thing moving. There was less than an hour before Augie Dann showed up, and we had a lot of ground to cover. "It's something I've always wanted to do."

"What is?" Oppenheimer asked. Like everyone else in the

room, he was watching one of the TV screens, which was re-playing the brunch he'd so enjoyed earlier that morning with his daughter and granddaughter.

"I've always wanted to do one of these Agatha Christie deals. Or Charlie Chan, in the movies."

"Oh, good heavens," Oppenheimer moaned. "You're not go-ing to announce that one of us is the murderer, are you?"

"As a matter of fact, I am."

CHAPTER
39

They all reacted about the way characters do in the Charlie Chan flicks, everybody mumbling at once, nothing in particular standing out from the babble. I nodded to Mister Li as he joined us, and noticed the icy look Oppenheimer gave him. The Doctor knew I hadn't figured out how to operate the system. He knew Mister Li had set the show in motion that everybody was watching now, the scenes being played out on a dozen screens all over the big room.

While they were all getting the protestations out of their systems, I swung by the open bar and spritzed some soda into one of the Doctor's big tumblers to use as an ashtray. When I'd lit a cigarette and taken a deep hit on it to collect my thoughts, I started talking, and the five people in the room got quiet and listened.

"I haven't quite nailed down yet who knows what, so I'll just pick a starting place and run through the whole thing. If part of it is old news to some of you, bear with me."

The scene on the screens around the room had progressed by that time to the point where Liz excused herself and not long afterward Carol passed out on the table. Li had done a bit of editing to speed things up, so it wasn't long before we were watching the Doctor buckling his "cyberspace" mask and gloves onto the inert form of his daughter. I was watching Carol in particular at that point, and she was coming alive on her pedestal. Her eyes opened wider and wider as the scene played out.

"Stop this!" the Doctor demanded, focusing a baleful glare on Mister Li. "Damn you, traitorous chink! Stop it this instant!"

"It's running on autopilot now, Doctor," Li answered, his face tight with the sting of the name-calling. "As if your wonderful brain were dreaming aloud, free association."

"Twaddle!" the Doctor spat, as he stormed off toward the blond wall and its automatic door.

I made a move to intercept him, but Li called me off with a wave of his hand. So I stood where I was and watched the Doctor bang head-on into the wall at full stride, caroming off into a tight circle, his knees sagging with the crack he'd taken to his head, both hands cupped over the fresh red knot on his forehead.

"I've sort of put everything on hold for a little while," Li explained to me quietly. "Nobody's going anywhere."

"This is kidnapping, Mister Kyle!" Liz announced, springing to her feet. "You can't keep us here against our will."

"Call the cops," I told her. "You can do that in a bit if you like. But for now, all of you just humor me."

"Look. Look." It was Carol, uncoiling off her pedestal and pointing at the big screen behind me. She was pointing at herself on television, at herself going through the motions of giving birth to a nonexistent baby. "Would you look? It's my dream!"

"Mister Kyle, you have no idea the harm you're doing here," Oppenheimer intoned, straightening to his full height again now that the pain in his head was easing. "You're taking enormous chances, I warn you."

"Yeah, Doctor. Think of it as one of those professional exceptions guys like us are qualified to make. And there's a good bit to come, yet."

Carol was mesmerized by the show, rigid on her pedestal, her mouth agape.

"Mother?" Liz sounded concerned, and went to Carol. She put her arms around her mom's shoulders. "Mother?"

"See, Doctor, the thing is, you weren't reinforcing Carol's memories of giving birth to Alan and Elizabeth at all," I said. "You were creating them. Or recreating them. The way I have this deal figured out, you've been tinkering with your daughter's mind this way for a hell of a long time. Maybe she was your original guinea pig, I don't know. But, in any event, she wasn't repressing anything when she had trouble remembering having the two kids, was she?"

"You're a dangerous man, Mister Kyle."

"Nothing compared to you, Pops. Alan and Elizabeth were adopted, weren't they? Where did you find them? Not through the usual channels, I wouldn't think. Too much red tape would cramp your style."

"You don't know what you're doing," Oppenheimer said, making it sound like a threat.

"Why? That was the question I've been asking myself."

A collective gasp from the little group greeted the next episode on our little in-house TV channel. It was Carol again, on a different day in a similar but different room, back in the "cyberspace" harness. She looked like a woman being visited in the night by an incubus, an invisible demon lover. Because what she was feeling as she gasped and cried aloud and writhed on the hard, flat lab table was obviously real, and there was no way for us to know what she was seeing inside the hood that covered her eyes, she was alone. There were only her and her father's machinery.

Tears streamed down Carol's face, and she shook her head from side to side as Liz comforted her.

"This, I believe, is how you planted the bogus history in her mind. Her husband left her alone when he died . . . no kids. That all came later. You did all that to her, didn't you, Doctor?"

Oppenheimer said nothing. He stood silent and tightfisted, glowering first at me and then at Mister Li, who had taken a seat on a pedestal off to my right and sat with his head in his hands.

"Doctor?" Liz looked up from her mother to accuse her grandfather with a wide-eyed glare. "Is this true? Is any of it true?"

"Yeah, kid," I assured her. "And a lot more."

Syd spoke up. "I think we've seen enough, Mister Kyle."

"Maybe, but there's a hell of a lot more to see."

The next few bits were things with Alan in them, puttering around a lab.

"Alan," the Doctor said, his voice almost reverent.

"That's right, Doctor," I said. "He was on to you, you know. He didn't have the whole thing figured out, but he was on the scent. Things might have worked out differently if he'd made one of those masterful exceptions you and I are so fond of. Too bad for him, he was going by the book, waiting till he had all the answers before he did anything about it."

"What do you mean?" Carol asked, lifting her head off Liz's shoulder.

"Alan was murdered," I told her. There was no easy or kind way to say it.

"No, no, no," Oppenheimer insisted. "Keep your facts straight, Mister Kyle. Suicide."

I didn't argue, and I watched the Doctor stagger from the wall where he'd been leaning to his daughter. He put his hand on her head as if to console her. Or control her—you can't always tell in these things.

"Carol," he said, his voice soft and full of concern for her. "I didn't tell you the truth about Alan. It was an overdose of an experimental drug he'd developed himself. Stopped his heart. I've no idea why. I didn't want you to be hurt. That's why I told you, told everyone, about the heart defect. It was senseless, and I wanted to spare both of you the pain. Mister Kyle, this little parlor game of yours has gone too far. Surely, even you can see that."

"Alan had gotten wind of the experiment you were running," I said, as if I hadn't heard Oppenheimer and didn't agree with him. "He knew that he and Elizabeth were your subjects, but he hadn't figured out the purpose of the whole thing."

"And I suppose you have?" Oppenheimer asked, sarcastic.

"You mean it's true?" Liz demanded. "It's true?"

"You don't understand, dear," Oppenheimer said, reaching out to her. But she pulled away. "It's very complicated. Very complicated, and delicate. You've no idea what you're toying with here, Mister Kyle."

"The trick is to assume the worst, and then keep pushing until something gives," I told him. "You'd be amazed what you'll come up with sometimes. Like the 'Oppenheimer Dilemma,' for example."

"What the hell . . ." the Doctor vapor-locked on me there, and didn't finish his thought.

I noticed Liz had backed away from her mother and the Doctor, and was edging toward the pedestal where Syd waited to take her in.

"You're a brain man," I said. "A psychiatrist, a biochemist. I had to ask myself, why would somebody like you go to all this trouble? A double adoption, programming your own daughter's mind with your dream machine. I knew you were trying to prove something with the two kids. Alan and Elizabeth. That helped the whole thing come together for me, see? Alan and Elizabeth. Not Liz, with an *L*. Elizabeth, with an *E*. *A* and *E*. Adam and Eve. Your method was showing through around the edges there, Doctor. But if you needed a couple of kids to experiment with, why brainwash Carol? That had to be part of the deal. She wasn't supposed to know, for some reason. She was supposed to think she was their real mother, to make the experiment work the way you wanted it to. So what if you drove your daughter crazy in the process? I guess you figured you were smart enough to do it without screwing her up too bad. And if you did, you could fix her, right? You're a shrink, a genius. You'd come up with some kind of treatment or chemical, or strap her down on your 'cyberspace' contraption until you put her back together again, wouldn't you? Besides, that was a bridge you'd cross later. The first order of business was your experiment with the two kids, wasn't it? What did you expect to prove? What were you after that you thought was worth all that trouble and pain?"

Liz spoke up. "Mister Kyle, I don't like this. I don't want to hear any more. I feel . . ." She put her hands over her mouth and threw up.

Syd embraced her and petted her and tried to convince her it would be all right.

"I beg of you, Mister Kyle," Oppenheimer pleaded. "Enough. Please don't pursue this any further."

I looked from Liz to the old man to Mister Li, who wasn't holding up much better than Liz. He returned my look without saying anything, but he was begging me to stop, too.

"Haven't you done enough?" Syd demanded. "Look what you've done."

"No." It was Carol. She got to her feet and shook herself free of her father. "No, Jack. Don't stop. I want to know all of it."

CHAPTER
40

"Good for you, Carol," I said. "But you'd better buckle up. It doesn't get any better from here."

The next scene up was a two-shot of Liz and her brother, Alan, horizontal. They were in a bed with twisted sheets and scattered pillows, grinding urgently to a payoff, at least for Alan. He was talking to Jesus and calling Liz's name.

The action on all those screens shouldn't have made Liz feel any better, but she stopped retching, and when she wiped her lips with her fingers, I noticed there seemed to have been more sound than substance to her illness. She watched herself, her eyes darting from one screen to another as she saw herself fucking her brother. I flashed on something I'd seen a hundred times in NFL games in sports bars: the running back or wide receiver returning to the huddle, his eyes looking up at the replay running on a big-screen TV up in the stands.

"Oh my God," Carol moaned.

"I . . . I . . . ." Oppenheimer was sputtering again.

What was playing didn't need any commentary, so I just watched with the others and lit a fresh cigarette. Alan said some nice things to Liz, then rolled over on his side and caressed her, his hand touching her hair and her face. She brushed his hand away and sat up in bed, then leaned down over him. His eyes closed and his head lolled back as she began to fellate him. In the background, I saw the posters of rock stars I'd never heard of, and one of the big speakers. They were in Liz's room, the one the Doctor kept for her because she liked to stay over.

Liz was caught up in her self-appraisal, or whatever was happening in her head. Now it was Syd's turn to sit bolt upright, mouth agape. And Carol looked from one of the screens to Liz and then to me, waiting to see what came next.

"That's how you persuaded Alan to devote his talents to making designer drugs, I suppose."

No response, not from anybody in the room. Finally, I heard Mister Li mumble something in Vietnamese that I didn't understand.

"And you had the connection to move the stuff. After all, the Tiger Boys were your Deep Ellum party pals. I guess they were impressed when they saw the quality of drug you could deliver. What went wrong there? Who got greedy, the Tiger Boys, or was it you? I figure Alan was doling the stuff out to you, a couple hundred tabs every time you'd let him spend a little quality time with you. Am I right? I'll take your lack of comment for a yes. Anyway, you started pressing him for more of the stuff, enough to make a major killing. I'm no expert, but I've been told that a shoebox full of the active ingredient of crap like that would bring a million dollars or more. The formula and instructions for making it—hell, the sky'd be the limit. Maybe that's what you were after from Alan, the whole how-to recipe for the stuff. That would have made you independent, wouldn't it? Then you wouldn't have to eke by on the trust-fund money when you turned twenty-one, or wait around for the Doctor and your mom both to die to get your hands on the estate. How'm I doing so far?"

"I'd like to see you prove any of it."

"That's not my problem, kid. You killed Freddy, too, of course."

"Don't be ridiculous," Liz snarled. Then she looked around at the others, who were staring at her. "He's bullshitting, y'all! He's making it all up!"

"See, Syd didn't hear the phone ring when Freddy supposedly called you the night he was murdered. If a call had come in, she'd have heard it on the kitchen extension. I don't think the bell was turned down, Syd, because I called the house this morning, and Lois answered. I could tell by the background noise that she was reloading the fridge. In the kitchen. And she heard it ring. So either Liz faked the call, or she called Freddy. That brings me to the sneakers."

"Sneakers?" Syd blurted.

"Shut up," Liz snarled at her. "Just keep quiet. He's guessing."

"Yeah. You see, Carol, there was a shoeprint in Freddy's blood, there in the closet. When I saw it, I figured it for a match with the Air Jordans the Tiger Boys like to wear. But it doesn't match up, I know that now. I do think it'll match your sneakers though, Liz. The ones you were wearing with the jeans and the SMU sweatshirt when you invited me over and showed me that lab journal of your grandfather's."

"What?" Oppenheimer came alive at the mention of the journal. Now, as I looked from one to the other of them, I could tell nobody wanted me to stop just yet, except maybe Liz.

"Alan gave it to her. I told you, he was on to you, but he hadn't put it all together yet when Liz killed him."

"Oh my God." It was Carol that time.

"Alan wouldn't give her what she wanted with the designer

drugs, and I'd speculate that he even threatened to blow the whistle on her."

"If only he had," Oppenheimer murmured.

"Alan was a pretty decent kid, in addition to being a genius, and maybe his conscience got to bothering him about the drugs. About bedding his own sister, too, for that matter. Anyway, he balked for one reason or another, and Liz slipped him a lethal dose of the very drugs he'd designed for her to get him out of the way."

"The experimental drug?" Oppenheimer wondered aloud.

"Yeah. It's like you told me earlier today; you change a molecule here or there, and it's a whole new deal. That's how the street chemists stay ahead of the law. They can diddle with a formula and make a drug that does what the market demands, but it's not exactly illegal, because the drug laws have to specify what's outlawed. And the chemists can swap around their formulas a hell of a lot faster than politicians can make new laws."

"The silly bastard. If only he'd confided in me," Oppenheimer moaned.

"I don't think he trusted you," I said. "And with good reason. You hadn't been exactly straight with him."

"This is all just such total bullshit!" Liz exclaimed, indignant.

"Back to the sneakers," I said.

"Right," she snapped. "The goddamned sneakers! If you'll recall, I wasn't wearing any sneakers when you took me away from Freddy's apartment, was I?"

"Or anything else. I do remember. No, you'd already given them to Syd because you'd seen the shoeprint, too. I don't imagine you were nearly as stoned as you pretended to be, either."

"But . . ." Syd began, then stopped short when Liz cut her a hard look.

"I haven't figured your part out in this yet, Syd. Did you go with Liz to Freddy's, or did you go over there for some reason after you'd called me?"

"I didn't know if you'd really go over there or not," Syd explained.

"Shut up, you idiot!" Liz snapped. "Don't say anything."

"I see. So after you called me because you really were worried about Liz, you couldn't just wait around the way I'd asked you to. Instead, you took a chance and went over to Freddy's yourself. I guess Liz was pretty pissed when you showed up, even more when you told her I was on my way over. Of course, she'd already stabbed Freddy to death by then, so she had to come up with a contingency plan on the spot. She gave you her shoes because they'd put her too near the body. She didn't have time to clean up things any more than she already had because she knew I'd be there any minute. So she gave her shoes to you and told you to haul ass for her house. How's that, pretty close?"

Syd didn't say anything. She just looked at Liz.

"Liz, I thought maybe you'd dumped the shoes around the apartment somewhere. But I talked to the investigator today, and none turned up. After things calmed down, you cleaned the blood off 'em, and I guess you figured keeping them would be safer than 'losing' them. That might attract suspicion. The thing is, it's not just bloodstains that can hang you. These days, with an old pair like that, the cops can trace a print by make and model, even match up wear points and I.D. a specific pair. You should have chucked 'em, kid."

"But, Mister Kyle," Oppenheimer put in. He was sitting on the pedestal Carol had vacated, and looked tired and confused. "Your theories about the blood, the night we had the lawyers over . . ."

"I'm afraid Liz threw me a curve there. I told you it looked like somebody had wiped her clothes in the blood on the floor, then daubed it on her hands. And I'll stand by that. The thing is, she did all that herself, after she'd washed the real blood spatter off."

"Wouldn't the real spatter still be on her clothes?" he asked.

"I don't think so. My guess is she wasn't wearing any when she killed him. That would make it easy to get close to him, and it's the best way to avoid awkward stains on your outfit. She was cleaning up before she called the cops. That and the business with the shoes and Syd here accounts for the delay in calling nine-one-one."

"But why in the world would she call the police?" Carol asked.

"Beats the hell out of me, to tell you the truth," I admitted. "The only thing I can come up with is she waited until she saw me coming, then made the call and left the phone off the hook to be sure I'd know the cops were on their way. That wouldn't give me much time to look the place over or decide what to do about the situation. It's a stretch, but we were all having to improvise under some time pressure that night. It was a woman who made the call, and I'd bet voice analysis will make a match on her."

"Why did she kill the man?" Oppenheimer asked. "Because he knew too much?"

"That's my guess," I said.

"And I suppose he wasn't really in the porn business?"

"Not likely. They'll probably trace the camcorder down and find out he bought it pretty recently. I imagine Liz gave him the money for it."

"But why did she want the video made, then?" Carol asked. "If she wasn't duped into it, if it was all her idea . . . I don't understand."

"The only way she could figure to get her hands on the stuff Alan had made for her, the rest of it or the how-to part, was through her grandfather. Obviously, she couldn't approach him directly, so she came up with this phony extortion racket.

Carol, you were supposed to go to your father for help; Freddy was on call to play the heavy, and Liz would have him demand Alan's stuff. If that didn't work for some reason, they'd have settled for cash. You'd have paid a million, wouldn't you, Doctor?"

He nodded.

"Do any of you believe this crap?" Liz stood up to plead her case and moved toward me. "I mean, he's just dreaming this shit up!"

"I forgot to mention the prints. They got two sets of latents off the knife. One was Freddy's. The other will turn out to be yours, I imagine."

"Bullshit!" she hissed. "I wiped off the goddamned kn . . ."

"Oh yeah," I said, when I saw that she'd caught herself and wasn't going to finish the incriminating sentence. "You're right. I got that part screwed up. They didn't find any prints on the knife at all. It had been wiped clean, like you said."

CHAPTER
41

" I could use a drink," Liz said, moving toward the bar, which was to my left and a little behind me. I took a step back to keep her in view. "Anybody else?"

Nobody was thirsty except me, and I planned to wait until I was back in my office with my birthday bottle of Johnnie Walker.

"This is all very confusing," Mister Li said, shaking his head.

"Very confusing," Carol seconded him.

"You're telling me," I admitted. "You should try keeping all this stuff straight. I had no idea being Charlie Chan was such hard work."

"Explain something to me, Jack," Carol said. She wasn't distracted now; she was clear-eyed and more focused than I'd ever seen her. "About Freddy. If he and Liz were in on the extortion together, why didn't she need him anymore?"

"You screwed that up," I told her, "when you went to Eddie about the videotape. You were supposed to have gone to your father. When Eddie brought me into it and I got the tapes back, the whole extortion deal got derailed."

"Oh, I see."

By my watch it was quarter to two, and I wouldn't have minded if Augie had shown up a little early. My little show hadn't quite gotten all I wanted done, but I didn't see how it was going to play much longer, and I was beat.

"But, Liz." Carol turned toward the girl at the bar. "What on earth did you need or want that you didn't have? To kill anyone for money . . . ?"

Liz ignored the woman who, for all the two of them had known, had been her mother until a few minutes before, concentrating on slicing a lime for her drink on the shelf in front of the bar in the wall.

"It wouldn't make any sense," Oppenheimer observed aloud from his seat on the pedestal. "She doesn't understand it herself."

"What do you mean?" Carol demanded.

"That's what the whole thing was about," the old man explained. "My dilemma."

"I was hoping you'd explain that for us," I said to encourage him to continue when he didn't seem inclined to say any more.

"I developed a psychoactive chemical," he said, sounding almost too tired to go into it. "This was before Mister Li came to work with me. It's been my life's avocation, a special project I haven't shared with anyone."

"What did it do?" I asked.

"Ah, there's the rub," he said, waving a finger in the air. "One of two things. One good, the other bad. And I'd hoped to learn why. That was why I arranged the experiment you've exposed today, Mister Kyle."

"Alan and Liz were your guinea pigs."

"Yes. I'm not ashamed of that. When you consider what a drug like this could do, its potential for millions of people . . . for mankind." He said that last part with a sardonic little laugh.

"What's the good news?" I prodded him.

"Alan was the exemplar. A prodigious boost in intelligence. It might have led to a generation of such brilliance that . . . the potential was enormous."

"And I suppose I'm the downside?" Liz asked, her drink in her hand.

The old man nodded. "I'm afraid so, little girl. And the worst of it is that until today, I'd failed to see it in you."

"I think you might get an argument about that being the worst part," I said. "But do go on."

"If you gave the drug to one subject, one of four results should occur. Either he would become a genius without defect, or he would demonstrate a severe mental aberration very much like sociopathy. You're familiar with the term 'sociopath,' Mister Kyle?"

"Euphemism for an evil son of a bitch."

"Precisely. I'd had both results in animal experiments. On occasion, much less frequently, I'd produced sociopathic geniuses. Relatively speaking, of course. I mean, we're talking about monkeys here. Very rarely, in numbers almost insignificant, the drug had produced no apparent effect. I'd thought that Liz . . ."

"On monkeys," I said.

"What? Yes. The logical next step was to use human subjects."

"If you say so. You needed kids for that?"

"Subjects at a formative age, yes. Application over time."

"Jesus Christ," Carol whispered. "My whole life is unraveling." She was shaking her head, with an odd smile.

"Alan and Liz," I said. We had ground to cover. "But Carol wasn't their birth mother."

"Of course not," Oppenheimer snorted. "That's evident."

"I am their mother," Carol insisted through clenched teeth, her jaws tight. "David made love to me, and my belly swelled.

I had morning sickness, terrible with Alan, not so bad with Liz. I remember . . ."

"You see?" the doctor cut in. "That's what she remembers. Nothing of what went on here."

"Yeah. You planted those memories in her, with your 'cyberspace' gear, like on those tapes we saw."

"Precisely. Oh, she married. She married a young man who took her away to some godforsaken . . ."

"New England," Carol said, more softly this time, as if she were seeing it in her mind. "He took me home to an old house where his family had lived since the Revolutionary War."

"And then he died," the doctor pointed out, as if lecturing a class. "Lost at sea or something."

"A car wreck. He'd worked late, and he was on his way home."

"In any event, she came back to me. And it was an opportunity I saw no reason to forfeit. Perhaps you can see my side of it."

"I doubt it," I admitted.

"The greater good, of course. We mustn't forget, after all, that Madame Curie was killed by her own experiments."

"Okay." I'd always been of the opinion that mankind was best helped one at a time, but there was no point in arguing. "It was important for your experiment that Carol should believe they were her natural children?"

"As a control for the environment/heredity subtext, to provide a neutral universe of parental variables to the . . . You wouldn't understand, any of you. But, yes, there it was important. For valid, scientific reasons."

"How old were they when you adopted them?" I asked.

"Eleven and twelve."

"What?" Carol shrieked. "That's impossible!"

"You see?" the Doctor demanded of me, smug in this proof of his virtuousity.

"No way," Liz put in. "I remember growing up in our house, the old one. I remember snowy winters. Goddammit, I remember Daddy!" She looked from Carol to Oppenheimer. "Don't I?"

"No." The old man smiled, showing his teeth in a way that did not connect with anything in his eyes, reminding me of a shark on one of those PBS specials. "Except as I have programmed you to remember."

"That's a little hard to swallow, Doctor," I said.

"I suppose so, and I don't think I'm being vain to say that I may be the only man in the world who could have made it work. You've no idea of the effort involved. Even Mister Li there, has only an inkling. We're talking about a complete deprogramming to start. Then hours in the lab, days in our little sessions, reconstructing three lives from nothing except my research design. If I were inclined to publish my results, there'd be a Nobel Prize in it, I can assure you of that."

Carol sank to the floor, a curious look on her face.

"Are you all right?" I asked her.

"I think I am," she looked at me with a puzzled smile. "I thought I was losing my mind." She laughed. "Because my life didn't seem real. I had these dreams . . . But of course, they weren't dreams, and . . ." The laugh cracked on her lips, and a tear traced down her cheek. "Now that . . . to hear him actually say that it was all . . ." She buried her face in her hands, and I couldn't tell after that if she was laughing or crying or both.

Liz cranked up, and everyone turned to look at her. She cried, her body shaking with sobs, great loud herky-jerking sobs and moans. Only Syd went to her, tried to comfort her at all. Carol sprawled on the floor as if she'd fallen off her pedestal in more ways than one. Oppenheimer sat looking at Liz the way he might have studied one of his lab monkeys. And I was content to keep my distance from the lot of them.

"Mister Kyle," Li said softly. "If I'd known how far this would go, I don't think I'd have gone along with you."

"Mister Li, if I'd had any idea, I would never have gotten mixed up in it to begin with."

"I was raped," Liz wailed, dragging the word "rape" out into half a dozen syllables that trailed off into another choking sob. "I don't care what anybody says, any of this bullshit about lab monkeys or any of it! Freddy raped me. And he was going to do it again, and that's why I killed him. It was self-defense."

"Don't say any more," Syd urged her.

"Doctor . . . Jack . . . you've got to help me. I didn't mean to do anything wrong. I . . . I'm all mixed up. I don't know . . . who I am or what I am. Please, Jack . . . you've got to help me."

"You won't need much of anybody's help," I said. I'd finally remembered Sam Spade's line to Brigid O'Shaughnessy: "'You're good. You're very good. It's chiefly your eyes, I think, and that throb you get in your voice . . .'"

She'd stepped away from the bar toward me, leaving her drink behind, and looked as if she might throw her arms out to me, offer herself to me more or less, plead with me one way or the other to help her again. Maybe she figured I'd bent the law for her once before, I'd do it again. And I think she must have figured that the two videos I'd seen her in hadn't hurt her chances any. I looked in back of her to make sure that she'd left the knife behind, as well as her drink. She had.

But when I quoted Sam Spade to her, that brought her up short. She'd probably never heard of Dashiell Hammett, but she knew it wasn't me talking, those weren't my words, and that told her that I was having none of it. So, quick as a wink, she changed tack in midstride and targeted her grandfather, or whatever Oppenheimer was to her now.

"You did it, too!" she cried. "You raped me, too. You violated me, crawled inside my head and fucked with my mind. How could you? How could you do that?"

Oppenheimer got to his feet as she came toward him, but there was nothing in his body language that hinted at remorse or any notion of comforting her. The tall, skinny old man came up on the balls of his feet as if he might dash for safety, and I could see the dank shimmer of fear in his eyes. I figured he knew her better than anyone, now that he had realized what she'd become. And he wanted no part of her.

Carol rose, too, and moved between Liz and her father, her hands out in front of her, her mouth open to speak. She said nothing, but took Liz in her arms.

In my peripheral vision, I saw Syd standing alone off to my left. She was covering her ears with her fists, and crying madly. Only Mister Li, who remained seated to my right, was still.

"Before anybody gets overexcited," I announced, "you all should know that the cops are right outside. They'll be trooping in here in a couple of seconds. So let's all just take a deep breath and get a grip on ourselves."

Liz tugged free of Carol and spun around. She stomped back to the bar and lifted the drink that she'd made.

"Guess I'd better finish this while I can," she said.

"You needn't get too worked up," I told her. "You're in for a hard time, but I wouldn't bet against you on beating the rap, not if the Doctor'll tell the truth and buy you a good—"

What I was about to say was "lawyer," but that was when the whole thing went to hell, and a lot of things happened at once. A bell and a buzzer announced the arrival of Augie Dann and whoever he'd brought with him, followed immediately by the sounds of their feet banging up the ramp to the door of the room where we were all standing. That distracted me a bit, but not so much that I didn't catch a blur of motion to my left that I knew was Liz. As I began to turn that way, the contents of the highball she'd made splashed into my face, burning my eyes.

Everything was slow motion after that, and as it usually does in that kind of a deal, my vision began to close down into a tunnel. I saw through my alcohol-burning eyes the form of Liz lunging toward me, with the knife she'd used to slice her lime in her hand.

I stepped back to my right and fumbled the revolver out from under my jacket. It wasn't exactly a quick draw, because my wrist was stiffly bandaged and sore, but I got the piece out in time. I leveled it on Liz and said something ominous, to let her know I meant business. That had the desired effect, as she froze, looking at me and the muzzle of the gun. The door opened, and I was aware without looking around of everyone's attention turning that way, toward Augie and the cops. Almost everyone.

Mister Li misconstrued whatever I'd said to Liz and thought that I was going to shoot her. Maybe it was because that was the way they did things in Vietnam. At any rate, he came flying in from my right and hammered the cutting edge of his right hand down hard on my bum right wrist. With a growl I couldn't help, I flinched as my knees buckled and the revolver flew free of my grip. It clattered on the floor as I saw Liz renew her attack. She came at me hard, swinging the knife from behind her right hip, and drove it home. But her luck was bad, and she got Mister Li instead of me.

The three of us, Liz, Mister Li, and I, were slammed together by the force of her charge, and my face was only inches from Liz's, so that I saw clearly the maniacal gleam in her eyes. She still had the knife, and I felt Mister Li crumpling to the floor between us. Before she could try for me again, I popped her with a short, sharp left fist, and I could see then that I'd shorted her wiring pretty good. The knife fell out of her hand, her knees buckled, and she fell into a sitting position on the floor beside Mister Li.

"A-i-i-e-e-e-e-!"

It sounded like one of those primitive death wails, something I'd heard on a TV news story once about some killing in the Middle East, and the dead man's women were doing that, giving out with a high-pitched keening note that split the air. I looked up from Mister Li's wound to see Syd standing in a wide-legged crouch, Leslie Armitage's nickel-plated revolver in her hand. She was pointing it at me.

"Police officer! Don't move!"

Augie and two other cops in suits were in the room, and they'd gone into shooting crouches of their own. Each of them, the three of them spaced in an unrehearsed L formation that improved the odds of a clear shot, had a bead on Syd.

"It's not fair. . . . It's not fair. . . ."

That was what Syd was saying, mumbling it over and over like a mantra. I located the knife Liz had stabbed Mister Li with and dropped it into my jacket pocket. Mister Li stirred at my feet as I turned toward Syd.

"Mister Kyle," he said.

"Take it easy, Li."

"Sorry, I didn't see the knife."

"Don't worry about it, just hang on."

It wasn't immediately clear whom Syd had in mind to shoot. The round black eye of the revolver's muzzle covered me more than anybody else in the room, but she jerked it here and there, taking in Carol and Oppenheimer a couple of times, too. They took note of that, and the next time she swung the piece back toward me, the old man took Carol by the arm, and they relocated hurriedly to the cover of one of his patented pedestals, where the two of them went prone to wait out developments. That looked like a smart idea to me, and I might have followed suit, but the thing was, it was my gun the kid was waving around, one that I'd brought into the deal. I had to do something.

"Put the gun down, lady," Augie commanded, his voice loud,

277

clear, and surprisingly steady. "Put it down slowly and back away from it. Nobody has to get hurt."

"Not fair . . . not fair . . ."

Without a lot of enthusiasm, I took a couple of steps toward her. She didn't back away from me, which was good. But she didn't lower the gun, either.

"Freeze, Jack. Don't be a hero," Augie told me. Good advice.

"Syd," I said. "Think it over for a second, will you? This doesn't make any sense."

"Do it, Syd. If you love me, you'll do it!"

Liz had cleared her head enough to deal herself into the act, and I thought about a kick to the head to put her out for a bit. But there was no telling how Syd would react to something like that.

"Shoot the son of a bitch, Syd. He can put us both in prison."

"Don't listen to her, kid," I said. "You don't want to kill anybody. Like I said, Liz probably beats the rap, and you're going to be okay, too. You didn't know any of this shit. You didn't kill anybody. And you didn't know about Liz's racket with Freddy or the Tiger Boys or any of it. All you did was you cared about her. You're not . . . culpable." It sounded like the wrong word, stupid and lawyerish, but I didn't want to say she wasn't guilty. I remembered from Hostage Negotiation School that you weren't supposed to use words like "guilty." "Don't make it any worse."

"Kill him!"

"I can't," Syd mumbled. She started to cry again. "I can't."

"You stupid, ugly dyke!" Liz was livid, and would have made a play for the gun herself except that I was blocking her and she didn't want to face the three cops.

"Drop the gun, lady," Augie commanded again. I knew this was a hell of a dicey deal, and that three trigger fingers were sitting on go. "Nobody has to get hurt here."

"You're worthless and stupid, Sydney. You're a freak and a fool and a pathetic loser. I never loved you, and I never will. You're a freak! The thought of you touching me makes me sick."

Liz had a pretty good instinct for the jugular, and Syd was taking the hits. I saw it in her eyes, and when she turned the gun on herself, I lunged at her.

We hit the floor hard, and the gun went off. Up close like that, it sounded like artillery, and the stench of cordite burned like hell.

CHAPTER
42

Augie and I had a lot of business to settle, and he wasn't through with me until damned near midnight Saturday night. Part of the delay was that I respectfully declined to be interviewed without my attorney being present. We got through to him on his twenty-four-hour pager, but he was none too eager to leave whatever Labor Day festivities he had going. When I told him to bring the bloody clothes from the murder scene with him, he bitched about having to stop by his office on the way downtown and get them out of his safe. When I told him money was no object, that Doctor Oppenheimer was treating, he brightened a bit.

In a stroke of dumb luck, nobody'd been shot at Oppenheimer's. I'd bungled my grab for the snubby, but got enough of it that the only damage done was a buried slug and a powder burn in the Doctor's white carpet.

As Augie saw things, I was in a hell of a lot of trouble, and that was pretty much the way I saw it, too. But the high-dollar lawyer earned whatever exorbitant fee he planned to bill Oppenheimer for, and things worked out quite a bit better than I would ever have been able to manage on my own.

The bottom line was, I gave a complete statement covering everything from the night that Eddie showed me Freddy's videotape in his hospital room right up until the steno walked into the interrogation room. In return I got a pass, immunity from prosecution. Later, the lawyer said that Augie and his boss, whom Augie bothered at home, hadn't been all that hot for me anyway. Augie's boss was a sergeant I knew from the old days. He and I had kicked down a couple of doors together way back when, and seen a thing or two. I didn't flatter myself that that had anything to do with the way things worked out, it was just one of those things. I wasn't clear if Augie and his sergeant worked directly for Eddie Cochran, or exactly who was on whose shift, and I didn't inquire.

Eddie would have some trouble to deal with when he got back on his feet, but nothing he couldn't handle. He'd known when he asked the favor of me that he was crossing a line, and he'd taken his chances because of the way he felt about Carol. He was a big boy.

We had all the interrogation rooms in the Crimes Against Persons offices busy that night, the whole motley gang of us, me and the Oppenheimers and poor little Sydney. Everybody except Mister Li. One of the officers rode in the ambulance with him to Parkland Hospital, and took his statement after he came out of surgery. The word from Parkland was that Mister Li would make it.

Along the way, in between rehashing all the speculation and theorizing I'd done at Oppenheimer's, Augie wanted to know about me and the Tiger Boys.

"The way I see it," I told him. "They knew there was a hang-up getting the rest of Alan's drug supply, and I don't guess they knew why. There's no telling what Liz had told them, to stall them. They probably didn't know who Liz really was, because I'm sure she handled everything through

Freddy. They must have been keeping an eye on his place, after he turned up dead, and they saw me. I'd bumped into them that first night, at the Art Bar, with Liz. So they wanted to know who I was and what my involvement was. That's why they jumped me and took all my stuff. They were trying to get a line on me."

"Makes sense. We'll get them."

"I'm sure you will."

By the time we'd gotten around to the Tiger Boys, we'd already worked through the more serious business, and Augie was warming up to me a little. For one thing, he appreciated it that I'd tipped him to Oppenheimer's video library and all the bugged rooms. I knew that everything that had gone on out there that day would be on tape with sound, and that would make his job a little easier. He saw the case on Liz about the same way I did. He'd clear the case on her, but getting a conviction would be a long shot. Maybe she'd plead out or plead insanity and turn herself in for treatment somewhere, not that it would do any good.

Liz's chances of getting away with murder had a lot to do with Sydney. Her parents had been called in, and Augie said he thought they were handling the whole thing as well as could be expected. Whether she'd ever testify against Liz was anybody's guess.

Alan's death was a dead end. Even if they exhumed the body and found an overload of the designer stuff in him, how would you ever prove Liz slipped it to him? Her lawyers would call it suicide, and that would be that.

The old man was a hell of a case, and Augie'd kicked that one upstairs. Somebody would take what he had to the District Attorney's Office, maybe see what the state attorney general had to say about it. The old son of a bitch had to be guilty of something. Morally, he was a lot like the underground chemists who tinker with illicit chemicals faster than the government can make laws. He'd come up with an evil so deep and new that I wasn't sure anyone had ever made a law against it. What's the rap for crawling into children's heads and rewiring their minds? Maybe he'd meant that business about the good of mankind or however he'd put it, or maybe he'd made a bargain with the devil. I hoped he wasn't a harbinger of things to come.

I knew I'd have quite a lot of testifying to do in the weeks and months ahead, and that I would do it cheerfully. That was part of the agreement my lawyer had worked out.

Carol was in the clear, and, for all she'd been through, I had a strange feeling that she was better off than when the whole deal started. I hoped that Eddie Cochran would see it that way.

About the last item of business we had to hash out was Leslie Armitage's gun. I'd had no business going around packing, and everybody agreed on that. The way things had worked out, Augie wasn't inclined to file on me for it. It would be a misdemeanor case, but one that carried with it a heavy fine and up to a year in the county jail. But the lawyer made a case that as far as anybody could prove, I'd only had the thing in Oppenheimer's house, which was of course private property, with the consent of the owner, and he didn't think he'd have much trouble beating the case. It was a stretch, but, like I said, Augie didn't have his heart in it, and that was one reason he and his boss went along with the immunity deal. But he did feel like he was obligated to let the state board know about it, which would have jeopardized my P.I. license, and my lawyer and I had to lobby long and hard to convince him that that was included in our deal for immunity from prosecution. That's so often the way it is—you beat your brains out over small change, when things like murder work themselves out, practically.

All in all, I counted myself lucky when Augie showed me out of his office at midnight. I was out of smokes, and he gave me one, even lit it for me. I was walking out a free man, more or less in one piece, and there was a lot to be said for that. And I hadn't had to hurt anybody very badly.

Of course, I'd had my butt kicked, all my stuff ripped off, and I was flat broke except for the four hundred dollars in accounts receivable for the surveillance job I'd wrapped up the evening I'd called on Eddie Cochran at Baylor, with a month's worth of rent and child support coming due. But when I considered all the alternatives, I didn't feel too bad.

"I'd like to ask you one thing," I said. After all, I'd been dishing out answers for most of the last ten hours. "If you don't mind."

"What's that?"

"Where'd you get a name like Augie?"

"I was the youngest of nine kids. I've got four brothers named Matthew, Mark, Luke, and John. My three sisters were named after the Maguire Sisters. By the time I came along, Mom was all out of ideas. So she named me for the month I was born in."

"It could have been worse," I said. "You could have been born in September, like me."

"You're right about that," Augie said with a soft laugh. "September, huh? What day?"

"Today, as a matter of fact. It's a couple of minutes past midnight."

"Well, then. Happy birthday, Jack."

I thanked him for that, and went with the uniformed officer he'd called to take me back to my car at Oppenheimer's. It was about one o'clock in the morning when I finally slumped into my chair back at the office.

There were a couple of phone messages. Della was on the tape, reminding me that she wanted me to meet someone at

Vincent's Monday evening. And my kid was on, too. It was nice of his grandparents to do that for me, to have him give me a call. The handmade birthday card he'd sent me was stuck in the frame of the photograph of him that I kept locked in my desk drawer.

I took the photo and the card out of the drawer and stared at them as I let the kid's voice play over and over on the tape. Then I pulled out what was left of old Johnnie Walker and drank myself to sleep.

CHAPTER
43

Somewhere around three o'clock Sunday morning I woke up with a backache and decided to get out of my chair and set up my cot. Out of habit, I walked a lap around my floor just to be sure everything was kosher, then I visited the men's room and turned in.

That was all I remembered until half-past eleven, when I finally got fed up with the dreams I was having and woke up again. It wasn't until I had sat up in the cot that I realized this was game day. The Cowboys were playing their last exhibition game at home. From inside one of the drawers of my file cabinet, I fished out my little portable radio and tuned in the pregame show. In the process, I discovered a forgotten pack of smokes. It may have been a reflection on how things were going for me that I got excited about that.

When I'd looked around and selected my freshest remaining dirty shirt and my only pair of jeans for my Sunday birthday outfit, I took the little radio along with my shaving kit and hobbled like an old man down the hall to the men's room.

I was about as fresh as I was going to be, and the coffee was steaming by the time the guys on the radio announced that it was almost game time. We were playing the Houston Oilers for the "Governor's Cup," or the bragging rights for the state of Texas, or some such rot. As I poured myself the first cup of coffee of the day, I heard thunder rumbling overhead. When I looked out the nearest window, the rain was coming down so hard I couldn't see across the parking lot to LBJ, and I was glad I wasn't one of the faithful thousands sitting out in the stadium with the hole in the roof. Not that I made a practice of going to home games. For what the tickets and parking cost, I'd pay my rent for a month.

There was a lot of banter with the radio guys about the rain and how it would change the complexion of the game, and all the usual jokes about the hole in the stadium roof and the new owner's plans to float some bonds to build a real roof for the damned thing, and kickoff was only a couple of minutes away when the elevator opened and off stepped Speed's friend Big Mac.

I'd forgotten how big he was, and he looked less than happy, as well as pretty wet. His glasses were fogged over, and his UNSOLVED MYSTERIES logo cap was soggy.

"Speak up, bud. Give me a clue," he said.

"Over here."

"Thanks."

He couldn't see where he was going, and he was carrying a pretty big load. There was a television set under one arm and some gadgetry in a bag over the other shoulder. All of this he dumped on Della's desk and wiped his glasses on his shirttail.

"Good morning," I said.

"Everyone's entitled to an opinion," he answered. "This your office?"

"Uh, yeah. Why?"

It didn't take him long to stick his head into my little one-roomer and reach a conclusion.

"Too damned little. Hell, there ain't room enough in there for me."

"Too little for what?" I asked.

"I'll just set this baby up out here," he said, ignoring my question.

So I stood by the supply closet drinking my coffee and listening to the first series of downs while he arranged the television he'd brought on Della's desk and went to work assembling whatever the gadget was that he had in the bag.

"What are you doing?" I asked.

"We're going to watch the Cowboys."

"The hell we are. The game's blacked out."

"Yeah, right." He grinned at me as if I were an idiot or a small child.

"It's started already, ain't you got it working?"

It was Speed, almost screaming, as he and Leslie battled their way through the stairwell door. It wasn't easy, because they were lugging a cooler between them, one of the family-sized hard-plastic ones you'd want to take if you and the family were going off to live in the woods for a week.

"I'm doing it, I'm doing it," Big Mac growled. "I'd let you rig it up, only I want the son of a bitch to be in color this time."

"Speed, Leslie. What are you doing here?" I said.

"Happy birthday, Jack. Have a beer."

"What?"

"There's no food here yet," Leslie couldn't help noticing.

"Yeah," Speed chimed in. "Who's bringing the food?"

"Don't look at me," Big Mac warned.

"Della's doing the food," Leslie said.

"That's right." Speed slapped his head as he handed me a cold can of beer. "Where is she?"

"Probably sittin' down in her car waiting for somebody to come help her schlep it up here. Or maybe she thinks the rain's gonna stop," Leslie offered.

"Did I miss something?" I asked. "What's going on here?"

"Boy, Jack, I gotta hand it to you," Big Mac said as he stepped clear of his gadgetry and turned on the television with a flourish. The picture was gorgeous, the Cowboys and the Oilers, as if we were there, with good seats. "You're a real sleuth. It's a goddamned birthday party, dumb-ass!"

"Ah, you guys," I mumbled. I didn't like this kind of stuff, but still, the Cowboys and beer . . . what is one to do?

"Yeah, happy birthday again, Jack." Speed toasted me with a beer.

"Many happy returns," Leslie joined in.

"Happy birthday, Sherlock." Big Mac made it unanimous. "Hey, Speed, how about a brew for a workin' man?"

"Thanks, everybody. I don't know what to say."

"Hold it down, Sherlock. The game's on."

"Right."

Maybe Della had been waiting down in the parking lot for the rain to stop or for someone to give her a hand, because she was the next to arrive, with soggy paper sacks full of food. Following her off the elevator was "Fast Eddie" Cochran in a wheelchair, propulsion provided by none other than Augie Dann.

"Hail, Hail, the gang's all here," Della sang.

Everybody said hello to everybody else, and Eddie introduced Augie around. There was so much noise being made that Big Mac threatened to plug his earphones into the set, since he was obviously the only one listening to the game.

"You do have the game on," Augie gushed. "But it's blacked out."

"Big Mac there is a genius with this stuff," I explained.

"Happy fortieth, Jack. You already got your birthday present last night," Augie said, smiling as Speed passed him a beer. "Immunity."

"I got no complaints, Augie."

"Yeah, Jack. Happy fortieth," Eddie sang out, wheeling himself in my direction.

"Thanks, Eddie, but I'm only thirty-nine."

"Pathetic, Jack. Take it like a man." Eddie grimaced. "I know I will, when the time comes."

"Forty, huh?" Big Mac looked up from the TV screen long enough to show me a wry smile. "I'da thought you were older."

"Happy birthday, Jack," Della said, bringing me a kiss on the cheek along with a sandwich and trimmings on a paper plate. "And many happy returns."

"You did this, didn't you?" I accused her.

"Of course."

"And I suppose you don't really have a blind date set up for me tomorrow night?"

"Ah, Jack. You sound disappointed."

"Not by a hell of a long shot, kid. And I mean that."

"You were getting so hinky," she explained, "that I had to come up with something so you wouldn't figure out we were planning this little surprise party. So I made up the blind date on Monday. It was a pickled herring."

She meant a "red herring," but I knew what she meant and made a big fuss over her for being so clever.

"Well, you should have known that we wouldn't let your birthday go by without a party," she said.

"You did last year," I reminded her. "And the year before."

"But this one's a milestone," she explained. "A man doesn't turn forty every day."

"But . . ."

"Yeah, Jack," Speed put in. "Today, you're officially middle-aged."

"Only if I live to be eighty. Against which, the odds are what I would call prohibitive."

"So what?" Eddie chimed in. "I never thought you'd last this long."

"Yeah," I said. "If I'd had any idea I was going to live this long, I'd have taken better care of myself."

My phone rang about the time the first quarter ran out, and I didn't mind answering it because the TV was rolling through its endless parade of commercials for tires, batteries, and beer. I thought it might be my kid calling again, wanting to speak to me in person. But it was Bill Scheiner. He had to yell into the phone to be heard, because of all the background noise. I finally understood that he was calling me from a pay phone at Texas Stadium.

"First of all, happy birthday," he said.

"How'd you know?"

"Della told me, when I called before."

"Oh. Thanks."

"I wanted to call and let you know," he went on, "that I have good news."

"Really?"

"Yes. I was talking to Mister Stewart about you."

"Stewart?"

"My boss, John Stewart."

"Oh, right."

"Your name came up at the tailgate party before the game."

"I'm flattered."

"The company has seasons tickets to the Cowboys. It's one of the perks I think you'll enjoy, Mister Kyle. You have children, don't you?"

"One, but . . ." I let my voice trail off, rather than go into the details.

"Well, I'm sure you'll get a kick out of bringing him—or her, for that matter—out to the games. We get to use the company tickets on a kind of a rotation basis. You should be able to see at least two or three of the regular season games, and bring the kid with you. How's that?"

"Great," I said, wondering if I'd really be able to have the boy over for a couple of weekends this season, how that would work out with my in-laws, and why Scheiner was sounding so positive about the whole job thing. So I asked, "Does this mean a decision's been made?"

"What? Oh, yes. I've gotten the cart before the horse, haven't I? That's what I called to tell you. As I said, your name came up at the tailgate party before the game, and Mister Stewart said that he'd decided to leave it up to me. He said he would let me pick the person for the position. How about that?"

"Sounds like he has a lot of faith in your judgment."

"I'd like to think so, Mister Kyle. Actually, the man he'd had in mind turned down the offer."

"Oh, I see." That seemed about right. I hadn't won anything in a long time, but I could live with a consolation prize.

"But that's not important. All that matters is for you to come in here and show him what you can do. I'm very confident that you'll get the nod to replace me come the first of the year."

"Sounds good."

"So, basically, the job's yours if you want it, Mister Kyle. What do you say?"

Play had resumed, and I looked out through my office door at the gaggle of friends who'd assembled for the occasion. They were enjoying themselves, with the game and each other, and I was flattered that they'd chosen my birthday as an excuse to get together and have a good time. Naturally, Big Mac's ability to get the Cowboys on TV had been a draw, but that was all right. It's the thought that counts. Also, I thought about my kid living with his grandparents on their farm outside Paris. It was a good place to bring up a little boy, and there were plenty of cousins and aunts and uncles for him there. But his grandparents had raised their kids, and deserved to take things easy and enjoy all that they had worked so hard for all their lives. It wasn't a permanent arrangement for Little Jack, and I didn't know how long it would be before his mom was free or in any position to take care of him. The odds of my getting custody were not good under any circumstances. As a fly-by-night private eye with no home address, I would no way ever be allowed to try to make a home for him. But as director of security, even assistant director? I figured that would trim the odds against me considerably.

"How soon would you need an answer?" I asked.

"Okay, Jack. I know it's a big decision for you. But we need to put this to bed. You can understand that."

"Of course."

"I'm out of here the first of the year. Naturally, I have some vacation coming, and there's the holidays, Thanksgiving and Christmas. Between you and me, I don't plan to be in the office much after the middle of November. I still try to make it out for deer season, you know."

"Don't we all?" I was lying there. I hadn't cared for going into the woods with a gun since I'd got out of the Marines.

"And there is a bit of in-service you'll need before you take over."

"I should hope so."

"All of which means you'd need to start by around the first of October."

"I see."

"At the latest."

"Uh huh."

"And if you were to decide for some reason to pass, we'd need time to find somebody else."

"Yeah."

"So I guess I'm saying we need your answer by the end of the week. How's that?"

"I'll let you know by next Friday."

"Fair enough. Well, I'd better get back to the game. You know, the 'Pokes can't do a thing without me."

"Yeah, get out there and cheer 'em on, Bill."

"I'll expect to hear from you Friday, Jack. Of course, if your decision is the right one, you can call sooner."

"I appreciate it. Thanks."

"Who was that?" Della asked as I stepped out of my office and lifted the lid of Speed's cooler to get myself another beer. From the look on her face, I surmised that she also thought it might have been my kid calling.

"It was a man about a job," I said.

"Anybody I'd know?" Eddie asked.

"Yeah, a friend of yours."

"So what's the deal?" he insisted. "Yes or no?"

"He says it's up to me."

"So that's a yes."

"I guess so."

"You're not sure?"

"I have until Friday to think it over."

"That ought to be plenty of time."

"Yeah, I guess so."

"It's a no-brainer, Jack." Eddie raised his voice a little. "For Christ's sake, what's the downside?"

"It's a big step," I said.

"Yeah, like up off the cold, wet street into an apartment you can call your own—or maybe even a house, for Pete's sake. And an office, with a steady paycheck and a secretary and a pension, and hospitalization."

"And Cowboy tickets," I added, smiling.

"Better yet. So what's to decide?"

"I don't know, Eddie. I guess I've gotten used to being my own boss, you know, and . . ."

". . . and scraping by, month to month, getting beaten up every once in a while. Yeah, I can see where a life like that would be hard to give up."

"I'll admit," I said, "on paper, it's not much of a comparison."

"Well, it's high time you started . . ." Eddie caught himself before he got up a full head of steam. "Never mind. You're a big boy. Do what you think's right."

"Thanks, Eddie. I probably will."

"Well, enough merrymaking for me," Augie announced.

"You're leaving?" I asked.

"Got a few things to do. I'm not on duty, mind you," he explained with emphasis, draining his one beer. "Just wrapping up some odds and ends."

"Might my friends the Tiger Boys be among them?" I asked.

"In a manner of speaking. Gang Unit's got Liz's friend ID'd. They're sitting on a couple of houses right now, with warrants in their pockets. I'll be surprised if we don't have him before the day's out."

"Glad to hear it."

"I only hope you'll make a good witness if it goes to trial," he said.

"I'll do my best."

"Well, so long, everybody. And happy birthday, Jack. Oh, and one more thing . . ."

"What's that?"

"I don't know what the deal is, but if that was somebody offering you a job on the phone just now, I'd strongly advise you to take it."

"Oh?"

"Yeah. Because, man, let me tell you, the way you operate, your luck's bound to run out one of these days."

"You're probably right."

On his way out, I walked along with Augie to ask him about getting Leslie's revolver back. He said if she'd come downtown during office hours and bring some I.D., he'd let her sign the papers and release it to her. I knew she wouldn't be real excited about vistiting police headquarters, but I also didn't want to impose on him anymore by asking for favors, so I told him that would be fine. I'd give her a ride if Speed was tied up on something.

When I turned from the elevator, I saw Eddie wheeling himself through the door of my office. He motioned with his head for me to join him, and I did, threading my way among the other four well-wishers, who were helping themselves to seconds on food and beer. When I got inside the office, Eddie was getting himself turned around to face me, and I eased the door closed behind me.

"How's Carol?" I asked.

"First things first," he said. "Here."

The envelope he handed me had the fat look, crinkled around the edges, that meant there was money inside.

"What's this?" I asked.

"A thousand dollars."

"Why?"

"Three days at two hundred, plus you got ripped off for a couple hundred in gear. If there's any extra, call it a bonus."

"You don't have to pay me," I told him.

"I know, and I didn't. That's from Carol."

"Oh."

"To answer your question," he went on, "she's in some kind of a marathon session with her shrink right now, over at her house. You have any idea what a shrink charges to make a house call on Sunday? On a holiday weekend?"

"I'm surprised she could find one," I said. "This all has to be pretty rough on her."

"Is the old man a son of a bitch or just plain crazy, Jack?"

"How the hell would I know? Maybe too smart for his own good. He engineered that big house of his to be like a brain, like he lived entirely in his own mind, see? And he never left the place."

"I know Carol hated to go over there."

"And with good reason, I'd say. She wasn't supposed to remember things, but I guess she did, one way or another."

"She thought she was losing her mind. She was getting her dreams mixed up with stuff that really happened."

"What does she have to say about it now?"

"She knows she's got a long way to go, but she sounded more optimistic this morning when I called than I've ever heard her," he said.

"That's good. Maybe all this was for the best, then."

"By God, I hope so."

"Me, too, because then you wouldn't have to kill me," I said.

"I'm stone in love with her, Jack. It makes me crazy sometimes. And being held prisoner by Miss Farmer wasn't helping any."

"I understand that. But there's one thing I've been puzzling about."

"What?"

"She never asked about you, man." I looked Eddie in the eye, half afraid I was stepping over a line, making trouble.

He laughed. "She didn't have to, Jack. She was in there with me more than old Miss Farmer, if you can believe that. She knew how I was doing."

The way he ducked his head and reddened, I knew what he meant, and it reminded me of *A Farewell to Arms*, the nurse snuggling with the wounded soldier.

"Okay," I said. "I guess that answers that."

"It was her way, too," he said. "She compartmentalized things in her life, kind of. She didn't mix my part with her kids, or her father. It makes sense, if you look at it from her side of things."

"Sure it does."

"Anyway. I appreciate what you did for us."

"And I appreciate the money."

"She can afford it."

"Eddie, I want you to know I also appreciate the deal with the job."

"I sure as hell hope you do, Jack. And I hope you have the good sense to tell the man you'll take it."

"You're right, I know. It's just kind of hard to see myself . . . I don't know. . . ."

"Coming in from the cold? Going straight? Hell, Jack, you'll get used to being somebody again. And, like I said before, maybe it'll do you some good as far as the kid's concerned."

"Wouldn't that be something?"

"Damned straight. And now, I'm going to be on my way. Happy birthday, partner."

"Can't imagine where you're rushing off to," I said.

"Yeah, I've got a ton of sick leave still coming, and Carol and I are going to see if we can nurse each other back to health."

"Sounds good. Need any help?"

"Nah, I've got to learn to operate this thing sooner or later."

"Okay. I'll watch you from up here. If it throws you, I'll come down and give you a hand."

"Fair enough."

I did push him out of my office and across the hallway to the elevator. Everybody told him good-bye and good luck, and then the door opened and he was on his own. I knew he'd make it all right, and he did, as I watched from a window and he managed to slide himself out of the wheelchair and into his car. He even got the chair stashed in the backseat, and then he drove away.

Big Mac stayed to the end of the game, then disassembled his hardware and lurched out with a belch and a big wave, a can of beer in each of his hip pockets. Speed and Leslie left a few minutes later, dragging their empty cooler between them. This time, I was able to convince them it was safe, and they took the elevator. That left Della and me. I told her how much

I appreciated the little party, the card everyone signed, and even the black balloons with the number *40* on them. She knew I usually didn't go in for that kind of thing, but I convinced her that I really meant it this time.

She started tidying up, collecting paper plates and empty beer cans for the trash. I walked into my office and settled into my chair. I looked out the window at the rain and the dark, ominous afternoon. Then I looked at the picture of my kid on the desk and the handmade card he'd sent me.

Della said something, but I didn't hear. I had a lot on my mind. I was thinking about Little Jack and American Southwest Motorfreight. I was thinking about calling Paris and hearing the little guy's voice.

FOR THE BEST IN PAPERBACKS, LOOK FOR THE

In every corner of the world, on every subject under the sun, Penguin represents quality and variety—the very best in publishing today.

For complete information about books available from Penguin—including Pelicans, Puffins, Peregrines, and Penguin Classics—and how to order them, write to us at the appropriate address below. Please note that for copyright reasons the selection of books varies from country to country.

In the United Kingdom: For a complete list of books available from Penguin in the U.K., please write to *Dept E.P., Penguin Books Ltd, Harmondsworth, Middlesex, UB7 0DA.*

In the United States: For a complete list of books available from Penguin in the U.S., please write to *Consumer Sales, Penguin USA, P.O. Box 999— Dept. 17109, Bergenfield, New Jersey 07621-0120.* VISA and MasterCard holders call 1-800-253-6476 to order all Penguin titles.

In Canada: For a complete list of books available from Penguin in Canada, please write to *Penguin Books Canada Ltd, 10 Alcorn Avenue, Suite 300, Toronto, Ontario, Canada M4V 3B2.*

In Australia: For a complete list of books available from Penguin in Australia, please write to the *Marketing Department, Penguin Books Ltd, P.O. Box 257, Ringwood, Victoria 3134.*

In New Zealand: For a complete list of books available from Penguin in New Zealand, please write to the *Marketing Department, Penguin Books (NZ) Ltd, Private Bag, Takapuna, Auckland 9.*

In India: For a complete list of books available from Penguin, please write to *Penguin Overseas Ltd, 706 Eros Apartments, 56 Nehru Place, New Delhi, 110019.*

In Holland: For a complete list of books available from Penguin in Holland, please write to *Penguin Books Nederland B.V., Postbus 195, NL-1380AD Weesp, Netherlands.*

In Germany: For a complete list of books available from Penguin, please write to *Penguin Books Ltd, Friedrichstrasse 10-12, D-6000 Frankfurt Main 1, Federal Republic of Germany.*

In Spain: For a complete list of books available from Penguin in Spain, please write to *Longman, Penguin España, Calle San Nicolas 15, E-28013 Madrid, Spain.*

In Japan: For a complete list of books available from Penguin in Japan, please write to *Longman Penguin Japan Co Ltd, Yamaguchi Building, 2-12-9 Kanda Jimbocho, Chiyoda-Ku, Tokyo 101, Japan.*

FOR THE BEST IN MYSTERY, LOOK FOR THE

☐ **THE PENGUIN COMPLETE FATHER BROWN**
G.K. Chesterton

Here, in one volume, are forty-nine sensational cases investigated by the high priest of detective fiction, Father Brown, whose cherubic face and unworldly simplicity disguise an uncanny understanding of the criminal mind.
718 pages   ISBN: 0-14-009766-X

☐ **BRIARPATCH**
Ross Thomas

This Edgar Award-winning thriller is the story of Benjamin Dill, who returns to the Sunbelt city of his youth to attend his sister's funeral—and find her killer.
384 pages   ISBN: 0-14-010581-6

☐ **APPLEBY AND THE OSPREYS**
Michael Innes

When Lord Osprey is murdered in Clusters, his ancestral home, with an Oriental dagger, it falls to Sir John Appleby and Lord Osprey's faithful butler, Bagot, to pick out the clever killer from an assortment of the lord's eccentric house guests.
184 pages   ISBN: 0-14-011092-5

☐ **GOLD BY GEMINI**
Jonathan Gash

Lovejoy, the antiques dealer whom the *Chicago Sun-Times* calls "one of the most likable rogues in mystery history," searches for Roman gold coins and greedy bird-killers on the Isle of Man.
224 pages   ISBN: 0-451-82185-8

☐ **REILLY: ACE OF SPIES**
Robin Bruce Lockhart

This is the incredible true story of superspy Sidney Reilly, said to be the inspiration for James Bond. Robin Bruce Lockhart's book tells the thrilling story of the British Secret Service agent's shadowy Russian past and near-legendary exploits in espionage and in love.
192 pages   ISBN: 0-14-006895-3

☐ **STRANGERS ON A TRAIN**
Patricia Highsmith

Almost against his will, Guy Haines is trapped in a nightmare of shared guilt when he agrees to kill the father of the man who will kill Guy's wife. The basis for the unforgettable Hitchcock thriller.
256 pages   ISBN: 0-14-003796-9

☐ **THE THIN WOMAN**
Dorothy Cannell

An interior designer who is also a passionate eater, her rented companion who writes trashy novels, and a rich dead uncle with a conditional will are the principals in this delicious thriller.   242 pages   ISBN: 0-14-007947-5

FOR THE BEST IN MYSTERY, LOOK FOR THE

☐ **A CRIMINAL COMEDY**
  Julian Symons

From Julian Symons, the master of crime fiction, this is "the best of his best" (*The New Yorker*). What starts as a nasty little scandal centering on two partners in a British travel agency escalates into smuggling and murder in Italy.
220 pages   ISBN: 0-14-009621-3

☐ **GOOD AND DEAD**
  Jane Langton

Something sinister is emptying the pews at the Old West Church, and parishioner Homer Kelly knows it isn't a loss of faith. When he investigates, Homer discovers that the ways of a small New England town can be just as mysterious as the ways of God.
256 pages   ISBN: 0-14-012687-2

☐ **THE SHORTEST WAY TO HADES**
  Sarah Caudwell

Five young barristers and a wealthy family with a five-million-pound estate find the stakes are raised when one member of the family meets a suspicious death.
208 pages   ISBN: 0-14-012874-3

☐ **RUMPOLE OF THE BAILEY**
  John Mortimer

The hero of John Mortimer's mysteries is Horace Rumpole, barrister at law, sixty-eight next birthday, with an unsurpassed knowledge of blood and type-writers, a penchant for quoting poetry, and a habit of referring to his judge as "the old darling."
208 pages   ISBN: 0-14-004670-4
